HOUSE
OF
ASH
AND
BONE

HOUSE OF ASH AND BONE

JOEL A. SUTHERLAND

tundra

Tundra Books, an imprint of Tundra Book Group,
a division of Penguin Random House of Canada Limited

*Publisher's note: This book is a work of fiction. Names, characters, places and incidents
either are the product of the author's imagination or are used fictitiously, and any resem-
blance to actual persons living or dead, events, or locales is entirely coincidental.*

Library and Archives Canada Cataloguing in Publication

Title: House of Ash and Bone / Joel A. Sutherland.
Names: Sutherland, Joel A., 1980- author.
Identifiers: Canadiana (print) 20220435162 | Canadiana (ebook) 20220435170 |
ISBN 9781774880968 (hardcover) | ISBN 9781774880975 (EPUB)
Classification: LCC PS8637.U845 H68 2023 | DDC jC813/.6—dc23

Published simultaneously in the United States of America by Tundra Books
of Northern New York, an imprint of Tundra Book Group, a division of
Penguin Random House of Canada Limited

The author wishes to thank the Ontario Arts Council for its support.

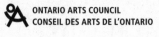
ONTARIO ARTS COUNCIL
CONSEIL DES ARTS DE L'ONTARIO

Library of Congress Control Number: 2022947059

Edited by Peter Phillips
Designed by Emma Dolan
The text was set in Adobe Garamond Pro.

Printed in Canada

www.penguinrandomhouse.ca

1 2 3 4 5   27 26 25 24 23

Penguin
Random House
TUNDRA BOOKS

To Colleen, my happily ever after.

PART ONE

ONE

Josephine sat completely still, pretending to be asleep, as the van cut through the dark.

When will we get there? she wondered.

The road grew more treacherous as it twisted through northern Vermont, hugging the Connecticut River. From above, Josephine thought, they'd look like a pair of giant snakes slithering side by side. Tall, scraggly pines—grown so close together that they ceased being individual trees and became one big blot of darkness in the night—loomed large at the sides of the road, blocking the low-hanging moon from view. Thick snowflakes filled the sky, making it difficult for Josephine's father to see the road.

Soft, sleepy music played on the radio.

The van's tires drifted off the paved asphalt and crunched loudly on the gravel shoulder.

"Shit," Mr. Jagger said under his breath as he yanked the steering wheel to the left, jerking the van back onto the road.

He took a deep breath and rubbed his face from top to bottom, as if trying to iron the wrinkles out of his skin—they'd gotten much worse over the past year.

"Whassat?" Mrs. Jagger mumbled. Her head perked up and she blinked three times.

"Nothing," Mr. Jagger replied quickly—a little too quickly to be believed. "Everything's fine. Just a bit of a tight turn back there."

Josephine stole glances at her sisters. Unlike their mother, they hadn't woken up. Elizabeth and Allison were seated in the back row with Josephine, their heads gently resting against one another. Mary was directly in front of Josephine, her head leaning on a balled-up jacket pinned against the window, and Louisa looked as comfy as ever in her baby bucket seat. Clutched tightly in her tiny fist was her lucky rabbit's foot.

"I think I fell asleep," Mrs. Jagger said.

Mr. Jagger shrugged. "You did. No big deal."

"I want to stay awake with you. How long was I asleep for? Five or ten?"

"More like fifty or sixty."

"Sorry."

The song playing on the radio ended, and "It's the Most Wonderful Time of the Year" started.

Mrs. Jagger groaned. "Seriously? Any radio station that plays Christmas music the day after Christmas should be taken off the air."

With a knowing laugh, Mr. Jagger drummed his thumbs along to the beat on the steering wheel. He didn't appear to share his wife's disdain.

As soon as the singer had crooned his affection for hosting parties, toasting marshmallows, and caroling out in the snow, Mrs. Jagger turned off the radio. "I can't listen to another word. I'd rather listen to the girls snoring the rest of the way. It can't be much longer, right?"

"Little less than half an hour, I think," Mr. Jagger said.

Josephine discreetly looked at her watch so her parents wouldn't notice she was awake. It was quarter past four. That meant they would pass through Canaan before five in the morning. Why her parents wanted to get there so early, she had no idea. It's not like the lawyer, Mr. Finger, would be ready to meet them—he probably wouldn't even be awake. What did her parents expect them all to do while they waited?

"Kids still asleep?" Mr. Jagger asked.

Her mother turned to check. Josephine quickly shut her eyes.

"Yeah," she heard her mother say. Josephine peeked through her eyelids when she guessed her mother was no longer looking.

About three hours earlier, long after the last of her sisters had dozed off, Josephine had given up trying to fall asleep too. She wished she could hit a switch and turn off her brain, close her eyes, and completely black out. It was a lovely thought—slipping into a void, leaving the real world behind, if only for a few hours. But her sleep was rarely so peaceful. Her dreams were too vivid, too real. Too weird. Not to mention the voices she heard too often . . . so she'd spent the past few hours pretending to sleep so she wouldn't have to talk with her parents, thinking about stories she'd like to write, and watching the world pass by in a gloomy blur.

There was something kind of thrilling in catching quick glimpses of country houses as they sped past. Sometimes, if an interior light was turned on, Josephine could see someone through a window. She found it fascinating that, all across the country, people lived in small houses in the woods, far from restaurants and movie theaters and shopping malls. Far from neighbors—far from other humans. She'd lived her entire life in the same house in Amherst, not too far from downtown Buffalo. That was home. Out here in the wilds of Vermont? That was . . . well, Josephine wasn't sure yet, but she found it odd in a way she couldn't quite express.

They passed a row of houses, each shrouded in darkness. Trees whipped past, then a few more small houses, then more trees, then . . .

Josephine sat up a little straighter in her seat. She thought she'd seen something—

"Don't get your hopes up," Mrs. Jagger told her husband, her voice sounding distant to Josephine's ears.

—something in the woods—

Mrs. Jagger continued. "If this doesn't work out, we'll be fine. We'll figure something out. We always do."

—something following them.

"I know," Mr. Jagger said.

Josephine rubbed her eyes and looked outside again. There was nothing there—definitely nothing following them.

Too little sleep, she thought. *I hope my kids don't think I'm a failure.*

That second thought—*I hope my kids don't think I'm a failure*—wasn't her own.

It was her father's, sent directly into her head, without his permission or even his awareness. Josephine was overtired and had let it slip through her defenses and enter her mind.

She pictured an imaginary net covering her brain, hoping her father's would be the only thought she'd hear for the rest of the drive, and closed her eyes once more. Her mother might look back again to check on the girls, and Josephine didn't want her parents to know she'd heard their conversation. Keeping her eyes closed also had the added benefit of not seeing things in the woods that weren't really there. Just in case, she pulled her noise-canceling headphones over her ears. She didn't put them on to listen to music—she put them on as an extra precaution. She'd worn them for years, every night while she slept, ever since the day she'd discovered the full extent of her . . . abilities.

Why would we think you're a failure, Dad? she wondered. *The library shouldn't have let you go, and besides, it's only been . . .* she counted the months, her optimism fading a little when she nearly got to double digits. *Something better will come along.* She wished she could tell him that, but then he'd know. Know what she could do. Know what she *was.*

And no one could ever know.

She spent the next thirty minutes trying not to think about anything.

The van slowed down and Josephine cracked her eyes open in time to read a sign on the edge of a town.

WELCOME TO
CANAAN, VERMONT
EST. 1782

They'd arrived. One week of vacation in Canaan. Elizabeth and Allison, the eldest two of Josephine's three younger sisters, currently still sleeping with their heads pressed together, hadn't been impressed when their parents broke the news a couple of days before.

"Where's Canaan?" Allison had asked with a tone that made it sound as if she'd just swallowed a mouthful of bile.

"It's in northern Vermont, just south of the Canadian border," Mrs. Jagger said. "That's kind of neat, right? Maybe we could go to Quebec for a day trip. You love maple syrup, and I could practice my French."

"We don't have passports."

"Well, no. That's true. We don't."

"And Vermont makes a ton of syrup too," Allison added sarcastically, "so we wouldn't need to visit Canada."

"That's the spirit!" Mrs. Jagger said, missing her daughter's tone.

Allison sighed dramatically. "Of all the places in the world, why are we going to Canaan?"

Their mother exchanged a look with their father, then said, "Your dad's great-aunt Melody—"

"Mercy," Mr. Jagger interjected.

"Right, Mercy. She passed away. And he's her last surviving family member. So her house, technically, is now our house. And we thought, well . . ." Mrs. Jagger laughed and blushed a little. "I don't know why I'm having such a hard time getting this out. We thought we'd spend the week between Christmas and New Year's there, like a getaway. A vacation."

"A vacation?" Elizabeth said dryly. "In Canaan? Who vacations in Canaan?"

"I can use the time to work on my book," Mr. Jagger said. He bounced Louisa gently in his arms. "Your mother can enjoy the peace and quiet. And you girls can explore. There's woods all around—it's very secluded. The closest neighbors are far away. Elizabeth, you can play guitar or sax or drums all night long and no one will call the cops."

"I don't have a drum kit," Elizabeth said.

"You can bang on the pipes. And Allison, think of the scenery. Think of the views you can paint."

"But Christmas Eve?" Allison said. "You decided to tell us this on Christmas Eve?"

"Would you rather we'd waited until Christmas Day?" her father said. "We just found out about the house yesterday." *Hell, I just found out my grandmother had a* sister *yesterday.*

It was another one of her father's thoughts that Josephine had heard unintentionally. She had promptly sealed her mental net and focused on her *own* thoughts. She, for one—maybe the only one—was excited about the news. The trip would be an adventure, and it wasn't like Amherst was any more exciting than Canaan. And, like her father, she could use the time to write. They could spur each other on, maybe even swap stories and critique what they'd written. She pictured the two of them going for walks in the snowy woods before returning to the house to warm up by the fire as they spun tall tales deep into the night. It sounded perfect.

Mary, Josephine later found out, was also excited about the getaway. "There will be *nothing* to do out there in the middle of nowhere," she told Josephine, with a wry twinkle in her eye, before they'd gone to bed on Christmas Eve. "We'll be forced—against our wills—to hang out."

Josephine laughed and gave Mary's shoulder a playful shove. "How *awful*."

In June, Mary would be the first of the Jagger girls to graduate from high school, and Josephine would finish eleventh grade. Their mother had homeschooled them both until they started public high school in ninth grade. Allison and Elizabeth, in fifth and sixth grades, respectively, had a few years left of homeschooling before going to high school, like their older sisters. While Josephine was excited to be nearing her final year, she was depressed when she remembered Mary would be leaving home to go to college in September. Only fifteen months separated them in age, so they had spent nearly every day of their lives together. Although it would still be crowded, the house was destined to feel quieter, and a little less lively, once Mary moved out.

Shortly after they passed the Canaan town limit sign, as if in response to Josephine's thoughts, Mary snored loudly, the sound muffled by Josephine's headphones. Josephine felt as if enough time had passed since she'd let her guard down and heard her father's thoughts, but just to be safe, she didn't remove her headphones completely. Instead, she slid them back slightly, uncovering her right eardrum. Enough to hear, but close enough to quickly cover both ears again if she needed to.

Canaan was quiet and dark. Streetlights lit deserted roads and sidewalks. A thick blanket of snow covered roofs and tree branches. The van's tires crunched loudly over the unpaved street that appeared to be the town's main thoroughfare. Josephine had the same feeling she had whenever she walked into a darkened room and turned on the lights only to discover someone was trying to sleep, which happened a lot in her household. She felt a little like an intruder. She felt like she shouldn't be there.

"You feel that?" her mother asked her father.

"Are you cold? I can turn up the heat."

"No, it's not that." Mrs. Jagger shivered and rubbed her arms. "Never mind."

Does she feel like an intruder here too? Josephine wondered.

Mr. Jagger covered his mouth with a fist and yawned. "So. This is Canaan."

"This is Canaan."

The van stopped at a T-shaped intersection. After a few moments, Josephine began to wonder what her father was waiting for. Why was he hesitating? There was no one in sight—just a scattering of small houses, a motel to their left with a glowing neon VACANCY sign, a restaurant dead ahead, and to their right a place called Wayne's Lanes & Jo's Grille, advertising "Pizza, Bowling, Lounge." Just when Josephine began to wonder if her father had fallen asleep, he turned left.

"That's the motel," Mrs. Jagger said as they passed it.

"I thought we'd drive by the house first."

"The lawyer won't be there yet."

"I know, but curiosity is killing me. I figured we could head out there quickly, and then come back. Just to check it out before the girls wake up. I don't think it's far."

Mrs. Jagger rubbed the back of her husband's head. "Well, if you're not too tired, go for it."

They passed more houses (some big, most small) and businesses (a convenience store, a gas station, a mechanic's shop). Before much longer, they left Canaan's beating heart. *If you can call it that*, Josephine thought. The highway cut a path through thicker and darker woods with no sign of life. The farther they drove north, the more isolated Josephine began to feel.

What happens if there's an emergency? she wondered. *How long would it take an ambulance or the police to help us?*

"The GPS says our turn is coming up," Mrs. Jagger said.

"Yeah, but I don't see a street sign," Mr. Jagger responded.

They passed a narrow, overgrown road that didn't appear to be paved. Josephine didn't see a street sign either.

"Shit," Mr. Jagger said. "I think that was it." He turned the van around, then pulled onto the unmarked road. Josephine bounced around in her seat as the van drove over potholes and tire ruts.

"Not what I expected from a road called All American Highway," Mr. Jagger said, his voice undulating with every bump and jostle.

The road bent to the west, revealing the entrance to a driveway ahead on their right. The driveway was even more overgrown than the road itself, and there was no house in sight, but the flag on the GPS indicated that it was their destination.

"Do you want to check Google Maps on my iPad just to make sure this is the place?" Mr. Jagger said.

"The GPS is never wrong," Mrs. Jagger countered. When it came to directions, her faith in their GPS was comically unwavering.

Mr. Jagger shrugged and turned onto the driveway. His shoulders tensed as he tried to keep the van from sliding into the ditch. The driveway bent and the trees parted, like a curtain pulling back to reveal a stage set for a play.

Comedy or tragedy? Josephine mused, ready for her adventure to begin.

The house was large, imposing, ornate, and black as the night. It was surrounded by tall, gnarly trees. The snow glowed in the moonlight.

But that's not what commanded Josephine's attention.

There was a stranger standing between the Jaggers and their new house.

TWO

"Who is that?" Mrs. Jagger said.

Josephine couldn't be sure, but there seemed to be a slight note of concern in her mother's voice. Josephine felt a little concerned too. She removed her headphones and held them on her lap.

"No idea," Mr. Jagger said. "It's so early. Maybe we're at the wrong house."

Mrs. Jagger double-checked the GPS and shook her head. "According to this, we're right where we're supposed to be. Should I wake the girls?"

The stranger—a man—hadn't moved. He'd given no indication that he'd seen them pull up, but they were only ten or fifteen feet apart and the van's headlights were shining directly in his face. His head was downturned, his eyes blocked from view by the brim of his hat. His long, forest-green coat didn't look especially warm, but the man didn't look cold.

"No, not yet," Mr. Jagger said. "Wait in the van. I'll go find out who he is and what he's doing here." It was clear by his tone that this was very low on the list of things he wanted to do.

"Are you sure? What if he—?"

"He's probably a neighbor checking up on the place. Maybe my great aunt—or the lawyer—paid him to help with the yard work and upkeep. I'm sure he's harmless."

He doesn't look like a handyman, Josephine thought. As to whether he looked harmless or not, she hadn't yet made up her mind.

Mrs. Jagger sighed and took her phone out of her pocket. "I'm going to be ready to call 9-1-1, just in case. If he says or does anything weird, get back here immediately."

With a final nod, Mr. Jagger said, "Lock the doors," and slipped out into the night.

A gust of frigid air blasted into the van in his wake, stirring Josephine's sisters but not waking them.

Her father trudged through the snow, slowly approaching the man. The stranger still hadn't moved. Mr. Jagger stopped midway between the van and the man, then raised his hand in greeting.

"Hello there," he said, his voice faint from where Josephine sat. "Can I help you with something?"

Josephine's insides felt like they were twisting into a big, tangled knot. She covered her eyes with her hands—not to hide, but to think. Doing so always helped her focus, especially in tense situations. She contemplated waking her sisters, talking to her mother, or joining her father. There was no reason to continue pretending to sleep, and with every passing second, her guts wrenched a little tighter, so she decided to talk with her mother. "Mom? I don't like this."

Mrs. Jagger turned quickly and faced her daughter. "Oh, Josie. I thought you were asleep." She cast a quick glance through the windshield. The man still hadn't moved or spoken. She looked back at Josephine. "Don't worry. Everything's fine."

"Who is this guy? What's he doing here so early?"

"Your father is talking to him. He'll figure it out and then we'll go to the motel."

"I said, can I help you with something?" Mr. Jagger asked the stranger, his voice louder.

Josephine shook her head. "Something's wrong. This guy gives me the creeps."

Mrs. Jagger forced a smile that quickly wilted. She looked at her phone and sighed, as if she'd just realized how little good it would do, out in the middle of nowhere, if things went bad fast. "He gives me the creeps too," she admitted.

With her anxiety rising fast, Josephine felt like she needed to do something other than just talk with her mom. She went through her options again, then settled on something she hadn't considered before. She decided to lift the mental net off her brain and try to pick up on the stranger's thoughts.

Immediately, Josephine heard her mother's panicked thoughts, loud and clear. *What should I do, what should I do, oh God, what should I do?*

Then she heard her father's thoughts, less loud but still quite clear. *Is this guy deaf or something? I think I could take him if it comes to that, but what if he has a weapon? I should have brought something heavy, like a tire iron, just in case.*

Josephine reached out to the stranger, poking, prodding, and probing. Silence. It was like scanning for a station on the radio and coming up empty—nothing but static hiss. But then something cut through and entered her mind. Only, not a voice.

A heartbeat.

Thump-thump. Thump-thump. Thump-thump.

"What the fuck?" Josephine said quietly. She'd never heard anyone's heartbeat before. Was it the stranger's?

Allison woke up and raised her head, waking Elizabeth.

"Where are we?" Elizabeth asked sleepily.

That woke Mary, who groaned loudly and rubbed her face. At least Louisa remained asleep—like most babies, she had a wicked, ear-splitting cry when woken early.

The heart Josephine heard kept beating.

Thump-thump. Thump-thump. Thump-thump.

The man still hadn't moved.

He's a statue, Josephine thought. *He's not real.* Maybe he wasn't. What a relief that would be. But Josephine had lived through enough challenges to have learned that life had a way of kicking you when you were down, and fairy-tale endings seldom existed outside of picture books and Disney cartoons.

Now that her sisters were awake, Josephine's head was beginning to fill with too many thoughts. She prepared to put the net back over her brain, but she tried one last time to hear the stranger.

The heartbeat faded and shifted slightly. *Thump-thump. Thump-thump. Thump-thump.* Maybe it wasn't coming from the stranger. It now seemed to be farther away, behind him. *Thump-thump. Thump-thump. Thump-thump.* The heartbeat was in the house. *Thump-thump. Thump-thump. Thump-thump.*

An old woman's voice penetrated Josephine's skull. *Merry meet, Josephine*, she said, her voice soft and grating all at once.

Josephine shut things down immediately. Her palms were sweaty and she was short of breath. *What the hell was that?*

Mary noticed that something was wrong with her sister and asked if she was okay. Josephine nodded, unable to speak. For a moment, she thought she could still hear the heartbeat despite her net, before realizing she was hearing her own heart beating in her chest, pumping blood into her ears, making her feel a little dizzy.

Her father turned around and looked at his wife with a perplexed expression. *What's with this guy?*

While Mr. Jagger's back was turned on the house, the man finally moved. He slipped a hand into his coat, reaching for something concealed within.

"Mom!" Josephine shouted, pointing at the man. Her headphones fell to the floor. "He's going for something!"

Mary, Elizabeth, and Allison all sat bolt upright and looked around in panicked confusion. The baby woke and started to wail. Their mom whimpered, an awful, helpless sound that frayed Josephine's already taut nerves.

Their dad turned back to face the man, but it was too late. If the man meant to harm him, he could. He would.

"Ben!" Mrs. Jagger shouted.

Mr. Jagger jumped in alarm and ran back to the van.

The man didn't pursue him. He remained where he stood, holding on to whatever he held inside his coat.

A few feet from the van, Mr. Jagger slipped on the icy driveway. His feet flew out from beneath him and he rocketed forward. His head struck the driver's-side corner of the front bumper with a loud *thwack*! He fell to the ground, out of sight.

Mrs. Jagger and her four elder daughters screamed. The baby's wails reached frantic heights.

The man ran to the side of the van where Mr. Jagger had fallen. He was old, but surprisingly fast.

Mrs. Jagger opened her door and rushed outside. Josephine unbuckled her seatbelt and got to her feet. Something hard crunched loudly underfoot, but she hardly noticed as she passed in front of Mary and through the sliding door. Mary followed her.

"Get away from him!" Mrs. Jagger shouted, shaking her phone at the stranger, punctuating every word, as if threatening to strike him with it.

The man crouched over Mr. Jagger, who was lying on his back in the snow. Josephine couldn't see her father's face, only his torso and legs. He wasn't moving.

"He's bleeding," the man said. His voice was smooth, like silk. He didn't sound panicked or concerned.

"Who are you?" Mrs. Jagger asked. She moved behind the man, facing the girls.

"I'm Damon Finger," he said. He raised his head and, upon seeing the looks of confusion on the faces of Josephine and Mary, added, "The lawyer in charge of Mercy's estate."

He had an odd look about him, with eyes set slightly too far apart, a protruding chin, and deeply wrinkled skin. The lenses of his glasses were filled with reflected moonlight. Josephine felt uneasy in his presence, but she realized that what he held—the thing that had pushed everyone over the edge—was nothing more than an envelope.

"Help me get Benjamin inside," Mr. Finger said.

Mr. Finger and Mrs. Jagger carried her husband—still unresponsive—by his arms and legs into the house. Mrs. Jagger had asked if they should leave her husband where he was and call an ambulance in case he had injured his neck, but Mr. Finger said his neck appeared to be fine and he'd be at risk of hypothermia if they left him lying in the snow. Mary opened the door for her mother and the lawyer, and then she, Elizabeth, and Allison followed the adults through the darkened doorway. Josephine had offered to get Louisa out of her car seat.

The howling wind blended with the baby's cries, each competing to be heard above the other.

"Shh-shh-shh," Josephine said softly as she unbuckled Louisa's shoulder straps. "It's okay. Everything's going to be fine." She sounded like her mother—not entirely confident.

Maybe her words worked, or maybe Louisa was getting tired of crying, but her wails turned to whimpers.

"That's a good girl," Josephine said. She handed Louisa her lucky rabbit's foot and cradled the baby against her chest, shielding her with the flaps of her unbuttoned coat. Since the lawyer had already arrived and her father was injured, she doubted they'd check into the motel back in town like they'd originally planned. Which meant Josephine could come back out to the van for everything later, once things had settled down . . . but she couldn't leave her backpack. It contained the book she was currently reading and her road snacks (a half-empty bag of crushed Cool Ranch Doritos, a handful of fuzzy peaches, and an unopened box of Nerds). *Nothing but the essentials*, she thought jokingly, momentarily forgetting her anxiety.

But her mood darkened again when she spotted her headphones. They were on the floor of the van in front of her seat, cracked in half. *No, no, no. Fucking hell, no*, she thought in a panic. *I must've stepped on them. They're broken, useless. How am I going to keep my family's thoughts out of my head while I sleep?* She covered her eyes to think. A worse possibility than hearing her parents' and sisters' thoughts dawned on her. *What if . . . what if I accidentally hurt someone with my mind again?*

Her mood darkened further as she took her first few steps toward the house. A bright red circle had stained the white snow near the front of the van, and there was a streak of blood on the bumper. Josephine couldn't believe her eyes, but there was a rabbit sitting in her father's bloodstain, its nose and whiskers twitching. It looked at her calmly and then bent its head down to the red snow, and . . .

"Are you *eating* that?" Josephine said, her voice high-pitched with disbelief. "Get out of here!"

The rabbit didn't flinch, so Josephine took a few threatening steps toward it. Finally, it bounded off into the woods, leaving a bloody trail of pawprints in its wake.

It couldn't have been eating Dad's blood, Josephine reassured herself. *Bunnies eat lettuce and carrots and dandelions.* She shook her head. The wind picked up again, chilling her to the bone.

Josephine turned and marched quickly, head down, shielding her face from the wind. But she slowed and eventually stopped as she approached the house. In the commotion of their arrival, she hadn't really gotten a good look at it yet.

It was large, at least four or five times bigger than their home in Amherst, with an exterior made almost entirely of wood as black as coal.

A lump of coal, she thought. *Some belated Christmas present.* It was more a joke than disappointment. Despite the odd things that had happened that morning, Josephine was still excited about the week ahead. The house had a vibe that promised mysteries waiting within, pulling her forward as if by invisible strings. As she walked—a little like a marionette, the house her puppet master—she continued to take in more details she hadn't noticed before.

From where she stood outside, the house was divided into three sections, each topped with a triangular roof. The door was dead center and the windows, seven in total, were made of tri-panel glass that reminded Josephine of cats' eyes.

Trees crowded in on all sides of the house, swaying with the wind and creaking loudly. If one of the bigger ones cracked and fell in the wrong direction, it could do significant damage. Josephine shoved the thought aside and thought how warm and cozy the house looked, shielded from the outside world. Even the snow couldn't quite reach it; the ground around its walls was barren, yellow grass and weeds clawing up the sides.

The house shimmered, a weird trick of the light, and for the briefest of moments, it had looked almost invisible.

You need sleep, Josie, she told herself.

She walked to the front porch and paused. Before entering, she felt she needed to do something. She lifted her net and listened. Half expecting to hear a heartbeat—or worse, a woman's voice—she heard nothing but the wind and Louisa babbling. Somewhat reassured—*the heartbeat and voice were probably just in my imagination*—she netted her brain, stomped the snow off her shoes on the stone stairs, and absentmindedly gripped the S-shaped door handle. She yelled in alarm and withdrew her hand in a flash. The handle was a brass snake, but for a moment she had thought it was a real snake. Josephine laughed nervously.

Mom's going to hate that, she thought as she pulled the door open. *But Dad's going to love it.*

He'd better be okay, or I'm going to kill that lawyer. She knew her father's accident wasn't Mr. Finger's fault—not really—but she couldn't stop herself from blaming him.

The door opened with a loud groan. She'd expected the interior of the house to be cold and dark, but found it to be the complete opposite. It was warm and bright, with wall-mounted lamps running along both sides of the front hallway and lit candles of all shapes and sizes on a foyer table. There was a cheerful purple door at the end of the hall that appeared to lead to the basement, and a wooden staircase leading up to the second floor. The air was rich with the comforting smell of woodsmoke. Josephine heard a crackling fire in the room to her left.

But she didn't hear anything else. No chatter, no footsteps, nothing. It was as if her family had entered one house and she'd entered an entirely different one. She held Louisa a little tighter and kicked off her shoes. She opened her mouth to call out before she spotted a shadow to her right, silently staring at her.

Josephine flinched before she realized the shadow was only her second-youngest sister, Allison. She was standing in a doorway, leaning against the frame.

"You're jumpy," Allison said.

"Yeah, well, it's not every day Dad—"

Allison abruptly pushed off the doorframe and walked past Josephine, interrupting her as she passed. "Took your time, too, didn't you? Get lost on the way in from the van?"

I was only out there a minute or two, Josephine thought, not bothering to say it out loud. It was obvious her sister wasn't in a listening mood.

"Where's Dad?" she asked instead.

"This way," Allison said over her shoulder as she casually walked into the room with the fireplace.

Josephine dropped her backpack on the ground, then followed her sister into a large family room. Sitting on a couch facing the fire were her parents. They smiled when they saw her.

"Josie, there you are," Mr. Jagger said. He removed his arm from his wife's shoulder, stood up, and plucked Louisa out of Josephine's arms.

"You're okay?" she asked.

"Of course I'm okay," he said with a wide smile and a slight frown.

When he didn't say anything else, Josephine said, "It's just, you fell. You hit your head on the van's bumper." She studied his face. There was a small red circle, not quite a bruise, above his left eye.

"Did I?" he asked, still smiling in confusion. He raised Louisa up to eye level and repeated the question in his baby voice, a voice that irritated all four of the elder daughters—and their mother—in equal measure, but Louisa adored it. She squealed in delight, her entire face beaming.

"Yeah, you did," Josephine said, resisting the urge to take Louisa back so she could force her father to sit down and tell her what was going on. "Really bad. I thought—"

Her father's smile faltered as he picked up on the urgent tone in his daughter's voice. "Oh, right. I remember now. That was nothing more than a bit of a slip on some ice. Sorry I scared you, but the good news is, I'm a-okay." He sat down and placed Louisa on the couch between him and his wife.

"Baba," Louisa said, her first and only word.

Mrs. Jagger handed the baby a bottle of milk. "I knew you'd want this. Had it ready to go."

Louisa squealed in delight, said *baba* one more time, then drank.

"Mom?" Josephine said, looking for some backup. Or at the very least, an explanation. Had her father hit his head so hard that his memory had been affected?

"Yes, dear?" Mrs. Jagger said pleasantly.

Josephine shrugged. "You saw what happened."

"Of course I did."

Josephine sighed in relief. She was beginning to feel like she was going crazy.

Mrs. Jagger placed a hand on her husband's shoulder. "Your dad slipped on some ice, but he's okay. A-okay. It was nothing."

Her words were close to a mirror image of what Mr. Jagger had said, making Josephine's cheeks flush in frustration. But why? Why was she getting so upset? She didn't want her father to be hurt, and here he was, telling her he was fine. She should be happy and relieved about that, and she was, but . . .

Josephine looked at her father's forehead again. The red spot had faded, like a magic trick. Here one minute, gone the next. "The lawyer said something about it being lucky your neck wasn't broken, and when I walked past the spot where you fell, I saw . . . ," she said feebly, the last thread of her memory coming to an end. What *had* she seen? She couldn't quite remember.

She covered her eyes with her hands. *Think, think, think . . .*

"Ah, yes, the lawyer," Mr. Jagger said. "Mr. Finger helped me inside, made me this tea"—he picked up a brown plaster mug as if toasting Josephine—"and is giving your sisters a tour of the house as we speak. Maybe he'll show you around after we take care of some paperwork." He blew on his tea and took a sip, then sighed contentedly.

My sisters, Josephine thought. *Allison led me here, but then where did she go?* Josephine sat down on a chair beside the fire. Outside, early morning daylight was beginning to wake the forest. She checked the time—it was 7:37 a.m. That couldn't be right. What time had they arrived in Canaan? She thought it had still been dark, maybe five or six in the morning. It was as if the past hour or two had simply vanished. *Don't be stupid*, she thought. *The drive must have taken longer than you thought, that's all.*

Regardless, why had the lawyer been waiting outside so early when they weren't due to arrive at the house until that afternoon? It was as if he had been expecting them.

Let it go, Josephine—let it all *go*, she thought. But the thought had come with an odd sensation in her brain, as if it hadn't been created there but planted. Was she hearing her father's thoughts? Her mother's? No, it couldn't have come from them—she hadn't removed her mental net. The thoughts continued before she could question them any further, and she accepted they must be her own. *It's fortunate Mr. Finger was there. It's fortunate Dad wasn't more severely injured. And it's fortunate—very fortunate indeed—that this house came into our lives precisely when it did.*

Don't forget how excited you are about this house.

Josephine nodded. "Maybe, if I'm lucky," she said to her parents, not really remembering what they had been talking about—something about the lawyer, and a tour of the house—but not actually caring anymore either. She stifled a yawn and realized she hadn't slept all night.

The room was warm, her chair was soft, and her parents were okay. A-okay. Everything was going to be all right. She shut her eyes and drifted into a deep, defenseless sleep without remembering to first put on her headphones—without remembering they were broken in the van. Without remembering that by falling asleep without her headphones, she was putting her entire family in grave danger.

THREE

Josephine woke with a start, mumbling loudly and clutching at her shirt. For a moment, she thought she'd been abducted, taken from her home in the middle of the night and held captive in someone else's house against her will.

"Holy shit," Mary said, startled. She was sitting on the couch across from Josephine. "You okay?"

"Where am I?" Josephine asked.

"Everything is cool. We're in Canaan, remember? The new place?"

It slowly came back to her. They had left home yesterday afternoon. Their mother had said they should wait and leave early Sunday morning, like they'd originally planned, but their father was too excited and anxious to get on the road, so they had started driving late on Christmas Day. Their plan had been to drive through the night and rent two rooms in the local motel for a few hours of shut-eye before driving to the house to meet the lawyer, but Mr. Jagger had decided on a whim to go see the house first. The lawyer had been there—*so very fortunate*, Josephine thought—and had helped them all inside.

And she had dreamt. Something dark and terrible. Images flashed through her mind. There had been a stranger. Her father had hurt himself. There had been blood.

My headphones, Josephine thought. She'd fallen asleep without them. That explained her dream—her nightmare. She couldn't keep her brain protected with her mental net while she slept, so wearing her headphones through the night helped keep nightmares at bay. Other people's dream-thoughts were typically louder and more potent than their waking thoughts, and that messed up her subconscious mind. But she didn't only sleep with the headphones for her own protection—she wore them to protect those she loved. Years ago, before she understood the full extent of her abilities, she had accidentally royally fucked up one of her closest friends, Helen, with nothing more than her mind. That was when Josephine discovered that, in addition to being able to hear other people's thoughts, she also had the power to get into people's heads and ruin their lives. It was a dark and terrible secret, one she'd never told anyone and something she had worked hard to suppress and control. Her family knew she wore her headphones at night but didn't know why, and had given up asking years before.

"Canaan, yeah, right, I remember now," Josephine told Mary as she leaned back into the armchair, trying to relax but still tense. "Is everyone okay? Nothing bad happened while I was asleep, did it?"

A look of concern flashed across Mary's face. "Well . . ."

"What?" Josephine asked, a feeling of dread washing over her.

"You did miss lunch," Mary said, smiling.

Josephine sighed in relief. "Guess I was really tired."

"You think so?" Mary said sarcastically. "You've been snoring like a baby for three hours."

Josephine's stomach ached in response. She patted her belly. "I'm starving."

"Relax, I made you a sandwich." Mary pointed to a PB&J on the coffee table between them.

The word *thanks* had barely passed Josephine's lips when she lunged for the sandwich and took her first bite. A small dollop of raspberry jam squirted out and splattered on the edge of the plate.

"I'd say *ew*, but we were all as hungry as you," Mary said.

"It tastes *so* good," Josephine said. "The peanut butter, the jam, the bread . . ."

"I know! One of the best sandwiches I've ever had. Top three, at least."

"Did Mom and Dad go out for groceries already?"

"No, Dad said the engine light was on in the van and he didn't want to drive around searching for a grocery store. But it didn't matter, because the kitchen was already stocked. Lawyer brought it all over, I guess."

The van, Josephine thought, *something about the van*. She looked at the splatter of red jam on the edge of her plate . . . that seemed to have some connection to the van's bumper, but she couldn't fathom what. It didn't matter. The taste of the sandwich made everything else seem unimportant. The lawyer was beginning to grow on Josephine. "He still here?"

Mary shrugged. "Don't think so."

"He was going to give me a tour."

"No worries," Mary said, picking up Josephine's plate and standing. "I'll give you a tour. Oh no!"

"What is it?"

"Your plate. I got jam on my sweater!"

Josephine knew how much Mary loved that sweater, and how much it had cost. She had saved up for it for months. "That sucks," she said.

Mary sighed. "Yeah, it really does." She had on a tank top beneath, so she removed her sweater, careful to not make a bigger mess of the jam. "It means your tour is going to begin in the laundry room. How exciting."

It wasn't terribly exciting, not by any stretch of the imagination, but the laundry room was more modern than Josephine had expected. The washing machine and dryer were new and expensive-looking, an ironing board came out of a cubby built into the wall, and there were a variety of cleaning products neatly arranged on wooden shelves. Mary found a can of stain remover and sprayed her sweater after carefully wiping away the jam.

"Mind if the next stop on the tour is my room?" Mary asked. She rubbed her exposed arms—they were very pale and covered in goosebumps. "It's chilly in here."

"Sure," Josephine said. She shifted her backpack from one shoulder to the other, having picked it up from the foyer on their way up, and followed Mary along the second-floor hallway. "How many bedrooms are there?"

"One for each of us. Well, Louisa has a crib in Mom and Dad's room."

"Five bedrooms," Josephine said in awe.

"How perfect, right? It's like it was meant to be."

Meant to be. Josephine had the same feeling, but she didn't want to get too attached to the house. At the end of the week, they'd be heading back to their comfortable but crowded home in Amherst. The thought already made her a little sad, but it fled from her mind the moment Mary opened her door and they stepped into her bedroom.

"Fuuuucckk," Josephine said, stretching the word out in a hushed tone.

The room was huge. Three or four times larger than the room she and Mary shared back home. It even had its own fireplace nestled between two large windows on the west wall. The furniture was solid wood and covered in intricate carvings. There was a writing desk, a makeup table, and a sitting area with soft chairs by one of the windows. There were enough dressers to hold not just Mary's clothes but the entire family's, and at the center of it all was a four-poster bed with silk curtains.

"Whose room is this?" Josephine asked. "Cinderella's?"

"Don't know, don't care," Mary said with a wide smile. "It's my room now, at least for the week. Wait until you see your room. Elizabeth, Allison, and I left it especially for you." She crouched in front of her suitcase and rifled through her clothes in search of a sweater to put on over her tank top.

Josephine walked slowly around the room, allowing her gaze to wander. Charcoal sketches of forest scenery adorned the walls. Hidden in the roots of a gnarly tree in one sketch was a small goat. Josephine tried to recall what a baby goat was called. A kid? Cat's eyes peered out of a bush in another piece, and a dark bird nested in a tree. The grass was sketched in an odd, swirling pattern. It looked like the letters *D* and *G* were hidden in the bottom right corner. Josephine found *DG* hidden in the rest of the pieces, too, and realized they must be the artist's initials.

"Has Allison seen these yet?" Josephine asked, nodding at the artwork. "She'll appreciate them."

Mary didn't hear her. She sighed and started looking through the clothes she'd dumped on the floor. Josephine continued wandering around the room.

On the fireplace mantel, beside a large brass plate that held a pile of white crystals ingrained with black and blue flecks, was a matching brass bowl. Josephine lifted a small pouch out of the bowl and held it to her nose. It smelled sweet, like flowers.

"Lavender," Mary said.

"Huh?"

"It's lavender. Our late great-great aunt must've loved the stuff, because there's a pouch of it by the fireplace in every bedroom."

A fireplace in every bedroom, Josephine marveled. She nodded and placed the pouch back in its bowl. She took a deep breath and let the air out slowly. It was like she was breathing out a plume of negativity she hadn't even realized she'd been carrying. She felt better than good; she felt great.

Check the closet, she thought out of the blue. She turned around and, for the first time, noticed a door in the wall opposite the bed. It looked like it might lead to a secret room or a hidden tunnel, but she had the unshakeable feeling that it was exactly what she was looking for.

The closet, Josephine thought. *Why do I want to check Mary's closet?*

Why she had thought to check the closet didn't matter, not really. What was in the closet mattered. At that moment, it was the *only* thing that mattered. The voice in her head had convinced her of that.

She brushed the thought aside and crossed the room. Her fingertips were drawn to the closet's doorknob as if by magnets. The doorknob was pleasantly warm to the touch. She turned it. The door swung open effortlessly. Inside was darkness. A string dangled from the ceiling. Josephine pulled it—

Click-click!

—and overhead, a lightbulb turned on, revealing what waited within.

"Mary?" Josephine said. "Have you seen this?"

"Hm?" Mary stood and turned to face her sister. "No. No, I hadn't."

It was a large wardrobe that didn't match the rest of the furniture in Mary's room. The wardrobe's wood was the deepest red, as dark as freshly spilled blood.

Mary joined Josephine and opened the wardrobe's doors. She gasped.

It was filled with the most beautiful clothing Josephine had ever seen.

Mary reached in and pulled out the first top her fingers alighted on, a black silk wrap blouse with a hint of blue woven into the fabric. She slipped it over her head and smiled so wide her cheeks dimpled.

"Fits perfectly," she said.

"You look killer," Josephine said.

"Thanks! What else is in here?" Mary opened the three drawers one after the other. The bottom two were filled with shirts and pants and dresses, but in the top drawer was a jewelry organizer packed to the gills with necklaces and bracelets, rings and earrings. Gold, silver, gemstones, pearls. Everything glittered and gleamed in the light of the hanging bulb.

Mary lifted the top tray and discovered a second tray, equally full, beneath it. She laughed out loud and Josephine joined her. It was a literal treasure trove.

"I was right," Josephine said. "This *must* have been Cinderella's room. Enjoy your newfound riches, m'lady." Josephine made a bow.

"There's more expensive jewelry and fancy clothing in here than I'd have reason to wear in a lifetime, let alone a week. Feel free to use any of it too." Mary returned the jewelry tray and took a step backward, stopping in the closet's doorway and gazing at the wardrobe in awe.

Josephine smiled and waved a hand in the air. "I don't think I'd appreciate it half as much as you. You and this room—this wardrobe, in particular—were made for each other."

From behind Mary's shoulder, a dark shadow with black hair and white teeth leered at Josephine.

Josephine sucked in a choking gasp of air.

In the blink of an eye, the shadow disappeared.

"What is it?" Mary asked in a panic, her eyes wide and terrified. She turned around, saw nothing, and turned back to face her sister. "Josie, what's wrong?"

Josephine's heart pounded inside her chest—*thump-THUMP-thump-THUMP-thump-THUMP*—filling her ears with each beat and her cheeks with blood. She took a deep breath, shook her head, and managed to smile.

"I don't know," she said. "I thought I saw . . . something."

"What, like, a person?" Mary scanned the room a second time, still concerned.

Josephine shook her head again. "No, of course not." She looked at the snow-covered pine trees through the window. "It was just a bird flying by outside."

But it hadn't been just a bird. It hadn't been just a shadow either.

It had been a woman. A pale woman with long, black hair. A smiling woman with plenty of teeth, but no eyes.

Just empty sockets, Josephine thought with a sick feeling in her gut. She felt like she might throw up. *Just two deep holes ringed by blood and flesh and bone.*

"Just a bird," she added quietly.

Mary laughed in relief. She pushed Josephine's shoulder playfully. "You scared the shit out of me."

"Hopefully you'll find some clean underwear in there," Josephine said, pointing at the wardrobe.

"Gross," Mary said. "I hope you don't freak out every time you see a bird or a squirrel or, heaven forbid, a bunny. In case you hadn't noticed, this house is in the woods."

"The woods?" Josephine said, her tone dripping with sarcasm. "Seriously? I didn't see any woods outside. You're kidding, right?"

"Scout's honor," Mary said, raising her hand. "With trees and rocks and rivers and lakes and everything."

"Well, I'll steel my nerves for the next animal crossing," Josephine said. "C'mon. Let's go check out my room. I hear it's pretty cool."

"Who told you that?" Mary said with half a grin, playing along with Josephine's feigned ignorance.

"Little birdie."

"Same one that flew past the window?"

"Ha ha."

Josephine followed Mary to the door and cast a quick glance over her shoulder. The wardrobe shone in the light of the closet, sticking out like a sore red thumb, but at least she didn't see anyone hiding in plain sight. All the same, being alone in the room made Josephine's heart beat a little harder again. "Wait up," she called to Mary, joining her in the hallway.

"That's Mom and Dad's room down there," Mary said, indicating the door at the end of the hall.

There was a hatch in the hallway ceiling near their parents' door. "Is that the attic?" Josephine asked, pointing up.

"I guess," Mary said with a shrug. "But it's not one of the stops on our tour. Probably just filled with cobwebs and dust, anyway. This room is Allison's."

Josephine caught a glimpse of Allison's room, directly across from Mary's. It was a little smaller but looked just as beautiful. The one wall Josephine could see was covered in paintings like the ones in Mary's room.

"Next up is Elizabeth's room," Mary said.

"The *best* room," Elizabeth said as she popped out of it. "I've already unpacked, so don't even think about asking me to trade." She squinted and pointed at Mary and Josephine with exaggerated force.

Josephine rolled her eyes and said, "You know I'm older than you, right?"

"Not only have I unpacked," Elizabeth said, her eyes darting left to right, making it fairly obvious she was looking for another reason to lay claim to her room, "but I just farted in there. Twice. Big ones."

"Seriously?" Mary said with a look of disgust. "What's wrong with you two?"

"What?" Josephine and Elizabeth both said, trying to hold back their laughter.

"You're gross, both of you," Mary said, but she looked like she was trying her best not to laugh too. "If we didn't look so much alike—"

"*I'd think I was adopted!*" Elizabeth said, mimicking Mary's voice and finishing her sentence. The oldest Jagger sister said this every time her younger siblings did something that irritated or disgusted her.

The dam broke, and Elizabeth finally released her pent-up laughter, then Josephine and Mary joined in. Josephine knew Mary appreciated her sisters' sense of humor, even if she'd never be caught dead telling a fart joke herself.

"You seem to have warmed to this trip," Mary told Elizabeth once they had settled down.

"Yeah, well, it's not forever, right?" Elizabeth replied.

Neither Josephine nor Mary answered. Their parents hadn't told them anything official, but they both suspected this week might be a test . . . like taking a car out for a spin before committing to buying it.

"And besides," Elizabeth continued, "it's like I said: I got the best room. The closet is filled with every single instrument I play, plus a few I want to learn. Apologies if I keep you both up at night."

"Nothing but lullabies after eleven o'clock," Josephine joked.

"And this is your room," Mary said as she opened the door across the hall from Elizabeth's.

"Oh, yeah," Josephine said. She stepped inside and set down her backpack. "I could get used to this."

The room was nearly as large as Mary's, had an identical fireplace, and was similarly furnished, including the coziest-looking bed she had ever seen. Josephine wasn't a vain person or especially interested in possessing material things, but the thought of sleeping in her own room every night—no snoring, rustling, or sighs from her sisters—excited her. She could keep the light on and read late into the night if she felt like it, or write in her notebook without worrying she'd wake someone up with the scratching of pen on paper. Story ideas often got stuck in the crevices of her brain in the middle of the night and refused to leave her alone until they were written down.

And there were books in her new room. Hundreds, maybe thousands, all neatly arranged on antique bookshelves that filled nearly every free bit of wall space. Josephine spun around, slowly taking them all in. She felt torn by the desire to race to all four walls at once to examine the titles on each and every spine.

"See?" Mary said with a wry smile. "Told you this was the perfect room for you."

"You weren't kidding," Josephine said. She wanted to say more, but she was a little overwhelmed.

Why—or rather, how—is each room perfect for us? Seems a little too perfect, doesn't it? It was Josephine's own voice, but she quickly silenced it. Questions like that could wait. The books were calling to her.

She started toward the nearest shelf but was interrupted—

Check the closet.

—by a thought that made her turn and walk in a different direction, as if she were on cruise control. She opened her closet door and turned on the light.

Click-click.

Instead of a wardrobe, the light revealed a bookcase even more beautiful than the others. It was made from dark cherry-wood polished to a high sheen and covered in carvings of people and animals reading. The books on the shelves looked older than the books in the room, each bound in leather, their titles and authors stamped on the spines in gold foil. The letters reflected the closet's light as if writ in fire. Many—no, most—were classic fantasies and fairy tales.

Having grown up on a steady diet of Disney movies, Josephine's favorite type of stories were fairy tales. And then, all at once, she was thinking of Helen.

Don't think about her, Josephine told herself, but it was too late.

Helen loved everything Disney—the movies, shows, theme parks—more than anyone Josephine had ever known, even more than Josephine herself. They had been born seven days apart, lived on the same street, and had practically grown up together. Helen was Josephine's oldest and best friend. Until the day, when they were eight years old, that everything changed. They had fought. Helen had done something awful. And Josephine had retaliated. She had gotten into Helen's mind. She had influenced her, hurt her, damaged her. Helen never recovered.

Elizabeth flopped down on Josephine's mattress, jostling Josephine out of her memories, and said, "These beds are like lying on clouds."

Mary moved to the window and looked outside. "Did Allison tell you what she was up to?"

"No," Elizabeth said. "Why?"

"She's outside."

"Oh, yeah, now I remember." Elizabeth rolled off the bed and stood beside Mary. "Not too long ago, she said something about seeing a boy her age in the woods and wanting to go play with him."

"Huh," Mary said. "She's outside, playing, but I don't see a boy."

Their voices sounded muted and distant to Josephine, almost like they were speaking underwater at the far end of a lake. She shook her head, forcing out the memory of Helen, and focused her attention on the books in the closet. She pulled one off the shelf—*Through the Looking-Glass, and What Alice Found There* by Lewis Carroll—and opened it to the copyright page.

"Holy shit," she said.

That got her sisters' attention. They joined Josephine and peered over her shoulders at the book.

"What is it?" Mary asked.

"It's a first edition," Josephine said.

"So?" said Elizabeth.

"So, it's gotta be worth . . . I don't know, like, thousands of dollars."

"*Holy shit* is right," Mary said.

"You could sell it!" Elizabeth said excitedly.

"Are you insane?" Josephine said.

Elizabeth frowned, looking a little hurt and confused. "Well, what else are you going to do with it?"

"I'm going to *read* it," Josephine said, as if it were the most obvious thing in the world. Her eyes drifted over all the rare books from spine to spine, sending shivers up her own. "I'm going to read them all."

The late afternoon gloom gradually gave way to the pitch-black of a winter's early evening, all-consuming in the Middle of Nowhere, Vermont. Without streetlights or steady traffic or apartment buildings, the darkness seemed nearly sentient in the woods, a giant mass that consumed everything in its path—trees, animals, people—and hid them in its belly until morning. The moon tried to combat the darkness, but the clouds had other plans and blotted out its pale blue light.

Josephine sat in a cozy reading chair by her bedroom window, her legs draped over one armrest, reading *Through the Looking-Glass, and What Alice Found There* ("Beware the Jabberwock, my son! The jaws that bite, the claws that catch!"). A standing floor lamp cast a circular pool of soft light around her, making her feel warm, cozy, and safe.

But the darkness hadn't only consumed the woods; it had also consumed the house. And the light of her lamp could only fend off so much. For things hid in the shadows—a *shadow* hid in the shadows. A shadow with teeth. Watching. And waiting.

FOUR

A little less than two hours later, a rich aroma seeped into Josephine's room and made her perk up. It was the smell of something cooking. Dinner. Meat and vegetables. Comfort food.

Her stomach growled as she sat up. She caught her book before it fell and placed it gently on the armrest of the chair. She stood up, left the light of her lamp behind, and entered the darkness.

Josephine stepped into the hall. It was nearly impossible to see anything. The other bedrooms were closed—no light escaped between the doors and their frames. There didn't appear to be anyone else upstairs. A murmur of voices drifted up from the main floor, accompanying the smell of food.

Each stair creaked underfoot as Josephine made her way down. The smell grew stronger, but she couldn't quite place it. Steak? Roast beef? Pork chops? Lamb? It definitely smelled like red meat.

Her hunger grew as she walked through the foyer, past the purple basement door, through the empty kitchen, and into a formal dining room she hadn't yet seen. She wasn't comfortable in Great-Great-Aunt Mercy's house yet, and felt a little like an intruder, the same way she'd felt when they'd first driven through Canaan. Joining her family made her feel better.

Her father and siblings were sitting around a large wooden table. No one looked up or acknowledged her presence. They were shoveling spoonfuls of stew into their mouths, the greasy, reddish-brown broth dribbling down their chins and dripping back into their bowls with tiny *plop, plop, plops*. Even Louisa, seated in an antique highchair at the head of the table, was enjoying the stew as Mr. Jagger alternated between feeding himself and the baby. The slurping, squelching, sucking sounds nauseated Josephine. Not only that, but the smell had soured.

"Watch out, dear," a voice said directly behind Josephine, causing her to jump. She turned and saw her mother, who'd entered the dining room from the kitchen the same way Josephine had passed only a moment ago. But . . . the kitchen had been empty.

"Where'd you come from?" Josephine asked.

"The kitchen," her mother said.

Josephine frowned. Her head was beginning to throb. Things weren't lining up, like a puzzle with pieces that didn't quite fit.

Mrs. Jagger carried an old black pot with a handle. She placed it on a pad in the center of the table. The contents bubbled, and steam wafted up from the surface. Josephine crinkled her nose—the smell was now nearly intolerable, but still her sisters and father were lapping up the stew like starved dogs.

"Don't worry," Mrs. Jagger said. "I made plenty, so everyone can eat as much as they'd like."

Josephine picked up her spoon and dipped it into the pot for a taste. She brought the spoon to her mouth, blew gently to cool it, and hesitated.

"Go on, eat up," Mrs. Jagger said. When Josephine still didn't eat, Mrs. Jagger guided the spoon to her lips and tilted it, forcing the contents into her mouth. The broth was greasy and gamey, two flavors that would normally have turned Josephine off, but as soon as the stew hit her tongue, she felt near starved. She chewed a small morsel of rubbery meat and swallowed. Everything slid down her throat like a small, wet snake.

"What kind of stew is this?" Josephine asked.

"Merry meat," Mrs. Jagger said with a smile.

"What?" Josephine asked, confused.

Mrs. Jagger laughed. "It's ewe stew."

"Sheep?" Josephine peered over the edge of the pot. Her mother had never cooked with sheep meat before. Come to think of it, she'd never made stew before, period.

"No." Mrs. Jagger smiled and laughed some more, as if Josephine had said something unintentionally funny. "Not *ewe*. Y-O-U. It's you stew."

"What?" Josephine said, now more confused than ever. Her stomach clenched, but her mouth filled with saliva. She was simultaneously ravenous and on the verge of throwing up. She tried to cover her eyes to think but her hands failed to respond, and she couldn't peel her gaze away from the pot.

A large hunk of meat rose to the bubbling surface and rolled over, slowly. With mute horror, Josephine realized it wasn't a piece of sheep or lamb meat. Staring back at her—with all the life cooked out of it—was her own face.

It's you stew.

The skin melted and peeled off the skull—*her* skull—in the pot. Her eyes popped one after the other from the heat. Something that looked like a spider's leg—long and thin and black—was sticking out of the jagged flesh where she had been decapitated . . . and then that thing twitched.

"Help me," her head said with a wet cough, spraying a mouthful of stew that covered Josephine's face.

Josephine's mind snapped. Her stomach heaved. There was no time to run to the bathroom, so Josephine closed her eyes and vomited into the pot, bringing up the small piece of her own flesh she'd eaten. She opened her eyes and found she was no more than a few inches from her cooked head.

She retched, backed away quickly, and looked around in a blind panic. Her sisters and father were gone. Only her mother was still in the dining room, watching Josephine, smiling widely. But then her mother twisted and contorted and morphed into something else—*someone* else. The shadow woman.

Josephine expected her to lunge at her with a shriek, but the shadow woman simply stood, and stared, and smiled, which was infinitely worse. And then the walls of the dining room dissolved, and Josephine was lifted high up into the air as the shadow woman continued to smile wide, manic, and ugly.

Josephine woke with a start. The book flew off her chest and skittered across the floor.

"No," she said groggily, jumping from the chair by her window to retrieve the book. She picked it up and checked for damage. Other than a small dent in one of the corners of the cover, it seemed fine. She sighed and placed the book gently on the armrest of the chair, then . . .

Her bizarre, twisted dream came rushing back to her.

It's you stew.

Sick, she thought. *What the hell is wrong with you, Josephine?*
The answer came to her almost immediately. It was so obvious.
My headphones. I fell asleep without my headphones on again.

There was nothing she could do about that—not until she could buy a new pair back home—and it was little wonder she had been tortured by such an awful dream. Her unconscious mind was reaching out and latching on to every stray thought—the weirder, the better—and had twisted them into a nightmare.

Her eyes settled on a brass bowl like the one she'd seen in Mary's room. Josephine plucked a small pouch from the bowl and held it to her nose, inhaling deeply of the lavender contained within. She exhaled slowly and felt settled, then placed the pouch back in the bowl and left her room.

Only one door was open: Allison's. Light poured out into the hallway and Josephine could hear soft brushing sounds from inside.

Josephine poked her head in. Allison was in the corner, blocked almost entirely from view by a large canvas on an easel. Josephine could only see her sister's legs and the top of her head.

"Allison? Hey. How's it going?"

Allison didn't answer.

That's it, not there, nothing but everything, black, black . . .

It was Allison's rambling, nonsensical thoughts, common when she painted. Josephine pictured the net covering her brain. Once she could no longer hear her sister's thoughts, she entered the room and slowly approached her. Josephine called her name again but, like before, Allison didn't answer. When Josephine reached the canvas, she said her sister's name more loudly, but still didn't get a reaction.

It's like she's not even here, Josephine thought. *Or I'm not even here.* An uneasy feeling filled the pit of her stomach and spread through her veins. *Is this another dream?*

What if it's not Allison behind the canvas?

What if it's . . . the woman I've been seeing?

Slowly, so slowly, Josephine peered around the edge of the canvas.

Allison screamed, high-pitched and trilling, causing Josephine to yell as well.

"Josephine?" Allison said with an accusatory tone. She placed a hand on her collarbone. The harmony ball necklace she always wore rattled and chimed—a beautiful sound that seemed out of place at the moment. "What are you doing?"

"No need to freak out," Josephine said, her heart pounding in her chest. "Your door was open. The light was on. I said your name, like, ten times."

Allison slumped on her stool. "I didn't hear you. Guess I was in the zone."

Josephine tried to look at the front of the canvas, but Allison quickly leapt to her feet and stopped her sister. "It's not ready. I'd rather you didn't look at it yet."

Josephine wasn't surprised. Allison was always protective of her works in progress. She shrugged and said, "Sorry."

"It's okay," Allison said. Then, as if she felt a little bad for making a big deal out of nothing, she added, "I'm painting a picture of the house. It has a very expressive face."

"Is that what you went outside earlier for? To find inspiration for your painting?"

Allison looked confused and didn't answer, so Josephine continued.

"Mary and Elizabeth were in my room this afternoon and said something about you playing outside."

Understanding spread across Allison's face. "Oh, yeah. Right. No, I went out to play with Larry."

"Who's Larry?"

"Laurence," Allison quickly corrected. "Only his friends call him Larry. He lives nearby. I saw him in the woods this morning when I looked out a window and found him when I went out exploring. I also found an abandoned house west of here. It was pretty cool. I think I might paint it."

"So you and *Laurence* have become friends, huh?"

Allison nodded.

Josephine smiled. That made her happy. Of all the girls, Allison always had the hardest time adapting to change. If she had already made a friend, well, the week ahead would be a lot easier on her—on the whole family. And if the vacation in the house turned into something a little more permanent, all the better that Allison already knew someone in Canaan.

"Well," Josephine said, pointing at the back of the canvas, "I'm looking forward to seeing this whenever you're ready to share it."

"Probably in a few days. Like Dad said, there's so much out there I want to paint or sketch, and luckily, I found a ton of art supplies in the—"

"Closet?"

"How'd you know?"

"Lucky guess," Josephine said. "It seems like the perfect place for us, doesn't it? For a few days, at least."

Allison nodded. "It's growing on me. Anyway, I'm starving. Let's go see what Mom and Dad are making for dinner."

"Sounds good," Josephine said, then added, "as long as it's not stew."

"Why not?"

"I don't know," Josephine said. And she didn't. It seemed like, maybe, she'd had a bad dream, but that didn't make any sense. Who would have a nightmare about stew? She laughed and said, "Stew would be fine."

It wasn't stew. The girls' parents had made meatloaf with mashed potatoes, carrots, and green beans. Mrs. Jagger had also baked an apple crisp for dessert and found French vanilla ice cream in the freezer. Everyone raved about the meal and went back for seconds or thirds.

"I'm just going to assume that the reason everyone enjoyed dinner so much is because of my culinary skills," Mrs. Jagger said, "and not because Canaan clearly must have an incredible fresh food market."

Mr. Jagger bounced Louisa on his knee. She burped happily.

"High praise," he told his wife.

Everyone laughed.

And for a moment, they were all happy.

Josephine looked at her parents and sisters, sitting together in the family room, and wished she had the magical ability to freeze time. It was perfect, this house. Not only was it large and full of secrets and surprises, but its isolation forced them to spend extra time together.

Forced might be too harsh a word, Josephine thought. She took a sip of hot chocolate and wiped her upper lip clean with the back of her hand. *Encouraged might be better. If I were to ever say it aloud. Which I won't, but still.*

Her mind was beginning to ramble, reminding her how tired she still was, even after her nap.

It's way too early to go to bed, she thought. Curled up in a thick, soft blanket on the couch, she was too cozy to move.

Flames flickered and crackled in the fireplace, filling the room with an intoxicating mix of heat, warm light, and the smell of wood smoke. Shadows danced on the walls.

The wood popped like a gunshot, interrupting the comfortable, dreamy haze of the night.

The sharp sound broke the family out of the collective fugue they'd fallen into. They shifted and blinked, stretched and sighed.

Mr. Jagger was the first to speak. No surprise; the girls all knew he wasn't comfortable with prolonged silences.

"So, one day in," he said softly to not wake Louisa, who was asleep in his arms. "Is everyone still upset that we came here for the Christmas break?" He floated the question to the room, but made a point of looking at Elizabeth and Allison.

"I mean," Elizabeth said in a lighthearted tone, "I haven't checked to see if the guitar in my room is in tune yet, but yeah, this place seems all right."

Mr. Jagger smiled, then looked at Allison. "And how about you?"

A little to Josephine's surprise, Allison nodded. "I think it's going to be a fun week."

Their parents looked even more surprised than Josephine. They both raised their eyebrows and shared a look.

"Well, about that," Mrs. Jagger said.

"There's a chance," Mr. Jagger said.

"A *slight* chance."

"Yes, that's right, slight. Well, we're considering the option of potentially . . . moving here."

None of the girls spoke. Josephine had expected the news, but she hadn't expected her parents to officially propose it quite so soon. She couldn't imagine what her younger sisters were feeling.

"C'mon, girls," Mr. Jagger said, still focusing his attention on Elizabeth and Allison, "say something. It's not that bad an idea, is it?" He looked at Mary and Josephine for support.

When no one answered, Mrs. Jagger picked up where her husband had left off. "I think it's time your father and I were honest with you."

"Karen—"

"It's time," Mrs. Jagger repeated, cutting her husband off. "Maybe a little *past* time."

Mr. Jagger sighed but relented. Mrs. Jagger cleared her throat and ran her fingers through her hair—a nervous habit—before continuing.

"We're running out of money. The employment insurance checks only got us through the first few months after your father was laid off, and then we had to dip into our savings. We've talked about me getting a job in . . . I don't know, some store or restaurant, but that wouldn't stretch very far, and then Louisa would have to go to daycare, and Elizabeth and Allison would have to go to public school, and we'd rather not do that until you enter high school, like Mary and Josephine."

Josephine swallowed hard. It felt like a lump had formed in the back of her throat. She'd assumed from time to time that their finances must have been getting tight, but she didn't want to know the details. She'd been happy to remain blissfully unaware, but now her mother was laying it all out on the line.

"But then," Mrs. Jagger said, "fate smiled upon us for the first time in what feels like ages. This house landed in our laps out of the blue, and at such a perfect time that it seems, somehow, like more than coincidence. It feels like fate. We could sell it, but it would be much less expensive to live here than in Amherst, and your dad and I thought it would be the perfect place for me to continue homeschooling, and for him to finish writing his book while looking for work."

No one said anything for a moment. Mary was the first to break the silence. "I'm willing to give it a shot. What's the high school like here?"

"There isn't a high school, exactly," Mr. Jagger said. "There's one school for kindergarten to grade twelve."

"Seriously?" Mary said.

Mr. Jagger nodded. "Afraid so. I looked it up. There's fewer than two hundred students."

Josephine shrugged. "We'll be able to learn everyone's names real quick."

Mary didn't look convinced that was a good thing.

"It will take some getting used to," Elizabeth interjected.

"We know," Mrs. Jagger said.

"It's a really big change," Allison added.

"We know," Mrs. Jagger repeated. "And we haven't completely made up our minds yet, but if we do decide to move here instead of selling the house, all we ask is that you—all of you—keep an open mind and give it a shot."

"We wouldn't make this decision lightly," Mr. Jagger said.

Mrs. Jagger nodded agreement. "We just want what's best for the family."

Regardless of what her sisters might feel, Josephine agreed with her parents. Moving to Canaan *would* be best for the family. None of them felt any particular affinity for their hometown, and they had so much more space in Great-Great-Aunt Mercy's house.

A voice laughed in her head. *Oh, please. You don't want to move to Canaan because you don't like Amherst or because you like this house. You want to move here to get away from Helen. As long as you're both in the same town, you'll always be afraid that you'll turn a corner and see her, that you'll accidentally bump into her, that you'll look over your shoulder and catch her staring at you, watching you, following you . . .*

Josephine shook her head slightly and rubbed her face. She could try to ignore her own thoughts, but she couldn't dispute them.

"Besides," Mr. Jagger said, with the chuckle he usually reserved for setting up a dad joke, "if the local mechanic can't fix the van, we might be here a lot longer than a week."

A short while later, Mrs. Jagger said she was tired and excused herself to bed. Elizabeth and Allison went to their rooms soon thereafter, and Mary offered to take Louisa, sound asleep, up to her crib in their parents' room. That left Josephine and her father alone.

"Are you thinking what I'm thinking?" Josephine asked.

"If you're thinking about putting some characters through hell and back," Mr. Jagger said, "then yes, I am."

They both left to collect their writing notebooks. Most people wrote on computers or laptops—Josephine once read an article about an author who had written an entire novel on his phone during his morning commute—but Mr. Jagger had instilled in her a healthy respect for the art of writing with pen and paper. "It connects you to your words in a way a keyboard can't," he was fond of saying. At first, Josephine had been skeptical, but she found the more she practiced writing by hand, the more she liked it. She didn't know if she felt more connected to her words, but she did feel it helped her to slow down and ponder more often. If nothing else, she played a lot less computer solitaire, and that had a positive impact on her productivity.

When they returned to the family room, Mr. Jagger held a stack of paper and an old-fashioned typewriter that Josephine had never seen before.

"Where did you get that?" she asked.

"It was in my closet. I thought I might give it a go."

"You never type your stories."

"This is different." He held the typewriter up and looked it over reverentially. "It's not like writing on a computer and, to be honest, I've had a bit of writer's block for a while now. I have a feeling this is just the thing I need to shake things up and get my groove back."

He set it down on the table and started typing almost immediately.

Click-click-click-click-click-click-click-click!

Mr. Jagger laughed. "So far, so good!"

Josephine watched her father write for a moment and smiled. She didn't know what his story was about—he was as protective and secretive about his writing as she was—but it didn't matter. It felt so good to write with him in the glow of the dying firelight, with nothing but woods surrounding the house for miles around.

But then, that happy feeling was doused.

What if nothing comes of this? Mr. Jagger thought. *Writing is probably a waste of time. You're letting the family down.*

"You're not!" Josephine blurted out before she was fully aware that her father hadn't spoken, that she'd accidentally heard his thoughts again.

"What?" he asked.

"You're not . . . ," Josephine repeated as her mind struggled to think of a new way to finish the sentence. "You're not going to give me a sneak peek of what you're writing? Even if I promise to keep it a secret?" She smiled feebly.

He looked at her skeptically, then smiled and laughed. "No way. It's not ready yet. But who knows? If Canaan is as good for my muse as I hope it will be, maybe by New Year's Eve. Sharing a short passage with the family could be a fun way to ring in the new year."

"Fair enough, but I'll hold you to that."

"Deal. I need all the motivation I can get."

Josephine wrapped her brain in her mental net to ensure she wouldn't hear any more of her father's thoughts while they worked, and then threw herself into her latest story. It was about a girl who wakes up one day and discovers that her family is acting a little unusually; she begins to suspect that they might have been swapped with imposters. The minutes flew past as her pages filled with words and her father *click-click-clicked* away on his typewriter. Before she knew it, he was wishing her good night with a kiss on the forehead. He left, taking the typewriter with him.

Josephine put down her pen and rubbed her eyes. The room suddenly felt much colder and darker. She wanted to stay up and keep writing, just a little longer, but she liked the thought of going to her room and being closer to her sleeping family. As nice as it was to have so much space to spread out, she wasn't accustomed to it. Being surrounded by people was what she'd always known, and it would take some time to get used to being on her own. Especially at night.

Each stair creaked as she climbed them. The hallway felt longer than it had in daylight—her parents' door and the attic hatch seemed to stretch away from her as she walked to her own room. She paused and looked at her sisters' doors. Each was closed. All was silent. Josephine entered her room and closed the door.

Sleep was calling to her. It had been a long day. She placed her notebook on the bedside table and ran her fingertips along its familiar cover, then slipped between the sheets. The bed was warm and soft and felt as big as a boat. She started to drift off, but then an idea came to her. It was a little embarrassing, but no one needed to know.

She got out of bed and picked up her notebook, then crossed the room and opened the closet door. There was a very brief flash of movement on the floor, a trick of the moonlight that had looked to Josephine's tired eyes like a snake's tail slithering out of sight. Josephine turned on the overhead bulb, *click-click*, and stepped inside. The rare first editions seemed to call out to her, each vying for her attention. Josephine closed her eyes. She could've sworn she could just barely hear them whispering.

She shifted the books on one of the shelves to the left, making room for her notebook. It gave her a small thrill to see her own words sharing space with Carroll and Montgomery, Grahame and Alcott. Classic authors, her literary idols. She'd leave the notebook there overnight and—

Josephine rocketed forward. Someone had pushed her from behind. She collided with the bookshelf and a few books fell over. She spun around and saw someone she never would've imagined seeing in Canaan—not in a million years.

She saw her old friend, Helen.

"Have a nice night," Helen said. Her lips curled into a smile and she slammed the door shut.

FIVE

Questions filled her head, fighting for her attention. Josephine ignored them; they could wait. There'd be time to ponder what had just happened—and *how*—later. Her immediate concern was getting out of the closet.

She turned the handle and slammed her body against the door. It didn't budge. She took a small step back, her shoulder throbbing in pain. Another thing that would have to wait.

Josephine couldn't recall seeing a lock on the door. Had someone barricaded her in?

Not someone, Josephine told herself, *but Helen. Somehow, impossibly, Helen has followed you to Vermont and is holding you hostage in a closet, just like the good old days.*

Soft blue moonlight filtered under the crack of the door. There were two thin shadows on the other side blocking the light. Feet.

"Helen?" Josephine said. "I have no idea what you're doing here. I have no idea how you even got here. I don't know why you've trapped me in the closet. But I don't have any problem with you. I'm not even angry, not about this or anything that happened in the past. I just want out."

Helen didn't answer, but Josephine saw one of the shadows— one of the feet—shift slightly. That subtle movement curdled the marrow in her bones. It was another indication that this was really happening, that she wasn't imagining things.

"Helen?"

Panic and anxiety filled Josephine like ice water injected straight into her veins. Claustrophobia was rearing its ugly head. The chill worked its way into her chest. It was getting difficult to breathe. How much air was in the closet? How much time did she have before it ran out?

"Please let me out."

Still no answer.

"Please, please, *please*. Open the door."

Nothing.

The ice water feeling wrapped around her heart and squeezed with every beat. Josephine balled her fists as her panic tipped over the edge. She banged on the door with all her might and screamed as loud as she could.

"Helen! For fuck's sake, open the door right now!"

The shadow feet disappeared.

"I'll see you in the morning, Josie," Helen's whispery voice said from the other side of the door. "Then again, maybe I won't."

"Don't leave me in here!" Josephine said desperately. She tried the door one more time, but it still wouldn't open. A tear slipped down her cheek. She turned and put her back against the door, then slid down to the floor and sobbed.

Time passed. How much or how little, Josephine couldn't say. She cried, banged, yelled. None of it mattered. Helen didn't let her out. No one came to her rescue. Josephine drifted to sleep and woke with a pulse-pounding start, only to do it again, and again, and . . .

She was asleep when she first felt something tickle her forearm.

Josephine woke up, but kept her eyes shut. *You're not alone,* she thought, with a weight in the pit of her stomach.

She recalled thinking she'd seen something that looked like a snake in the closet.

That better have been a trick of the light, she thought desperately. *On top of everything else, I can't be stuck in here with a fucking snake.*

But then she heard breathing. A slight whistle of air, in and out, in and out, in and out, nearly imperceptible at first but impossible to ignore now that she had detected it. *Human* breath.

Open your eyes.

It was a command—someone else's thought—so invasive and powerful that she couldn't disobey it.

Josephine opened her eyes and immediately covered her mouth, stifling a sob.

The shadow woman was leaning over Josephine, her black hair dangling down, dragging across Josephine's skin.

Double, double, toil and trouble. The woman's thoughts penetrated Josephine's skull. She tried to cover her brain, but no luck. *Wakey-wakey with a tickle-takey.*

The woman's rhyme seemed to please her, and her smile widened. Even without eyes, she seemed to stare at Josephine. More than that, she seemed to stare *into* Josephine.

"Who . . . are . . . you?" Josephine managed to choke out, each word a coarse lump of sand that clung to the sides of her dry throat.

The shadow's smile faltered, just a little, then spread again. "You can see me?" she asked. Her voice was a strange mix, both playful and threatening, like honey-coated poison.

Josephine had heard that voice before. Back when they first arrived. With a heartbeat. In the house. *Merry meet, Josephine*, the voice had said. It hadn't been her imagination.

With a nod, Josephine said, "I can see you."

"Fascinating," the shadow said. "Simply fascinating. I *thought* you could. Yes, I thought you saw me standing behind your sister as you ogled my jewelry. But I didn't believe it. Not then. But now I do. And even still, it's hard to believe." Her smile grew even wider—impossibly wide. It was more a gash across her face than a pair of lips, unnatural and painful-looking.

Josephine's lip trembled, and she sucked in a few ragged, sputtering breaths, like a five-year-old child with a skinned knee.

"Is this real?" she asked, her voice sad, scared, and quiet.

"That depends," the shadow said. "The mind is a powerful thing . . . so powerful that it can trick itself. You can believe what you want. I can help you. I *want* to help you—you *and* your family. They can't see me. They will never know I exist. And you don't have to, either. Some say *the truth will set you free*. Ridiculous. The truth will weigh you down, drown you, tear you apart."

Josephine had no idea what the shadow was talking about. The fog of fear clouded her thinking, her vision, her brain. All she wanted was out. Out of this conversation, out of the closet, out of her own skin. She stared at the closet door and willed it to open, wished and hoped and pleaded for a way out . . .

The closet door rattled.

Was that me? Did I . . . ? No, it must have been Helen, or one of my sisters, or . . .

Whoever had rattled the handle, had the shadow woman noticed?

But the shadow kept talking, rambling, hissing. "Dreams are better than reality. So are nightmares. Reality is horrifying. Dreams and nightmares—they aren't. Not once you wake up, anyway. Do you want to believe this is nothing more than a nightmare? I can make that happen. With a snap of my fingers." She rubbed her thumb and middle finger together for emphasis, but instead of a healthy *snap*, the sound was a brittle *click-click* of long nails, old bones, and leathery skin.

There was no air left in the closet. The walls were sweating. Josephine felt as if she would pass out.

"You don't even need to say anything. Just nod. But listen. If you want me back, if you need anything—*anything*—you call Dorcas, and I'll return. But for now, for this to be only happening in your mind, in your sleep, you nod your head. And you'll wake up in bed. And this will be a bad dream, slow at first to forget, but it will fade, it will be gone, and then . . ."

Josephine didn't wait for the shadow—for Dorcas—to finish her sentence.

She nodded.

She woke up.

Josephine sat up on the floor of the closet . . .

No, that wasn't right. She was sitting up in bed. *Her* bed. In her room. With early morning sunlight streaming in through the windows and the smell of breakfast cooking downstairs.

She rubbed her eyes and wondered why she had thought she was in the closet—

Her dream. No, not a dream—a nightmare. It had been awful, terrifying. She'd been trapped in the closet by her old friend Helen, a girl she hadn't seen in years, and then there'd been . . . someone else in the closet with her. A woman. A familiar woman, but try as Josephine might, she couldn't quite place her.

Where have I seen that woman before? She thought of all the interactions she'd had with adults other than her parents over the past week or two, but those had been few and far between, since she'd hardly left home during the holidays. The more Josephine tried to place the woman, the harder it became to picture her. Was there something . . . unusual about her eyes? Her mouth? Josephine couldn't remember, and by the time she'd slipped out of bed and walked to the bathroom, she'd not only forgotten about the woman, but about the dream entirely.

Click-click.

Gone.

"Morning, sleepyhead," Mr. Jagger said when Josephine entered the kitchen. He flipped two eggs out of a frying pan and onto a plate. "Nice of you to join us."

"Join you?" Josephine said, happily accepting the plate. "You make it sound like I had a choice. Breakfast smells ridiculously good. I feel like I was lured down here by some sort of dark magic."

"You were, and its name is bacon," Mary said.

Mr. Jagger smiled and continued to flip eggs. "Speaking of which, the bacon is on the table. So is toast, hash browns, fruit salad, coffee, juice . . ."

"I think Dad's trying to fatten us all up, like Hansel and Gretel," Mary said. She slid to the side so Josephine could pull up a chair between her and their mother.

Elizabeth and Allison, seated across the table, laughed.

"It's all this food," Mr. Jagger said, waving at the fridge and pantry. "I can't just let it go to waste."

"I'm not complaining," Mary said.

"Me neither. Is there any salt and pepper?" Josephine asked. There weren't any shakers on the table.

"No, I've checked every cupboard and drawer and there's none in the house," Mr. Jagger said. "But I don't think you'll need it. Try it and let me know what you think."

Josephine was skeptical—salt and pepper on her eggs was a staple. She cut into them and sopped up the runny yolk with some toast and bacon, then sighed as she chewed. "You're right, it doesn't need it. Please thank the lawyer for me."

"You can thank him yourself today," Mrs. Jagger said. "He's due to arrive later this morning."

"Think he'll bring some more groceries?" Allison asked.

"One can only hope," Elizabeth said.

"I think grocery shopping on an ongoing basis is probably a little beneath his salary range," Mr. Jagger said, and then he added, "but I hope so too."

"I swear, it's like your father and I never made you a decent meal before we came to Canaan," Mrs. Jagger said.

"Baba," Louisa called from her highchair. Mrs. Jagger handed her a bottle.

"At the very least, we can ask him where he shops," Mr. Jagger said. "I was able to get an appointment with a mechanic in town to look at the van's engine, and I could pick up a few more groceries at the same time."

"We should also ask the lawyer about . . . ," Josephine said, before allowing her words to trail off with a frown.

"Ask him about what, sweetie?" Mrs. Jagger asked with a curious smile.

Josephine shook her head. "I'm not sure," she said with a shrug. Her cheeks tingled with heat. She wasn't trying to cover anything up—she literally had no idea what she'd been about to say. She grabbed another piece of bacon and shoved it in her mouth.

"Maybe you shouldn't stay up so late writing with Dad," Mary said.

"I disagree," Mr. Jagger shouted with a dramatic wave of his spatula in the air. A piece of egg white sailed a few feet across the kitchen and stuck to the side of a cabinet.

"Careful with that spatula, dear," Mrs. Jagger said. "You're making a mess."

"Forget the mess," Josephine said. "Don't waste the food."

The doorbell rang.

Mr. and Mrs. Jagger exchanged a surprised look. Mrs. Jagger glanced at her watch and said, "If that's the lawyer, he's early."

"Who else would it be?" Mr. Jagger said. "We don't exactly know many people in Canaan."

Mrs. Jagger stood with Louisa, but Mr. Jagger waved her back down. "I'll get it," he said.

Déjà vu, Josephine thought, but what was familiar about this wasn't clear to her. *What is with me this morning?*

And then, like catching sight of something through a plume of smoke shifting in the wind, she had a glimpse of a forgotten memory. When they had arrived yesterday morning, her father had been the first to greet the lawyer.

It felt like it had happened a lifetime ago, but it had only been a little more than a day. Josephine found that hard to believe. *What have I done in that time? Napped, eaten, read, written, slept . . . that's about it.* She'd only seen the kitchen, the family room, the laundry room, the four bedrooms the kids had claimed, and the upstairs bathroom. There was so much house left to explore—a couple more rooms on the main floor, the entire basement, the attic—not to mention the surrounding woods. *I'll have to fix that today.*

A moment later, Mr. Jagger reentered the kitchen with the lawyer. Mr. Finger was dressed like the morning before, wearing a three-piece suit that was the same color as his slick gray hair. His glasses reflected the kitchen's light, obscuring his eyes.

"Good morning, Mr. Finger," Mrs. Jagger said. She stacked a few dirty plates on top of one another, including Josephine's—which still had some bacon and eggs on it.

"Hey, I was still eating that!"

Her mother either ignored her or didn't hear her. "I'm sorry about the mess," she told the lawyer.

"Never you mind," he replied. "I owe you an apology for the trouble of arriving earlier than expected. I was in the neighborhood, you see."

"Of course," Mrs. Jagger said, taking the plates to the sink. She placed them on the counter beside some candles and a box of matches. "It's no trouble at all. Would you like a cup of coffee? Something to eat?"

"I would," Josephine said under her breath, eyeing the sink where her food had been dumped with the dirty dishes.

"Thank you, but I'm quite all right," Mr. Finger said. "I trust you're all enjoying the food we stocked the pantry with?"

We? Josephine thought.

"Yes, thank you," Mr. Jagger said. "The girls can't stop raving about how good everything tastes."

"Ah yes, well, Canaan was founded a long time ago by farmers. And the locals have passed down farming techniques and recipes from generation to generation. They're quite proud of their homegrown crops and locally sourced meat."

"You speak like you don't live in Canaan," Mrs. Jagger said.

"I do now," Mr. Finger said. His face folded with a frown, deepening his already deep wrinkles. "I've lived here for some time, in fact."

"Where did you live before?" Mrs. Jagger asked.

"Massachusetts," he answered quickly, but he shook his head as if that wasn't quite right. "I moved here around the same time as your great-aunt, God rest her soul. Which brings us, of course, to the purpose of my visit." He raised his snakeskin-patterned briefcase, indicating the paperwork that was undoubtedly waiting within. "Shall we move this conversation to the dining room? No need to bore the children with the details of Mercy's estate."

Mr. and Mrs. Jagger agreed and took Louisa with them as they left the kitchen.

Mr. Finger hung back a moment. "I'm sorry we didn't have the chance to formally meet yesterday, Josephine," he said.

"That's okay," Josephine muttered, feeling vaguely uneasy, like she had taken a sip of spoiled milk. That was a good way to describe how the lawyer made her feel . . . like he was slightly *off* and his presence made her a little queasy.

Then she saw something that made her gasp. She covered her mouth.

Everyone looked at her with a mixture of alarm and confusion. Everyone except for the lawyer, who continued to regard Josephine without any change in his expression at all.

"You all right?" Mary asked.

"Yeah, I'm fine," Josephine said, trying to laugh it off. "I thought I saw something that wasn't there."

There was a brief and awkward pause before Mr. Finger wished them all a good day, gave Josephine one last brief glance, and left the kitchen.

Mary expelled a stream of pent-up air and swatted Josephine's shoulder. "You freaked me out. If you're going to see things that aren't there, will you at least do it quietly?"

Josephine laughed and nodded, but as soon as her sisters had stopped paying attention to her, she turned and looked behind her chair, just to make sure. There was nothing there. She could've sworn she'd seen—in the reflection of Mr. Finger's glasses—someone standing directly behind her back.

The shadow.

The shadow had a name, and it came back to her in a snap.

Dorcas.

Fresh air. That's what she needed. Exploring the rest of the house could wait. She needed to get outside.

It was a chilly morning, cold enough to make the snow crunch loudly under Josephine's boots. Large plumes of frosty breath streamed out of her mouth when she exhaled, but the sun was shining and that helped lift her spirits and clear her head.

There was a sloped cellar door jutting out of the ground on the east side of the house. Like the door inside leading to the basement, the cellar door was painted purple, although the paint was faded and peeling from the sun, snow, and rain. Beside the cellar door was a woodpile that looked like it had been there longer than the house. The edges of the logs were dark gray and covered in moss and lichen.

Josephine walked southeast with no real direction or purpose. It just felt good to breathe in clean air, which she found in abundance in the forest. The air smelled noticeably better than it did back in Amherst, where it was tainted by a mixture of exhaust from the highway behind her house and whatever was pumped out of the cement factory a little up the road. All she could smell now was fresh snow and pine trees. Her cheeks throbbed red and the tip of her nose tingled. It felt good. She felt alive.

She walked until she could no longer see the house when she turned to look for it, and then she walked some more. A few minutes later, she stopped. She could've sworn she'd heard something moving through the woods, crunching the snow in time with her step. She turned around but there was nothing there, not even a squirrel or a bird.

She moved on and immediately thought she heard someone following her again. *Crunch, crunch, crunch.* She stopped and heard . . . nothing. Was it some sort of echo, the sound of her own footsteps bouncing back to her?

"Hello?" she called, feeling a little silly. No one would answer. She was alone.

"Hey there, sis!"

Josephine flinched as someone leapt out from behind a pine tree. It was Allison, wearing her favorite green coat. Although it was concealed, Josephine could still hear the familiar chime of Allison's harmony ball necklace.

"Allison! Don't scare me like that!"

"Sorry," Allison said, her smile flipping to a frown. "You're super jumpy lately."

"Yeah, well, there's been a lot on my mind."

"Mine too. Like, where's Larry? Have you seen him?"

"Who's Larry?"

There was that overwhelming sense of déjà vu again. *I think we've had this same conversation*, Josephine thought. *Why can I barely remember it?*

"Oh, right, he's this kid I met yesterday. Lives nearby. His name is actually Laurence—only his friends call him Larry." Allison must not have remembered their previous conversation either, because Josephine now definitely recalled her sister telling her the very same thing only the day before. "We're playing hide-and-seek. He's better at hiding than seeking. Like, *super* good. I can never find him . . . not until he wants to be found. He's like a ghost or something."

Memories were coming back to Josephine slowly, piece by piece. She covered her eyes, which helped her focus, as Allison peered behind trees and snow-covered bushes. Mary and Elizabeth had said something about Allison playing outside with a boy, and Josephine had talked to Allison about it while Allison . . . while she painted.

"Well, have fun," Josephine said, deciding to drop it. She had come outside to clear her head, but now her temples were beginning to throb. "I haven't seen anyone, but I'm sure you'll find Laurence soon. He's just a boy after all, and no boy can stay hidden forever."

"Thanks, Josie!" Allison bounded off, her head whipping left to right.

Josephine laughed a little as she watched her sister prance through the snow like a deer on a mission. She carried on in the direction she had been heading before the chance encounter with Allison.

There seemed to be no end to the forest. It stretched in each direction as far as the eye could see. She broke through some thick brush, half expecting to see something new—a farmer's field, a neighbor's house, a country road—but was met with more forest. Which suited her current mood perfectly. Nowhere to go, nothing to do. She was free.

Josephine stopped and took a few backward steps. Something had caught her eye—an odd marking on a tree. Maybe nothing more than an irregular growth in the bark, but she was curious. She approached the marking and examined it more closely.

It wasn't created by nature. It was made by a person, no doubt about that. It was faded, dark, old enough to trick the eye into thinking it had always been a part of the tree. It was a carving of a star, like the stars she'd drawn when she was a little kid—one long connecting line that crisscrossed over itself. Five triangles forming the points, with a pentagon at the center.

A pentagram, Josephine thought.

She removed one glove and ran her fingers over the carved lines, then shivered and pressed her hand into her armpit to warm her fingers. The tree was colder than she had expected.

She suddenly felt like she was being watched. Josephine looked to her left and right. There was no one there, but she saw another carving on a tree about six feet to her left. She walked to the tree and discovered the carving was another pentagram, also created a long time ago.

Josephine looked farther to her left. There were nearly identical markings on at least three more trees that she could see. To her right, she saw the first marking she'd noticed, and two more beyond it.

It was like they were forming some sort of barrier in the woods.

"Hello," a girl's voice called out softly from behind.

"Allison," Josephine said as she spun around. "What did I tell you about sneaking up on me?"

But it wasn't Allison.

It was someone else. A stranger.

SIX

"Who's Allison?" the stranger asked. She looked the same age as Josephine.

"Oh, hey," Josephine said. "Sorry, I heard your voice and thought you were her. Allison is my sister."

"Sorry to startle you. You seem a bit on edge."

"You're not the first to say that," Josephine said.

"Having a bad day?"

"Not exactly," Josephine said. "More like a confusing day. My mind's been a little mixed up since we came here." Something about the girl made Josephine feel relaxed and at ease. She instantly felt like she could trust her, even though they'd just met and she didn't even know her name.

"I'm Dorothy, by the way," the girl said, offering her hand.

Josephine shook it. Dorothy's hand was ice-cold.

"Nice," Josephine said. "Like *The Wizard of Oz*."

"Would you believe I've never seen it? I always wanted to."

"I've watched it more times than I can count," Josephine said. "The book is even better."

"Isn't it a kid's book?"

"Yeah, but it's a classic, and you'd be surprised how violent it is."

"Really?" Dorothy asked. "I haven't heard that before. My childhood's a bit of a blur."

"Oh yeah, absolutely. Most classic children's books and fairy tales are pretty gruesome."

"You must be a big reader."

"Absolutely." Josephine thought of the closet full of rare books and realized she hadn't yet told Dorothy why she was in Canaan—she hadn't even told Dorothy her name. "I'm Josephine. My family and I are staying for the week in the house that way." She pointed northwest. "It used to belong to a distant relative, but she died, so it's ours now."

The girl turned to look in the direction Josephine was pointing. Her eyes widened. "The old place?"

"You know it?"

The girl nodded. "Of course. You can't grow up in Canaan without hearing a story or two about the creepy old house in the woods. I live nearby, that way." She pointed southeast, the direction Josephine had been heading.

Josephine laughed, hating the way it sounded a little nervous. "What stories have you heard?"

Dorothy scanned the woods and asked, "You sure you want to know? If I was staying there—"

"I definitely want to know," Josephine said, interrupting Dorothy. *I need to know.*

Dorothy lowered her chin and eyed Josephine sideways. She fidgeted and rubbed her right hand with her left. Josephine noticed a pair of small, dark, circular scabs on the side of her right forefinger. Her skin was red and looked like it might be infected. Dorothy shoved her hands in her pockets.

"All right, I'll tell you, but fair warning: I guarantee this is a hell of a lot more violent than any children's fairy tale you've ever read," Dorothy said. "The man who used to live there many years ago was a blacksmith and an alcoholic. One day, drunk out of his skull, he snapped and killed his wife and their baby girl. Used a sledgehammer and pulverized their skulls like ripe melons, then passed out on the floor beside their bodies. Woke up the next morning in a puddle of his own vomit and his family's blood. Although he was filled with regret, he was more concerned that he'd get caught, so he put their bodies on his anvil—first his wife, then his daughter. And . . . well, he used his tools—chisels, tongs, saws—to break their bodies apart, piece by bloody piece. They say he had to drink twice as much booze as the night before to get through it, but somehow he did. By the end, he had a pile of flesh and bones up to his waist, but he was still scared someone would find the remains and identify who they belonged to, so he . . . this next part is really fucked up."

"Go on," Josephine said, her voice cracking.

Dorothy took a deep breath. "All right. They say he lost the last shred of his sanity that day and shoveled the pile of gore into a large black pot in his basement. He boiled it down for days until the stew was good and thick, and then he ate it spoonful by bloody spoonful, until, eventually, his wife and child were no more."

Josephine felt her stomach churn, recalling fragments of a similar dream she'd had. *It's you stew.*

"What happened next? Was he ever caught?"

Dorothy shook her head. "He didn't live long enough. He killed himself."

"How?"

"Made a batch of fresh cement and sealed himself inside the basement wall." Dorothy fell silent and stood stock-still, then burst out laughing. "Crazy, right?"

Josephine felt her heart hammer, as if it had stopped beating some time before and had only just revved back to life. "Yeah, crazy." She laughed meekly.

"And obviously complete and utter bullshit," Dorothy said. "This town is boring as hell. Kids will do or say just about anything for a little entertainment, and what's more entertaining than a family story of murder, cannibalism, and suicide?"

I can think of a few things, Josephine thought. With a shrug, she said, "You certainly won't see anything like *that* in a Disney movie."

"Told you it was more violent than your beloved fairy tales!" Dorothy laughed some more. She looked at her watch. "Telling it sure does pass the time, though. Hey, your sister—Allison, right?"

"Yeah," Josephine said, curious where Dorothy was headed.

"Does she have hair the same color as yours, only shorter and curlier?"

Josephine nodded.

"And a bright green coat?"

Josephine nodded again, a sense of dread pooling in the pit of her stomach. Maybe it was just the blacksmith story rattling around inside her skull, but for some reason she was afraid Dorothy was about to tell her something bad.

"I saw her yesterday. Playing in the woods. Does she like to draw?"

Josephine exhaled in relief; she hadn't been aware that she'd been holding her breath. "Yeah, she's an artist. Of my whole family, she was the most upset about this trip, but I think the woods are growing on her quickly. She's already made a friend. Maybe you know him—he must live around here. Laurence?"

Dorothy's pale skin went one or two shades paler and her eyes widened. But she pinched her lips together and didn't say a thing.

"What is it?" Josephine asked. "You do know him, don't you?"

Dorothy shook her head violently, as if the very thought of knowing Laurence disgusted her.

Josephine laughed awkwardly. "C'mon. What's the big deal? He's just a boy. Right?"

"He's not *just a boy*," Dorothy whispered.

Josephine's mind raced ahead without waiting for Dorothy's words to keep up. Unchecked, she accidentally reached out and latched onto Dorothy's mind, hearing the girl's troubling thought so loudly it felt like her skull had been pierced by a needle: *He's not a boy at all.*

Startled, Josephine gasped in pain. She covered her brain in its net. Thankfully, her headache receded immediately, but Dorothy's unspoken words remained. *Not a boy at all?*

Dorothy continued before Josephine asked her what she meant.

"He's dead."

The ground seemed to shift beneath Josephine's feet, as if the earth had just tilted off its axis. She shook her head. She must've misheard Dorothy.

"He died. Years ago," Dorothy said. "I see him sometimes, in the woods, drifting between the trees. I didn't think anyone else could see him. I thought I was the only one."

"He can't be dead," Josephine said flatly. He couldn't be. There was no such thing as ghosts.

Not true, a voice in Josephine's head said. *You've seen a ghost yourself. A shadow . . .*

She shook her head. Her mind was filled with patches from peculiar dreams—*nightmares*—that were masquerading as memories.

"Ghosts aren't real," she said, more for her own benefit than Dorothy's. "My sister knows his name. She's . . . she's *talked* to him."

"I used to think ghosts weren't real too, but I soon realized Laurence wasn't a normal boy. I thought he must be imaginary, something in my head. But I saw him too often for that. And if your sister has seen him too, well, he can't be a figment of both of our imaginations, right?"

"But she's with him right now. They're playing hide-and-seek."

"Did you see him yourself?"

"Well, no, but—"

"You haven't seen him because he's not really *there*. Not like you and me and Allison. He used to live west of your house."

The abandoned house Allison told me about, Josephine thought.

"These woods are haunted," Dorothy said, looking around in a wide circle, "but most people can't see the ghosts. That's what my grandma says. She has the ability, and so do I."

Josephine scanned the forest, trying to convince herself that Dorothy's claims were nothing more than another story, like the blacksmith who killed and ate his family. Just another Canaan legend. If she could just find Allison and talk to Laurence, she could prove Dorothy wrong and put this shit to rest. She could—

Something Dorothy had just said sunk into Josephine's brain.

Most people can't see the ghosts.

Not ghost.

Ghosts.

She turned slowly to face Dorothy. She dreaded the answer, but needed to ask the question all the same. "You're telling me there's more than one?"

Dorothy said nothing. She looked sick to her stomach. Worse than that. She looked scared to death.

Josephine was growing agitated. Dorothy couldn't continue dropping vague tidbits without explaining herself—especially if Allison was in danger.

Oh, God. She hadn't considered that yet, not fully, not completely. *Is Allison in danger?*

"Dorothy, look at me," Josephine said.

Dorothy looked up. Her eyes were wet and her lips trembled as she spoke. "Forget I said that. Forget I said anything, okay?"

"No," Josephine said. "You have to tell me: Is there more than one ghost in these woods?"

The wind picked up, shrieking through the trees, rustling leaves and creaking branches.

"There are two," Dorothy said quietly. She immediately looked side to side, as if afraid one of the two might be listening.

Josephine saw another sudden flash from a nightmare. Dark hair. A wide smile. Black pits for eyes.

And she knew—whether she wanted to admit it or not—that the shadow woman wasn't just a part of her dreams. She was a part of her reality.

"Who is she?" Josephine said.

Dorothy frowned. "How do you know the other ghost is a woman?"

"I need to know who she is," Josephine said, more forcefully than before.

"Have you seen her too?"

Josephine nodded.

"Her name's Dorcas," Dorothy said.

Josephine had forgotten the ghost's name yet again. She repeated *Dorcas* in her head three times, envisioning the name being stamped into the grooves of her brain, hoping it would stick.

"She lives in your house," Dorothy continued. "Sorry, no. She *haunts* your house. She hasn't *lived* there for a very long time."

Josephine closed her eyes, swallowed, then looked at Dorothy again. "Do kids tell stories about Dorcas too?"

"No," Dorothy said. "None of my friends have ever mentioned her. I think I'm the only one who knows about her. Well, now you do too. And while I don't believe the blacksmith story, I know for a fact Dorcas is real."

"I have to go," Josephine said suddenly.

"What? Why?"

"Allison is out there somewhere, playing hide-and-seek in the woods with a ghost, and the rest of my family is home alone with Dorcas."

"Wait!" Dorothy said, scanning the woods behind Josephine's back. "Did you hear that?"

"What?" Josephine turned around but saw nothing. "I didn't hear—"

There was a crack of a twig and a crunch of snow.

"Someone is coming," Dorothy said.

A shiver spread up Josephine's spine.

"You can't go back that way right now," Dorothy said, "and we can't stay here."

Josephine nodded, suddenly feeling helpless and small, thankful she had met Dorothy. "Where should we go?"

"Follow me."

They ran for a little less than a minute before arriving at a small fort made from thick branches lashed together with rope. The jagged ends of each branch were dark gray, and the walls looked about ready to cave in on themselves. It could have been straight out of a fairy tale, the ramshackle dwelling of a goblin or a troll. The fort had no windows, and Josephine didn't see any way in.

Dorothy gripped one of the branches and swung a hidden door outward, brushing the snow on the ground aside like a child's solitary angel wing.

"Get in," Dorothy said. "Quickly."

Josephine caught sight of a country house not too far in the distance, a plume of smoke drifting lazily from its chimney, before she ducked her head and followed Dorothy into the fort.

The walls blocked the wind, but the gray darkness made Josephine feel a little uneasy. The ground was dirt, frozen solid, and there were toy trucks and mud-caked action figures strewn about. There were two wide logs near the back, standing up on their ends like stools. Dorothy sat on one and Josephine sat on the other.

"Who do you think that was?" Josephine asked. She wiped her nose on the back of her glove and tried to steady her breathing.

"I don't know," Dorothy said. "One of them—Dorcas or Laurence. Whoever it was, they were listening to us. And watching us."

Josephine sighed. "How is this my life now?" The appeal in visiting Canaan—in possibly living in Canaan—was waning fast.

"Welcome to Canaan," Dorothy said.

Josephine nodded. She couldn't think what else to say, so decided to change the topic. "Did you build this fort?"

Dorothy nodded. "Years ago, when I was a little kid."

"Cool. I would've killed for something like this when I was younger." A getaway, an escape, a place of her own.

"My dad helped me build it. My grandma too." Dorothy smiled. "She said every girl should have a safe place. Somewhere to go where she can be a kid forever."

"Like Peter Pan never growing old in Neverland," Josephine said.

"You're totally obsessed with fairy tales, aren't you?"

"Guess I've never really grown up either," Josephine said with a smile. Some kids back home teased her, called her a nerd and a bookworm like those were bad things. "My dad and I never built anything like this, but we write together."

"Is he an author?"

"Well, no," Josephine admitted. "Not officially. He wants to be, and he's a really good writer, but he hasn't had anything published yet. He's working on a new book. We're from Amherst . . . but he thinks he can get a lot of writing done here. Mom homeschools Allison and Elizabeth—she's older than Allison by a couple of years—while looking after our baby sister, Louisa. My older sister, Mary, and I are in high school. She's graduating in June, but I have one year left." She laughed, a little embarrassed. Something about Dorothy made Josephine feel like opening up, like they had already met. "I can't believe I'm telling you all this. You must be bored to death."

Dorothy laughed and said, "That's funny." She shook her head. "I'm not bored, promise. It's actually pretty interesting. You have a big family. It's just me and my parents, and my grandma when she comes to visit. If your dad hasn't had any books published, how do you buy, like, groceries and stuff?" A look of shock at what she had said spread quickly across Dorothy's face. "Sorry. I shouldn't have asked that."

"It's okay, I don't mind. Dad used to be a librarian, but his branch closed and he was laid off. He's been looking for another job, but it's been months."

"There's a small library in town," Dorothy said. "It's super old, but it's all right. I go there sometimes."

"Maybe I'll check it out sometime this week," Josephine said.

"Maybe your dad could get a job there, if you end up moving here."

Josephine nodded and shifted on her log, feeling a little like Absolem, the blue caterpillar in *Alice's Adventures in Wonderland*, sitting on his mushroom stool. *Don't tell Dorothy that—she already thinks you're a bit too much into fairy tales.*

A short silence passed between them. Josephine's thoughts turned back to the woods, and what lived in them. "Are you sure we're safe in here? It doesn't look too . . . solid."

"Positive," Dorothy said. She pointed to the door.

Josephine turned and saw a pentagram carved into it.

"That will protect us from Dorcas, and I wear this on me at

all times just to be safe," Dorothy said. Out of her shirt, she pulled a necklace with a small wooden pendant with a similar pentagram, then tucked the necklace back out of sight. "My grandma gave it to me a long time ago. She's the only person who believes me about Dorcas. She's always said that as long as Dorcas haunts these woods, I need to be careful."

That raised more questions, but first Josephine wanted to know more about the ghost. "What do you know about Dorcas?"

"She's evil," Dorothy said, her voice hushed. "Pure and fucking simple. Did you notice the pentagrams on the trees?"

"Yes."

"They go all the way around your great-great-aunt's house, encircling it. They were carved a long time ago by townsfolk to form a protective barrier."

"To keep her out?"

Dorothy shook her head and brushed a strand of her dark hair away from her eyes. "Not exactly. To keep her in."

In her house. In my house. "If no one else can see her but you and your grandma, how do you know? Did your grandma tell you?"

Dorothy nodded. "I also read about it in the library. I was there one day after school, killing some time, and I wandered into the local history room. There was an open book on the table—really big and old. The cover was made of red leather and its pages were yellow, like an old map. The words weren't typed, but handwritten in dark ink. The wind blew through an open window and the pages fluttered and turned, skipping ahead a bit. They stopped on a drawing. Of her."

Josephine drew in a sharp breath, a feeling of dread brewing in her stomach.

"I recognized her immediately, since I'd seen her before," Dorothy said. "In the woods. Always on the other side of the stars. Hiding behind trees. Looking out at me from the windows of your house."

A new, unexpected voice called out in the forest. "Pumpkin?"

"Shit," Dorothy said. "That's my mom. I hate it when she calls me that. You have to go. She's really weird with new people and—"

Josephine barely registered Dorothy's mom's voice or what Dorothy had just said. "What did you learn about Dorcas in the book?"

Dorothy spoke quicker and with more urgency. "She lived way back in the 1600s. Her full name was—is—Dorcas Good. And you might not believe this, but she was the youngest person accused of witchcraft during the Salem witch trials. I think she killed some people or put a curse on them or something, and she's continued sacrificing people ever since she died."

You call Dorcas, Josephine thought, *and I'll return.* "She was . . ." The words got stuck and she had to clear her throat before finishing her question. "A witch?"

Dorothy winced as if she'd been accused of witchcraft herself. "Allegedly. It makes sense, though, doesn't it? How many other people stick around after they die? How many other ghosts are repelled by pentagrams? And how many other people gouge their own fucking *eyes* out, but can still somehow *see*?"

"Cursing and sacrificing people . . ." Josephine reeled as her mind raced. "Shit. Shit-shit-shit. What if there's some truth to the blacksmith story? Maybe Dorcas got into his head and made him do what he did. And if so, what's stopping Dorcas from doing it again?"

"Your family's in serious danger," Dorothy whispered.

It was as if Dorothy had read Josephine's mind and said what Josephine herself was too afraid to say.

"Pumpkin?" Dorothy's mother called, sounding a little closer than before. "Are you out here?"

Dorothy looked frantic. "Look, your family is in trouble and my mom is strict and overprotective and a little bit psycho, so you have to go, like, now! Run!"

Josephine broke free from the terror that had frozen her. She left the fort and ran.

As she tore through the woods, the question she'd asked Dorothy nagged at her: *What's stopping Dorcas from doing it again?*

But with every bend of her knee and every pump of her fists, with every footfall in the snow and every pounding heartbeat, one word answered that question on a seemingly endless loop:

Me, me, me, me . . .

Josephine would stop her. Josephine would protect her family. Even if it killed her.

PART TWO

SEVEN

Josephine ran. Blurred thoughts, fueled by fear, whipped through her head. Her lungs burned and her heartbeat pounded in her eardrums. The trees flew past as she weaved around them. She didn't slow when she passed the star carvings or even as she approached the house. For an impossibly long moment, the house appeared to be retreating as she ran to it and then, just when she began to think she had lost her mind, she was suddenly on the front porch.

Josephine barged through the front door and collided with her father.

"Whoa!" he shouted as he struggled to keep his balance.

Josephine bounced and rolled off her father, tripping over his foot. She reached out and tried to grab hold of his arm, but she was moving too fast. She caught a brief glimpse of her mother and the lawyer standing behind her father, looking on helplessly, as the world tilted. The back of her head struck the edge of the hall table and stars flashed in front of her eyes—stars made up of five triangles and a pentagon—in a violent burst of blinding light before everything went pitch black.

Josephine woke up in her bed. She sat up suddenly, winced, and lay back down. Her head was pounding.

"Oh, thank God," her mother said. She was sitting at the foot of the bed.

"You're okay," her father said, and Josephine wasn't sure whether he was telling *her* that, or himself. Either way, he was clearly relieved. "I thought . . ."

I thought you might not wake up at all, Mr. Jagger thought. Josephine quickly slipped a net over her brain, shutting out any further thoughts.

"What happened?" Josephine asked. Things were hazy, but she had been with . . . what was her name? *The Wizard of Oz* . . . Dorothy. They had talked about the ghosts that haunt the woods—Dorcas and . . . Allison's new friend, Laurence. Dorothy's mother had called her, and someone was sneaking up on them, and . . . something else she couldn't quite remember, but all of it spurred Josephine into running home.

"You ran through the front door and straight into me as I was seeing Mr. Finger out," Mr. Jagger said. "You tripped over my foot, spun around, and hit the back of your head on the table. You passed out and we carried you up here."

Josephine tentatively touched the back of her head and felt a large bump, but at least her fingers came away dry. "Did you take me to a hospital?"

"No, we . . ." Mrs. Jagger shook her head, then frowned and finished her sentence. "Didn't."

"Um, do you think maybe you should have?"

Mrs. Jagger smiled, a half-grin that wasn't very convincing. "Well, I *think* we thought of it, but then . . . we thought you'd be fine. Right, dear?"

"That's right," Mr. Jagger said, nodding quickly to back up his wife. "You should be more careful, Josie."

Josephine sighed. "Like father, like daughter."

"What's that?" Mr. Jagger said in confusion.

"We both hit our heads."

Mr. Jagger laughed a little and shook his head. "I didn't . . . hit my head." He looked to his wife for confirmation. She looked as unaware as he did.

Dorcas, Josephine thought. *She's to blame for my parents' missing memories. She prevented them from taking me to a doctor. She's messing with everyone's heads, making timelines fuzzy, and who knows what else?*

Mrs. Jagger gave her husband a concerned look. "Maybe she hit her head harder than we feared."

"She hit it hard enough," he replied warily.

"I'm fine," Josephine said. "Really. I don't know why I said that. Maybe it was just a dream." *Maybe all of this, every single fucked-up thing that's happening, is just a dream.* It certainly felt like one, but she knew she wasn't that lucky.

"Are you hungry? Thirsty?" Mrs. Jagger asked. She pointed at the bedside table. There was a ham and cheese sandwich on a plate next to a glass of water.

Josephine drank half of the water and placed the glass back down. It helped with the headache, if only a little.

"Do you remember what got you all worked up?" Mr. Jagger asked.

"Let me think." Josephine covered her eyes. She remembered

plenty, but there was one thing she felt she was missing—something that had scared her more than anything. "Dad."

"Yes?" Mr. Jagger asked.

It was him. She was afraid of him. If Dorcas was in his head—and Josephine had no doubt she was—what might she make him do? "I don't remember," Josephine said. "Probably because I'm exhausted. Maybe I'll remember more in a bit."

Her father looked like he wanted to ask her further questions, but her mother cut him off.

"Of course," Mrs. Jagger said. She squeezed Josephine's hand and smiled with a mixture of relief and worry. "We'll talk more later." She and her husband stood up.

"Before you go, can you get me my writing notebook?" Josephine asked. "It's on the bookshelf in the closet."

"Of course," her father said, crossing the room to retrieve the notebook. He handed it to Josephine. "Going to keep working on your story?"

She nodded. "Maybe after a nap."

"Rest up. Feel better."

"Call us if you need anything."

Her parents stepped into the hall, took one last look at her, and then shut the door.

Josephine immediately turned to a new page and began to write.

Josephine put her pen down and made a fist with her right hand three times in a row, working the stiffness out of her fingers.

She'd filled a page with notes, but by the time she'd reached the bottom, she'd already forgotten what she'd written at the top.

Dorcas Good:
- Accused of witchcraft in Salem as a child. Dorcas killed some people or put a curse on them, has been sacrificing people ever since she died.
- Now a ghost, the shadow woman. I've seen her at least two or three times since arriving yesterday, but somehow keep forgetting. Dark hair, pale skin, wicked grin, <u>no eyes</u>.

Laurence:
- Allison's friend. Calls him Larry.
- Also a ghost.

Stars carved in trees:
- Forming a protective barrier, trapping Dorcas here, keeping her away from town. Same pentagram in Dorothy's old fort and on her necklace.

Dorothy:
- Lives with her parents beyond the pentagrams, grandma knows a lot about witches.
- Dorothy saw picture of Dorcas in the Canaan library, in an old book. Red leather? Local history room?
- Local kids tell a story about a blacksmith who lived in our house. Killed his family, cut them up, cooked them, ate them. Killed himself—sealed in the basement wall. Probably not true, but what the fuck do I know?

Josephine thought of something else she didn't want to forget and pressed the tip of her pen back to paper, then removed it. She had been about to describe not being sure she could trust her dad, but what if he found her notebook and read that?

Instead, she reread her notes. *"What the fuck do I know"* is *right.* Everything she had written was ridiculous, but she was afraid it was all true. And one of the things that scared her most was the way her memory seemed to be working against her, actively trying to purge itself of these facts, these things she'd been told and witnessed herself. If she couldn't remember, how could she do anything?

She needed to keep her notebook close at all times. She needed to write down everything.

Had any of her sisters seen anything unusual? Or were their memories failing them, too, just like her parents' memories were? She'd ask, but she'd need to be subtle, at least at first. If she started with, *Hey, have any of you seen a witch-ghost with no eyes hiding in the shadows?* and her parents overheard her, they would probably put her in the van and take her to the nearest psychiatrist. She also needed to talk to Allison about Laurence.

She got out of bed to go find her sister, and her notebook fell to the floor. As she picked it up, something caught her eye. The book had opened to the story she'd written the night before, only . . . it wasn't what she'd written. At least, not what she *remembered* writing.

With a sickening coil of anxiety clenching her gut, she sat back down on the edge of her bed and began to read.

Once upon a time, there was a young girl who moved to a land far, far away. She was a very special girl and had incredible abilities, but she was afraid she might not always be able to control them. She was afraid she might accidentally hurt her family or friends, so she ran away from home.

She settled in the kingdom's northern forest and built herself a house. But since she didn't have boards or bricks or nails or screws, she built her house out of gingerbread and icing and candy that was thrown away from the village bakery at the end of each day. Every night, when all the town was asleep, the young girl would sneak through the woods under the light of the moon and take as much as she could carry. It took her many years, but eventually, her gingerbread house was complete.

Time passed and the young girl became a young woman. She avoided all contact with other people, fearful that they might discover her secret abilities and she in turn might accidentally harm them. She ate nothing but gingerbread and icing and candy, and she snuck back into town to steal more to rebuild her house every now and again. For a time, all was well.

But more time passed, and the young woman became a middle-aged woman. And she grew sick of sugar and spice and everything sweet.

"Rabbit stew," she would often say aloud, sitting alone in her gingerbread house. "What I wouldn't give for a simple, hearty rabbit stew."

Even more time passed, and the middle-aged woman became an old woman, and she couldn't stomach the thought of taking one more bite of her house. That's when she had a wicked thought.

"Children love gingerbread," she said with a cackle.

The old woman set to work. She broke off pieces of her house and collected them in her basket. And then, under the light of the moon, she snuck through the woods, leaving a trail of gingerbread crumbs leading from the town to her house.

It wasn't long before her plan bore fruit. The next day, a small boy wandered to her doorstep, eating gingerbread crumbs as he went. When he saw the gingerbread house, his eyes went wide and he dropped the last crumb he'd picked up. Without hesitating, the old woman flew through her front door and put a curse on the boy. In a puff of smoke, he was changed into a plump rabbit.

The old woman grabbed the rabbit by the ears before he could hop away and threw him in a pot of boiling water. The rabbit thrashed about in silence, but the thrashing didn't last long. The old woman seasoned the stew and let it simmer for three hours, making the meat nice and tender. Once it was ready, she ate the rabbit stew—every last drop. It tasted better than anything she had ever eaten, but she felt a twinge of guilt. The rabbit stew hadn't actually been rabbit, had it? She cast the thought aside.

"That was good," she said, "but I vow to never, ever do it again."

However, time passed, and the old woman grew older. And hungrier. Try as she might, she couldn't get the taste of the stew out of her mind. And before long, she snuck back outside and laid another trail of gingerbread crumbs between her house and the town. The next day, the old woman ate another pot of rabbit stew, every last drop.

This time, she didn't feel a hint of guilt.

By the time the next full moon rose, the old woman had become an old, plump woman. And she began repairing her house not with gingerbread and candy, but with rabbit skins and bones.

Late one night, sitting by the fire and picking bits of sinew out of her teeth, the old woman gazed into the crackling flames and smiled. But then a sudden thought drifted through her mind.

"Am I a witch?" she asked the darkness.

She shook her head and wiped her greasy palms on her dress.

And then, as if someone was speaking directly into her head, the darkness answered.

"No, you're not a witch. You're an old woman, who used to be a middle-aged woman, who used to be a young woman, who used to be a young girl. And you're still the same person you've always been.

"You're still Josephine Jagger."

Josephine dropped the notebook as if it were a poisonous snake. She half expected to see it transform before her eyes and slither away into the shadows, but of course, it didn't. It lay on the floor at her feet, pretending to be an inanimate object that couldn't hurt her, but she knew better.

Sticks and stones will break my bones, but words will never hurt me.

Josephine shook her head. Falser words had never been uttered in the history of clichéd expressions. Words had the power to bite, to scratch, to tear her apart from the inside out.

You're still Josephine Jagger.

She'd written those words. And they had stabbed her like a knife in the back. Why would she write herself into her own story, and as the villain, no less? How could she have penned an entire story without remembering writing a single word of it?

Dorcas, her instinct told her. Dorcas had crept up behind her while she wrote, held her hand, and guided the pen across the pages. Or worse, maybe she had slipped into Josephine's mind and worked her charms from within. And then, when the story was complete, she must have cast a spell and wiped Josephine's memory. But why? Dorcas would have known that Josephine would find the story and would have no recollection of writing it.

Just to mess with me. Josephine was beginning to believe that Dorcas liked getting into people's heads and toying with them, like a cat with a cornered mouse, playing with it before eating it.

She wrinkled her nose. It was an apt description—a little too apt. What else was she and her family to Dorcas than a meal to be played with?

Dorcas had all the power.

Not all *the power*, Josephine thought. *I know who she is.* She picked up the notebook. *And I have a way to make sure I don't keep forgetting who she is.*

It was a start, but she needed to do more. She just didn't know what else she *could* do.

While developing a plan, Josephine decided she should get to know the house a little better. It was time to complete her tour.

The first stop was the only bedroom she hadn't yet seen: her parents'. Josephine crept along the upper hall with her note-book clutched tightly to her chest.

She pushed the door open. It groaned.

"Hello?" she said. "Mom? Dad?"

As far as she could tell, the room was empty. Hard as it was for her to believe, the primary bedroom was even larger than the rest of the bedrooms. Large, ornate furniture, a wide fireplace, and amateur paintings in gaudy frames on the walls. Without moving in for a closer look, Josephine was willing to bet the initials DG were signed in the bottom-right corner of each.

Inside a crib at the foot of the bed were a few of Louisa's belongings: her favorite blankie, a toy rattle, a rubber giraffe, a pacifier with a duck on it.

"What the . . . ?" Josephine said in dismay.

Peeking out from beneath the giraffe was a baby's foot, a jagged shard of broken bone jutting out from its bloody stump.

Josephine took a step away from the crib and closed her eyes tight. *What has Dad—no, what has* Dorcas *done to Louisa?* She took a steadying breath and then dared another look. *Oh, thank Christ.* It wasn't a dismembered baby's foot but Louisa's lucky rabbit's foot. She let out a deep sigh of relief.

On her way out of the room, she caught sight of the closet. The door was open a crack. There appeared to be a wardrobe within, its reddish hue capturing Josephine's attention and drawing her closer out of curiosity. She looked over her shoulder to verify that she was still alone, then stepped into the closet and turned on the overhead bulb.

Click-click.

She ran her fingers over the smooth surface of the wardrobe, then opened its door.

The typewriter her father had used the night before was sitting on one of the shelves.

I wonder what he actually *wrote*, Josephine thought, thinking of her own story—of gingerbread and witches and kids cooked in pots. *Scratch that. I don't want to know.*

But too late—she caught sight of the page sticking out of the typewriter. It wasn't his novel. It was his work experience.

So I'm forced to write myself as a cannibalistic witch and Dad gets to type up his résumé? Josephine thought with a smirk. *Hardly seems fair.*

She remembered that she wanted to recommend that he apply for a job at the Canaan library.

Guess he's way ahead of me.

The rest of the shelf space was filled with knickknacks, trinkets, and collectibles, but nothing of any particular interest. Josephine was about to close the wardrobe when a pile of small dolls caught her eye.

Josephine picked up the largest one, roughly the size of her hand. It was smooth and a little sticky, like a candle. It was, she realized, made from wax that had been molded and shaped by hand. None of the dolls wore clothing, but their facial details had been intricately carved. Josephine was gazing into the tiny, pinhead-shaped eyes of the doll she held when it hit her.

She was holding her father.

She counted the remaining dolls. All together, there were six. One larger than the others, four medium-sized, and one the size of her thumb.

It's my family, she thought in perplexed horror. *Dad, Mary, Elizabeth, Allison, Louisa . . . and me.*

Josephine picked up the Josephine doll. She had a mouth—*my mouth*—a nose—*my nose*—and ears—*my ears*—but in place of eyes, the doll had two large *Xs.*

She shoved the Josephine doll back onto the shelf with the others, shut the wardrobe, turned out the light—*click-click*—and quickly closed the closet door.

"What are you doing in here?"

It was Helen.

No, it was her mother. Why had she thought it was Helen? That was especially odd since she hadn't seen Helen in years . . . had she?

The memory hit her suddenly. Yes, she *had* seen her. Helen had trapped her overnight in her own closet. Josephine made a mental note to add that to her notebook later.

"Mom," Josephine said, "you startled me."

"I could say the same about you," Mrs. Jagger replied. "I didn't think you'd be out of bed yet, let alone snooping around my room." She said it with a hint of a smile, but to Josephine, her lighthearted expression felt a little forced.

"I'm not snooping, just . . . checking things out. There's still so much I haven't seen yet."

Mrs. Jagger nodded. "Did you find anything interesting?" Her eyes darted to the closet door and back to her daughter.

Josephine pictured her dead-eyed doll but quickly shook her head and looked away. "No, not really. Nice room, though. Like all the others. It's quite the place, this house." She noticed an odd bulge in one of the pockets of her mother's jeans. It looked like she had something hidden within.

Mrs. Jagger followed her daughter's sight line, looked at her pants, then quickly slipped a hand into her pocket as if to conceal whatever she had hidden there. She smiled innocently. "It is. Well, if you don't mind, I think I'm going to take a nap. All this country air . . ." She laughed. "It's going to my head."

"All right, Mom. Love you."

If her mother heard her, she didn't give any indication that she had. Instead, she stopped at her dresser, held a pouch to her nose—*lavender, no doubt*—and inhaled deeply. Then she lay down to sleep.

Josephine frowned as she closed the door. It was only then that it dawned on her that one member of her family was absent from the wax doll collection in the closet. Her mother.

EIGHT

Walking down the staircase, Josephine had to stop and steady herself against the banister. Her head was a little fuzzy, and it felt like the ground was tilting slightly. She envisioned the next stair down suddenly disappearing the split second before her foot stepped on it, sending her tumbling into a black hole, a yawning tunnel lined with sharp teeth that would swallow her whole and keep her prisoner deep within the bowels of the house for eternity with only the blacksmith for company.

"You okay, Josie?"

Josephine exhaled forcefully and jerked her head up. Her father, walking up the steps toward her, took a staggering step backward and grabbed the handrail to steady himself.

"Holy shit," he said, "I almost fell."

"What happened?"

"I don't know. It felt like there was a gust of wind, like someone flew past me. Or rather, like someone flew straight *into* me. Weird." He straightened his hair and cleared his throat.

Josephine peered over her father's shoulder. There was no one behind him. No one she could see. Had Dorcas just passed by them? Josephine hadn't sensed her . . .

Did I somehow knock Dad back?

No, impossible. It couldn't have been me. I've never moved any-thing with my mind in my life.

But then she remembered something she thought at the time had been a dream, but more likely had actually happened. She had fallen asleep in her closet after being trapped in it. Dorcas had woken her up. Josephine had looked at the door, willed it to open, and then . . . the handle had rattled.

"Where's Louisa?" she asked, both to change the subject and out of sudden concern for her sister.

"Huh?"

"Louisa. Mom's sleeping upstairs, so if you don't have her—"

"Your sister is with her," Mr. Jagger said, adding, "Mary."

Josephine sighed in relief, and then wondered why she'd been so freaked out that her dad didn't have Louisa. She and her sisters regularly looked after the baby.

Her lucky rabbit foot. I panicked when I saw it, thinking Dad had done something awful to Louisa before I realized my mistake and Mom entered the room.

"Are you okay?" her father repeated.

"Yeah, I'm fine. It's just . . ."

"Just what?"

It's just so, so much. Josephine sighed. It felt like everyone she cared for was in danger and the world was slowly crumbling all around her. "Does Mom seem okay to you today?"

Mr. Jagger smiled in relief, as if he'd been afraid she was going to say something worse.

If only he knew just how bad things really are, Josephine thought.

"I think she's been under a lot of pressure," Mr. Jagger said. "You know, with me losing my job and her homeschooling your younger sisters and looking after Louisa, and now with this trip and this house. But I think this place is going to be so, so good for her. For all of us. It came along at just the perfect time, didn't it?"

I've heard that before. "Yeah, I guess it did."

Mr. Jagger's eyes caught sight of Josephine's notebook. "Going to do some writing?"

Right, my notebook, Josephine thought with a jolt. *I was going to write something in it . . .*

"That's the plan," she said.

"Cool. Maybe I'll join you later. My book's not going to write itself, you know."

Only, it might. Your story might end up going places you never imagined.

"Speaking of things not writing themselves," Josephine said in a rush, hurrying down the stairs, "an idea just came to me and I want to get started before I forget it."

"Good luck," her father called out as she ran away.

Josephine heard her sisters' voices coming from the family room and kitchen, so she turned left at the bottom of the stairs and entered the dining room. She sat down at the table. It was the first occasion that she'd spent any significant time in the room outside of her nightmare—*it's you stew*—but her focus was on writing down her thoughts before they disappeared. The fact that she'd already begun to forget what had happened in her parents' room by the time she'd reached the stairs was troubling.

She placed her pen down on the notebook to rub her eyes and clear her mind. It rolled onto the table, which was long enough to seat her entire family plus a few guests. Josephine tried to grab the pen, but it fell off the edge, hitting the floor with a hollow *clink*. She got down on her hands and knees and peered under the table. The tip of the pen was visible behind the central supporting leg. Not wanting to crawl through the dust, Josephine stretched out her arm and reached behind the table leg.

Her fingers touched something that crinkled. She recoiled her hand instinctively. Whatever she'd touched had felt like fine paper. There was a hint of brown dust on her fingertips.

What the . . . ?

Before the more logical portion of her brain could voice its concerns, she blindly reached again and picked up whatever she had touched. The moment she saw what it was, she dropped it with a gasp and wiped her hand on her pants.

It was a snake.

But snakes slithered, and this one didn't move. They were scaly, not dried-out. And this snake only weighed as much as an empty plastic bag.

Josephine realized it wasn't a snake, but a snakeskin.

Gross, she thought in disgust. She pushed the snakeskin back under the table with the toe of her shoe.

Footsteps approached. Josephine turned just in time to see Elizabeth walk through the foyer. She wore a rainbow-striped sweater and was playing a flute. Mary walked behind her, wearing one of the dresses she'd found in her closet and holding Louisa's hands up in the air as the baby took tentative steps and squealed in delight.

"What's up?" Mary asked when she spotted Josephine.

"Not much, just writing a bit," Josephine said. "Where's Allison?"

"Where else? She's out playing with her new best friend."

In a stage whisper, Mary added, "I think she has a crush on him."

"Can we talk about that?"

"Sure," Mary said. "As long as you don't mind joining in our parade first. It's Louisa's new favorite game."

Elizabeth struck up her tune again and continued on, leading Louisa, Mary, and now Josephine in a circular path through the dining room, the kitchen, a sitting room, a small office, and into the family room. The girls sat on the couch and chairs, and Louisa, Elizabeth, and Mary laughed in joy. Josephine had a view of the dining room from where she sat. She could see the edge of the table, but the snakeskin was blessedly out of sight. Just thinking about it made Josephine shudder.

"So," Mary said. "What should we do next?"

"I wanted to talk to you, remember?"

"You did?" Mary looked genuinely confused.

"I said so, like, three minutes ago. In the dining room."

"Yes. Right. I remember," Mary said, but nothing in her tone made Josephine believe her. "What's on your mind?"

Josephine thought for a moment, then retrieved her notebook from the dining room and reviewed her notes. "Allison," she said. "And Laurence."

"What about them?" Elizabeth asked.

Where to start?

Laurence: Allison's friend. Calls him Larry. Also a ghost.

Jumping in like that wouldn't do. Josephine knew she needed to broach the subject gently or her sisters would think she was joking, or that she was having some sort of breakdown.

"Have either of you actually seen Laurence yet?" she asked.

Mary and Elizabeth exchanged a look.

"I haven't," Mary said. "Have you?"

Elizabeth shook her head. "No, but so what?" she asked Josephine.

"Don't you think that's a little weird?" Josephine said.

"No, not really," Elizabeth said. "We've only been here a couple of days. And they play outside in the forest, not in here with us. Are you jealous, Josie?"

"What?" Josephine asked, genuinely confused. "What do you mean, jealous?"

"You're seventeen and you've never had a boyfriend."

"Elizabeth!" Mary said with a serious tone and a reproachful look.

"It's true," Elizabeth said with a shrug.

"Trust me, I'm not jealous," Josephine said with a sigh. Elizabeth's comment hadn't bothered her—plenty of boys had asked Josephine out and she'd turned them all down—but she wanted to get back to what was important, and that was Allison's safety. "What has Allison told you about Laurence?"

Mary shrugged. "Just that she made a friend. She told us his name, obviously. And that they like to play hide-and-seek in the woods."

That reminded Josephine. *I saw them—well,* her—*playing hide-and-seek this morning.*

"I still don't see what the big deal is," Elizabeth said.

"I met someone, too," Josephine said. "A girl about my age named"—she glanced quickly down at her notes—"Dorothy. She lives in the next house east of here, about a fifteen-minute walk away. She knows Laurence. She said . . ." *Just say it.* "Well, she said he's dead." Josephine laughed awkwardly, her eyes void of mirth. "She said he's a ghost."

There was a long, awkward pause in which Mary and Elizabeth stared at Josephine. Louisa broke the silence with a burp.

"C'mon, Josie," Mary said as she wiped a small dribble of spit-up off Louisa's chin. "You don't actually believe that, do you?"

"I don't know," Josephine said. "Why not?"

"Well, for starters, that's fucking crazy. And second, *that's fucking crazy*. There's no such thing as ghosts."

"How can you be so sure of that?"

"Do you know anyone who has ever seen one?"

"Yes!"

"Other than this girl you just met."

"No, but—"

Elizabeth interrupted Josephine and jumped into the conversation.

"How do you know this *Dorothy* isn't the ghost?" Elizabeth's tone made it sound like she wasn't fully convinced Dorothy existed at all. "We might not have seen Laurence, but we haven't seen *Dorothy* either." This time she added air quotes with her fingers when she said *Dorothy*.

"You can stop saying her name like that," Josephine said, a touch defensively. "*I* saw her. *I* talked to her."

"And Allison has seen and talked to Laurence," Mary said gently, with a mothering smile that was a touch more mature than her years.

Josephine sighed in resignation. "You have a point." Maybe Laurence wasn't a ghost. Perhaps Dorothy simply had an overactive imagination. Perhaps she was just messing around with Josephine. But even if that explained Dorothy's claim about

Laurence, Josephine felt certain that Dorothy had been telling the truth about the house, and about Dorcas.

Josephine wanted to meet Laurence for herself. Just to be sure.

Elizabeth played a few triumphant notes on her flute and said, "Of course we have a point. You're a storyteller, after all."

"So?"

"So, you're used to making things up. Your imagination is as big as this house, maybe as big as this entire state, which explains why your head is always in the clouds." She played a few notes that Josephine immediately recognized as the opening of "When You Wish Upon a Star" from *Pinocchio*.

Josephine had to laugh despite the undercurrent of anxiety she'd felt all day. She threw a pillow at Elizabeth to get her to stop playing, and all three of her sisters, including Louisa, joined in the laughter.

Elizabeth placed the flute on the coffee table and Josephine stared at it for a moment, her mind wandering. Her sister had been right; her head often *was* in the clouds.

But that's when I do all of my best thinking.

"It's weird . . . ," Josephine said.

"Oh no," Mary said with a grin. "What now?"

Josephine collected her thoughts. "What are the odds that our great-great-aunt Mercy played music, and loved reading and writing and drawing and painting, and had a taste for expensive clothes . . . and just happened to be the exact same size as Mary?"

"Given that she's one of our ancestors," Mary said, "I don't think it's surprising at all. We're an artistic family, and I'm a common size."

"Yeah, I guess," Josephine said.

Mary frowned. "Are you okay, Josie? Do you like it here?"

Josephine nodded. "I do. It's great." She'd already revealed enough to realize saying anything further, at least right now, was pointless. She needed more proof of Dorcas's existence before telling her sisters that she suspected the house was haunted by the ghost of a witch. Telling them about Laurence hadn't gone over well.

She stood up. "Time to get back to writing," she said, a white lie. She wanted to be alone and explore the house a little more. "If either of you see Laurence, come find me. I'd like to see him with my own eyes, just to prove he's not dead."

She had intended it to be a joke, but Josephine's smile faded when her sisters looked back at her in confusion.

"What are you talking about?" Mary asked.

"Not dead?" Elizabeth added.

They had no idea what she meant. They'd already forgotten what they'd just talked about.

Dorcas.

"Never mind," Josephine said.

Other than the attic, there was only one area of the house Josephine hadn't seen yet.

The basement was a dark pit lit only by the ground-floor hallway light behind Josephine. She stood in the purple doorway, her shadow stretching thinly down the stairs, wondering if she really, truly wanted to venture into the depths on her own.

There wasn't a light switch at the top of the stairs, or a string hanging from the ceiling. She spotted a large flashlight on the first step beside the wall. She picked it up and pressed the button.

The light didn't turn on. Josephine smacked the side of the flashlight with her palm a few times. With the third smack, it flickered to life.

Great, she thought sarcastically. *I've got a good feeling about this.*

She shined the light from side to side, slicing her shadow with every pass. Something small and bony at the bottom of the steps retreated from the flashlight's probing beam—and just then, the flashlight turned off. Josephine resisted the urge to scream. She shook the flashlight. It sputtered back on and she shone it at the ground, realizing there was nothing at the bottom of the stairs. What she thought she had seen had been a trick of the light, but it gave her pause.

Stop being such a baby and take a step.

She took a step. The top stair groaned loudly under her weight.

And another.

She did as she was told.

Keep going.

With every creaky step, it got a little easier to continue. But then she reached the ground and froze. Her limbs seized momentarily, as if encased in cement. The air was thick, making it a little difficult to breathe. She'd expected it to be cold, but instead, it was hot and humid and smelled . . .

It smells meaty. And rancid. That was as close as she could get to describing the thick odor that filled her nostrils. There was also a hint of ash. That kind of made sense in a basement like this, but rancid meat? It was like something had died years ago and was still decomposing.

The uneven ground beneath her feet wasn't concrete or wood, but dirt. The walls were made of stone. And she still couldn't see a light switch. There wasn't a single window in the basement. The flashlight revealed a second set of stairs that went up to a sealed cellar door leading outside—she remembered seeing the faded purple cellar door when she went for her walk. Her flashlight passed over a shovel leaning against the wall in the corner and old shelves that held a mix of jars and boxes and loose items—a lifetime or two of accumulated junk.

Maybe more—much more—than two lifetimes, Josephine thought. *The Salem witch trials took place sometime in the late 1600s. Dorcas would've died in the 1700s. There might have been six or seven families who lived here in between Dorcas and Great-Great-Aunt Mercy.* Josephine had a feeling not much about the house had changed since Dorcas had been alive. Had each successive owner kept the same furniture in the rooms, the same art on the walls, the same junk in the basement?

Josephine continued to scan the basement when she suddenly realized she wasn't alone. Someone shined a light back at her. It couldn't be her parents, Mary, or Elizabeth—they were all upstairs.

"Allison?" she asked. "Is that you?"

No one answered.

Because it's only me, Josephine realized. She had shined her flashlight into a mirror. Like every other piece of furniture in the house, it was an antique, a free-standing mirror supported by two wide, wooden feet. The glass was covered in a sheet of dust and strands of matted cobwebs. There was a patch of small, brown mushrooms sprouting out of a crack in its wooden frame.

Mirror, mirror, not-on-the-wall, Josephine thought as she stared at her dusty reflection, *is this the creepiest basement of them all?*

The mirror answered back. It whispered, a brief and strangled sound—words, but nothing Josephine could decipher.

My imagination again, she told herself. But she had a feeling that wasn't true. It hadn't been her imagination.

Josephine's heart began to beat heavily in her chest.

Thump-thump.

Was someone else in the basement with her?

No one else is here. I would've heard them come down one of the sets of stairs.

Maybe it was an animal scurrying through the dirt. Yes, an animal taking shelter to escape the cold of winter. That's what the sound had been. An animal.

Because if it wasn't an animal, and it wasn't her family, the only other explanation she could fathom was that she had heard a ghost.

She shined the light at the ground and turned in a circle, searching down low for the raccoon or opossum or whatever else might have been skulking about in the dark.

The light passed over something small and white. Josephine pointed the flashlight at it. It *was* an animal, she had been right, only . . .

Thump-thump.

The animal was dead. Long dead. It had no fur, no flesh. Only bones.

A rabbit, Josephine thought. *Of course it's a rabbit.*

And it wasn't the only one. As she scanned the floor, the beam from her flashlight uncovered a trail of rabbit bones leading to a pile a few feet high. There must have been two or three—no, four or five dozen rabbits, maybe more—in that unceremonious heap. And beside the pile of bones was some sort of black pot, large and round and—

Thump-thump.

Josephine spun around on the spot. She'd felt eyes on the back of her neck.

There was no one there.

But she couldn't shake the feeling that she was being watched.

Thump-thump.

Thump-thump!

Thump-THUMP!

Something moved across one of the walls. It slipped into a thin crack between two stones. There and gone before she could get a good look, but she had seen just enough to know what it had been. Fingers. Human fingers. Sticking out from within the wall where the fingers—*and the body*—must surely have been concealed.

Holy shit. The blacksmith story is real.

"Stop it," Josephine commanded in as firm a voice as she could summon. *Don't be ridiculous. It was an insect retreating from the light. That's all.* But nothing she told herself calmed her jackhammer heartbeat.

Thump-THUMP!

Her heart pounded against her chest painfully, filling her ears with its beat, nearly drowning out all other sounds. But not quite.

She heard the whisper again, a low moan that became the word " . . . *me.*"

Thump-THUMP!

It was the mirror. The whisper had come from the mirror.

Thump-THUMP!

No, not from the mirror.

Thump-THUMP!

Behind the mirror.

Thump-THUMP!

Josephine's entire being screamed at her to stop, to turn and run out of the basement as fast as her legs could carry her, but her shaking hand acted without her permission and swiveled the mirror on its rusty hinges.

Thump-THUMP!

Hidden behind the mirror—

THUMP-THUMP!

—embedded in the stone wall—

THUMP-THUMP!

—was a faint outline that looked like . . . like a mouth . . . and a nose . . . and an—

THUMP-THUMP-THUMP-THUMP-THUMP-THUMP!

An eyelid.

The eyelid opened.

"Help me," the stone face said.

Josephine screamed, dropped the flashlight, and ran out of the darkness.

NINE

Josephine slammed the purple door shut, crossed the hall, and dropped to the floor. With her back against the wall, she stared at the doorknob and waited for it to turn, for the door to creak open, for the stone man from the wall to lurch out of the basement.

It didn't happen, but in the dead silence, she thought she could still hear her heart beating behind the door, down below, fading away to nothing as if she'd left it in the basement to slowly die.

Thump-thump. Thump-thump. Thump-thump. Thump . . .

"Josie, are you all right?" It was Mary. She was standing beside Elizabeth in the hall, near the entrance to the family room. "I'd just gotten Louisa to fall asleep in her crib. You nearly woke her."

"What's wrong?" Mrs. Jagger asked in a panic as she and the girls' father rushed down the stairs from the second floor. "It sounded like someone was being murdered."

"There's someone in the basement," Josephine said. *The blacksmith. The blacksmith the kids say killed his family. He's real and he's trapped in the walls of our basement.*

"Is it Allison?" Mr. Jagger asked.

"No, someone in the walls."

"Maybe it was an—"

Josephine cut her father off, anticipating what he was about to say. "It wasn't an animal. It was a man. I saw him with my own eyes, and he talked to me."

There was a collective silence, thick and weighty, as Josephine's family exchanged worried looks with one another. Whether they were concerned about what she saw or about her mental state, Josephine couldn't say.

A little from column A, a little from column B . . .

She proactively netted her brain. She didn't want to accidentally hear a single word of what her family was thinking.

"All right," Mrs. Jagger said in a reassuring tone. "All right. Let's go downstairs and check it out."

Her sisters and father exchanged another set of looks, and this time Josephine thought her family—even Mr. Jagger— looked a little afraid of what might be hidden below. Her mother opened the door and walked down into the dark, followed by Mary, then Elizabeth.

"Don't think you get to stay up here," Mr. Jagger said when Josephine didn't stand. "If your mother and sisters and I are going to be murdered by a stranger hiding in the basement walls, you're going to be murdered too." He smiled.

Reluctantly, Josephine picked herself up off the floor. She looked down the steps and watched as her mother and sisters were swallowed by the darkness. She took a deep breath and followed, her father close at her heels. She didn't want to venture back into the basement, but at least she wasn't alone.

A shiver racked her body once she'd stepped off the last creaky stair. Something was off.

It's cold, Josephine thought. Her breath clouded with every exhale. *And it no longer smells like meat and ashes.* Instead, it smelled like a typical unfinished basement—musty and wet.

"I wish I had a sweater," Mary said, wrapping her bare arms around her body.

"Me too," Elizabeth replied.

"Where did you see the man?" Mrs. Jagger asked.

"In the wall behind that mirror," Josephine said, pointing.

"*In* the wall?" Mrs. Jagger asked. "Or near it?"

"In it."

Her mother's expression was skeptical, but she didn't push the subject any further.

Mr. Jagger shrugged and picked up the flashlight Josephine had dropped. The light cast sharp shadows on his face, obscuring his eyes in black pools. He approached the mirror, his feet crunching through the dirt.

Mary and Elizabeth retreated a few steps and stood shoulder to shoulder with Josephine. They looked at each other and reached out for Josephine's hands. She clutched them, thankful for the comfort. Mrs. Jagger stood alone.

Mr. Jagger gripped the mirror's frame—it was once again blocking their view of the wall, even though Josephine was certain she hadn't left it like that. He hesitated for a brief moment, then swung the mirror aside and shone the light at the wall.

"Oh, dear God," he said with a sharp intake of breath.

"What?" Mary and Elizabeth said in unison.

I knew it, I knew it, I knew it, Josephine thought.

"It's a spiderweb," Mr. Jagger said. "Right here on the wall. A nest, actually. Big one too."

Mary and Elizabeth crept closer. Josephine followed.

"See?" Mr. Jagger said, shining the light at what he'd discovered.

The nest was large, larger than Josephine would've ever imagined finding this far north—it looked more like the type of nest you'd find in a southern rainforest, or maybe Australia. It was gray and had a wide black hole near its center.

"I bet this is what you thought was a face," Mr. Jagger said. "That hole kind of looks like a mouth, or an eye, and—"

Something moved in the darkness of the hole.

No one said anything.

Mr. Jagger frowned and kept the flashlight trained on the hole in the nest. The light shook in his trembling hand.

A fat barn spider with hairy brown legs crawled out of the nest and perched on the lip of the hole, as if regarding the human intruders in contempt.

Mr. Jagger laughed in relief, but stopped abruptly.

A cluster of tiny spiders spewed out of the hole and skittered across the wall in all directions. Babies. Hundreds of baby spiders.

Mary and Elizabeth screamed, but not Josephine. She'd seen worse.

At least Louisa isn't here to see this, Josephine thought. *She'd be scarred for life.*

Her sisters' screams were cut off by another scream, this time from the top of the stairs. It was Louisa, standing in the hallway and crying.

The baby took a wobbly step forward. One more step and she'd tumble. The stairs were too steep. The fall would kill her.

Josephine was the first to act. She raced up the stairs three at a time.

Louisa stepped down onto the top stair and lost her balance. She fell.

Josephine reached her just in time to catch her. Louisa wailed in fear and Josephine held her tight. *How did you get out of your crib?* Josephine wondered. *How did you get all the way down the second-floor stairs without hurting yourself?*

Even more alarming than those questions was the realization that Louisa had appeared the moment Josephine had thought about her. *As if I summoned her . . .*

My abilities are putting my family in even greater danger, she thought with the weight of a sinking stone. *I'm as big of a threat as Dorcas.*

The stairs creaked one after the other as her mother ran up them. Mrs. Jagger ripped Louisa out of Josephine's arms and glared at Josephine.

"See what this silliness of yours has done?" she shouted. Without waiting for a response, she stepped into the hallway and disappeared.

Her sisters passed her, followed by their father.

"I swear I saw a face," Josephine said in desperation. "It wasn't that spider's nest. It was near it, right there behind the mirror, and it said . . . it said . . ."

What had it said? Josephine was already beginning to forget.

Her father stopped, his back to Josephine. He sighed and ran a hand through his hair. The flashlight lay forgotten on the floor at the bottom of the stairs—Mr. Jagger must've turned it off and dropped it when Louisa had fallen, and hadn't bothered to pick it up.

"It said *something*," Josephine insisted. "You believe me, right?"

Mr. Jagger turned and faced her. "I don't . . . I'm not sure what to believe." He looked like he was about to add something else, but instead shut his mouth and walked away.

Josephine made a fist and bit down on it, stifling a frustrated yell, then sat at the top of the stairs and recorded everything that had happened in the basement in her notebook. She had to protect them . . . maybe even from herself.

Some time later—Josephine wasn't sure whether she'd been writing for twenty minutes or two hours—the front door swung open. The wind shrieked as Allison stomped her feet on the front step, freeing snow and ice from her boots. She stepped inside, holding a sketchpad, and closed the door. She hung her coat on a rack and tossed her hat and gloves in a pile on the ground next to the heating vent.

"Allison," Josephine said. "I've been looking for you."

"Well, here I am," she said cheerily. "You found me."

"Can we talk?"

"Sure." Allison frowned and clutched her necklace nervously. "What about? Are you okay?"

"I'm fine," Josephine said with a shake of her head, a motion that threatened to expose her white lie. She pointed at the front door. "Have you been playing with Laurence all this time? Is he somewhere near?"

Allison looked at Josephine with squinted eyes. "No, he left a while ago. I've been drawing. Why?"

"That's what I want to talk with you about."

"Can I take this up to my room first?" Allison held up her sketchbook.

"Of course. I'll come with you."

They walked upstairs to Allison's room and Josephine closed the door behind them. They sat on the foot of the bed and Allison placed her sketchbook down between them.

Josephine tried to think of the best way to begin the conversation—*I think your new friend is a ghost*—but Allison spoke first.

"I know what you're going to say," she said quietly.

"You do?" Josephine asked, surprised.

Allison nodded. "And it's not true," she said, her volume rising to a near-shout.

Josephine didn't have any proof that Laurence was a ghost, just Dorothy's word, but the fact that Allison was immediately so defensive made Josephine suspicious.

"He's not my boyfriend, okay?" Allison said, her cheeks turning a bright shade of red. "I just met him and we're just friends and boyfriends are totally gross anyway."

Josephine had to laugh. "Why did you think I was going to say that?"

"Elizabeth told me you thought Larry and I are boyfriend-girlfriend."

Technically, Elizabeth and Mary had also joked about Allison and Laurence being an item, but Josephine didn't bother sharing that detail. "I believe you, and to be honest, I don't care if you are interested in him or he's interested in you, except . . ."

"Except what?"

Except it might be a little difficult to date a dead boy.

"Have you seen where he lives?" Josephine asked.

Allison puckered her mouth and looked up at the ceiling. "I don't remember, but no, I don't think so."

"Have you met his family?"

After a moment of thought, Allison shook her head.

"Has he told you the name of his school, or any of his friends, or anything else like that?"

"We just talk about the woods and my artwork and whatever game we're playing, okay?"

"Okay," Josephine said, her hands held up in surrender. "What has he said about your drawings? Do you mind if I look?"

Allison said she didn't mind, so Josephine opened the sketchbook.

"He said I'm really good," Allison said.

"He's wrong," Josephine said as she flipped through the pages, looking over her sister's forest illustrations. "You're *amazing*." Josephine knew her sister was talented beyond her age, but her most recent drawings were light-years beyond her previous work. The snow seemed to sparkle, the branches of the trees appeared to sway in the breeze, and the drawings were so vivid that Josephine felt a chill from looking at them. She could hear the wind. She could smell the pines.

Allison smiled. "Thanks. He seemed to like that one in particular."

Josephine had stopped at a sketch of their house. Where the other drawings were peaceful and serene, this one was violent and angry. The page was filled with dark lines that had been drawn and redrawn so forcefully that the paper was torn in places. Shadows floated past the house's windows and the outer walls swelled like a pair of lungs. She thought she heard a faint hiss when her eyes fell upon the snake-shaped door handle. The sound was replaced by Josephine's heartbeat, as loud in her ears as it had sounded in the basement.

Thump-thump. Thump-thump. Thump-thump.

But her heart wasn't beating as hard as it had before. It wasn't beating hard at all.

The heartbeat is coming from the drawing, she realized. *It's coming from the house.*

"Has Laurence told you anything about the house?" Josephine asked, ripping her eyes from the page. "Anything at all?"

Allison bit her lips and frowned, clearly thinking hard. Finally, she said, "I don't remember."

"Think a little harder. It's important."

Allison looked around the room as if trying to jog her memory, then looked at her sketchbook. Something clicked—her eyes widened and her mouth formed an O.

"What? What did he say?"

"I can't tell you," Allison said, shaking her head. "He made me promise I wouldn't repeat it. It doesn't really matter, anyway, because it was silly."

"You have to tell me, Allison," Josephine said. She was trying to keep calm, but her voice rose an octave or two. "I don't care if it seemed silly. It's important."

"No, no." Allison refused to meet Josephine's eyes. She stood up to leave.

"Yes!" Josephine yelled, standing quickly and grabbing Allison's wrist to prevent her from leaving. She accidentally knocked the sketchbook off the bed and a few loose sheets scattered across the floor. One caught Josephine's attention, and she released Allison's wrist.

It was a drawing of the shadow woman. Surrounded by darkness. Pale skin. Long black hair. Wicked grin. No eyes. Dorcas.

Josephine scooped it up and held it in front of Allison's face. "Have you seen this woman?" she demanded.

Allison backed away, rubbing her wrist. "You hurt me."

"Have you seen this woman?" Josephine repeated loudly.

Allison seemed to notice the sketch for the first time. "No! I've never seen her before. I've never even seen that *drawing* before."

"It was in your sketchbook," Josephine said. "Who else would've drawn it?"

"I don't know!" Allison yelled, reaching her breaking point. "All I know is I didn't do it!"

"You must have forgotten . . ." The truth dawned on Josephine, so clear it practically shone. She pointed at the drawing of Dorcas. "She *made* you forget."

"What?"

Josephine looked straight into Allison's eyes and decided to cut to the chase. "She's a ghost, Allison. This house is haunted."

Allison snatched the drawing out of Josephine's hand. "Get out of my room."

Josephine sighed, but she didn't argue. What would be the point? There wasn't anything she could say to convince Allison of the truth. "All right," she said, backing out of the room, into the hallway. "Forget everything I said." She closed the door and headed down the stairs, knowing that after a few minutes Allison would, indeed, have forgotten everything she had said, whether she wanted to or not.

After dinner, Josephine remained in the kitchen with her parents while her sisters took Louisa into the family room. She helped clear the table and put the leftovers in the fridge. Their dinner conversation had been light and breezy; Allison hadn't acted upset about the way Josephine had treated her or anything she had said in her bedroom; Mrs. Jagger hadn't said anything further about catching Josephine snooping in her closet; and no one had mentioned what happened in the basement—not the spider's nest or Josephine's claim of having seen a face in the wall or the giant flashing neon question mark of how Louisa had gotten out of her crib all alone and walked down the upper staircase safely before nearly falling down the basement stairs.

She worried that, had she not written everything in her notebook and reread her notes a few times throughout the afternoon, she probably wouldn't have remembered any of the terrifying things that had happened since they'd arrived either.

Mr. Jagger sang The Police song "Every Little Thing She Does Is Magic" as he washed the dishes. He handed them to his wife to be dried, pausing briefly to kiss her.

Josephine gagged loudly and said, "Gross."

Her parents ignored her.

"You don't sing as well as Sting," Mrs. Jagger said.

"Hey, c'mon now," Mr. Jagger protested.

"You didn't let me finish! You don't sing as well as Sting, but you're cuter than he is."

"I'll take it," Mr. Jagger said with a smile.

Mrs. Jagger shrugged. "Well . . . *as* cute, at least."

"Ouch, but I'll still take it."

It was, Josephine had to admit, a nice moment. She wished she could enjoy it, but she couldn't. She cleared her throat loudly to get her parents' attention, and then she floated a proposition.

"I know this house is larger and nicer than ours—"

"About that," her father said, interrupting her. He spoke quickly, his evident excitement spurring him on. "We've decided that it wouldn't make sense to sell it."

"Especially since you girls all love it so much," Mrs. Jagger added.

That's debatable, Josephine thought. She opened her mouth, but her father cut her off again.

"We haven't told the others yet," he said. "We wanted to tell you first."

"Why?" Josephine asked, genuinely perplexed.

Her parents shared a look, then Mrs. Jagger said, "Of all of us, you seem to have the most personal, special connection to this house." She laughed and blushed. "It sounds silly and I can't really explain it, but your father has noticed it too."

He smiled and nodded in agreement.

"It's like this house chose you," Mrs. Jagger said. "Like you were always destined to live here."

Josephine was at a loss for words. Nothing her mother had just said made sense, and yet . . . maybe it did.

It's like the house chose me.

But what's it going to do to me? What is Dorcas *going to do to me?*

She couldn't end up like Dorcas or Laurence, or worse, like the face in the basement wall. Was it actually the blacksmith? Or someone else?

Whoever he was, Josephine had temporarily forgotten what the stone man had said, but it came back to her now.

Help me.

She had to do something. Her eyes lit upon the box of matches on the kitchen counter. She picked them up as an idea formed in her head.

No, not *formed*. The idea was *planted* in her head.

And Josephine—she was too drained to realize that distinction. Her guard was down and so was her net.

"Well, say something, Josie!" her father said.

"Something," Josephine joked. *Act casual,* she thought. *You don't want your parents to pick up on anything, to question you, to put a stop to your plan.* "I'm a little cold, and tired. I think I'm going to light a small fire in my room and go to bed."

She turned and left before her parents could say anything else.

She shook the box as she walked up the stairs. The matches rattled like bones in a miniature coffin. Josephine wasn't going to light a small fire—she was going to light a *big* fire. Big enough to put an end to all her family's troubles, whether they could remember those troubles or not.

After all, she had to do *something*. The voices in her head had told her so.

TEN

It happened in a daze.

Josephine opened her bedroom door, her face half obscured by shadow. She stood as still as a statue. Her mind was blank, her head empty. She was acting purely on impulse, but not an impulse of her own.

Something on the ground slithered in a figure-eight pattern around her feet and disappeared into the hallway's shadows.

She entered her room and closed the door.

She looked at the fireplace. It was wide and dark, a giant mouth, hungry, waiting to be fed.

She crossed the room soundlessly and placed her notebook and the box of matches on the fireplace mantel. She entered the closet. There was no need to pull the light's string. There was no need to use her eyes. No need to see. Her fingers did that for her. They danced over the spines that stood at attention on the shelves like toy soldiers.

"Ah," Josephine said, when her fingers found the book they'd been searching for.

Clutching the first edition of *Through the Looking-Glass, and*

What Alice Found There to her chest, Josephine slowly returned to the fireplace.

Do it right, she thought. *There's no rush.*

She placed the book on the fireplace grill. Without taking her eyes off the book, Josephine picked up the matches, removed one, and held its head to the striking surface on the side of the box.

Through the Looking-Glass, and What Alice Found There was no longer a rare and valuable book, no longer a story Josephine wanted to read, no longer a world she wanted to fall into. It was a sacrificial lamb, nothing more. But all the same, her hand hesitated.

It's what must be done.

Burn the house.

Burn the witch.

Burn my family.

Burn everyone to ash and bone.

It's what must be done . . . to save us.

She struck the match. The phosphorus ignited, the sulfur and potassium chlorate fed the flame, and flickering firelight made her eyes glow in the darkness. Tears—not of happiness or sadness, but of righteousness—ran down her cheeks.

Josephine laughed, held the flame to the corner of the book, and waited for the fire to catch, and spread, and consume.

But it didn't. The flame burned the matchstick to a blackened, curled nub. The heat reached the tips of her forefinger and thumb and she tossed the charred match to the back of the fireplace.

The book was undamaged. There wasn't even the slightest burn mark where Josephine had held the flame to it. She struck another match and watched as the book failed to catch fire, then struck another match and another, each with the same result.

She stood and entered the closet, quickening her pace, and brought back a stack of books. She tossed them into the fireplace and tried to burn one after the other. And one after the other, each refused to ignite.

With a frustrated grunt, Josephine dropped her head to her chin. Her notebook, sitting on the floor beside her knees, caught her attention. She had left it on the mantel . . . or had she? No matter, it was there now, right in front of her, just when she needed it most. She picked it up and studied its cover, then laughed again. It would do perfectly.

She placed it open on top of the other books, lit the last match in the box, and touched the flame to a corner of one of the notebook's pages.

I knew you'd figure it out, Josephine thought in a voice not quite her own. *Clever girl.*

The notebook caught fire immediately. The flame grew and spread and devoured, satisfying its endless hunger.

Dorcas killed some people or put a curse on them, has been sacrificing people ever since she died.

The words practically jumped off the page. It was one of the notes Josephine had written in the notebook, and it was about to be destroyed by the fire.

Dorcas sacrifices people, Josephine thought, coming quickly back to her right mind. *And now she's trying to sacrifice my entire family, using me as her puppet.*

"Oh, shit," she said. She picked up the notebook and swatted at the flame with her hand. When that didn't work, she tossed it to the floor, ripped the duvet off her bed, and smothered it. Her heart ached as she pulled the blanket back. The fire was out, but the corner of the notebook was burned. A thin strand of smoke drifted up through the air. The blackened paper crumbled at the touch and drifted to the floor like snowflakes.

The damage was done, but it could have been worse.

I nearly killed my entire family.

She squeezed the notebook to her chest, leaned forward, and cried. A vision of her parents and sisters trapped inside the house as flames licked at the walls and brought the roof down on their heads tortured her mind.

"No," she said forcefully. "No. I didn't nearly kill everyone. Dorcas did." She looked around the room. It appeared to be empty, but Josephine felt that Dorcas was somewhere, watching, waiting. "I know what you're trying to do. And I'm not going to let you do it. Do you fucking hear me? I'm not going to let you!"

Saying it out loud diminished her fear and hardened her resolve. She decided she needed to learn more about Dorcas and the house, and she knew where she needed to go to do that.

The Canaan library.

But that would have to wait until the next day.

It was late, and a headache's early tentacles were creeping through her brain, poking and prodding, exploring, squeezing, throbbing. She walked to her bed and lay down heavily.

Her last thought before she fell asleep was of her notebook. She slid it under her body and cradled it protectively, then closed her eyes and was gone.

Josephine's dreams were predictably macabre, filled with images of rabbits and wax dolls and fire and blood and bones. Her eyes opened, only they didn't, not really—Josephine had a feeling that nothing she was experiencing was real, that she was still asleep and her subconscious was at the wheel. She was in her room, lying in bed, staring at the closet. The door was open, but the light was off, so Josephine couldn't see the bookshelf within.

She rolled over and wished she could dream of her home back in Amherst rather than this nightmare house. Wasn't it bad enough that she had to spend her waking time there? Couldn't she at least have a little peace at night?

Click-click.

The closet light turned on.

She rolled over quickly and looked. But the closet was still pitch-black.

I could've sworn I heard the string, she thought, then remembered it was just a dream. Dreams were weird, but they couldn't hurt her.

She rolled back onto her stomach.

A minute or two of dream time passed.

Click-click.

Josephine looked at the closet. The light was still off.

Fine, you want to be like this? she asked her dream, as if it were a sentient being. *I'll keep my eyes on the closet. Let's see you pull the string without turning on the light now.*

Click-click.

The light turned on this time.

Dorcas stood within the closet.

Click-click.

Lights out. Darkness. Dorcas was gone.

Josephine lurched into a sitting position and hugged her knees to her chest.

It's just a dream, she reminded herself.

Click-click.

The light turned on, but the closet was empty.

Click-click.

Darkness.

Dreams can't hurt me, she thought desperately.

Click-click.

The closet light didn't turn on. Instead, light spilled across the bed from a different source within the room.

Josephine turned her head slowly.

A bedside lamp had turned on.

Click-click. The closet light turned back on.

Click-click. The room's main overhead light turned on.

CLICK-CLICK! All the lights turned off at once and the room was plunged into absolute darkness.

Just a dream, Josephine insisted, *just a dream, just a dream, just a dream . . .*

She closed her eyes tight and never wanted to open them again. She felt childish, but she also didn't care.

Footsteps fell, cutting a slow, gentle path across the room from the closet to the bedroom door. The door opened with a painful, drawn-out *creeeak*. Although she had kept her eyes closed, she had a good idea who had just left the room, but where was Dorcas going? Why had she tormented Josephine with the lights just to walk away a moment later? It didn't make sense.

It's just a dream. They rarely do make sense.

"Unnnnhhhhh . . ."

It was a low, sleepy groan, and it had come from one of her sisters' bedrooms.

Josephine slipped out of bed. It might just be a dream, but she felt compelled to check on her sisters and make sure they were okay.

She walked through the dark and stepped into the hall. Allison's door was open. The others were closed. She wanted to enter, but settled for a peek through the doorway, telling herself she didn't want to intrude but aware that was a lie. She was afraid.

Allison tossed and turned in her bed, her eyes shut tight and her forehead beaded with sweat. Her duvet and bedsheet were bunched up at her feet.

Dorcas glided through the room. Her bare feet were an inch off the ground. The witch came to a stop beside the bed and looked down at Allison. She clasped her hands together and smiled.

How does she see without eyes? Josephine thought with a sickening feeling in her gut.

After a moment of silent meditation, Dorcas placed a hand on Allison's forehead.

Josephine was overcome by the sudden desire to charge into the room, but she couldn't move—she was rooted to the floor where she stood. She tried to open her mouth to scream, but her lips felt like they'd been stitched together.

Allison stopped thrashing and fell still at Dorcas's touch.

Dorcas slowly leaned forward, so close to Allison that her thin lips nearly brushed the side of the young girl's face. She whispered something directly into Allison's ear, into her head, into her mind. What she said, Josephine couldn't hear.

Dorcas finished and stood up straight. Allison sighed in relief, then continued sleeping, only now more peacefully.

Still smiling, Dorcas turned to face the door. Josephine broke out of her trance and hid in the hallway, no longer eager to be seen. She considered running but was afraid she'd be heard, so she pressed her back up against the wall and tried not to panic. She was too exposed for her liking, but it was the best she could do with the time she had.

Dorcas slid out of Allison's room and closed the door. Josephine shut her eyes. She couldn't bear to watch. She bit her lips together hard enough to taste blood. Her body trembled so violently she was afraid Dorcas would be able to hear her vibrations. Surely she'd be caught, surely Dorcas would kill her, surely she'd boil her body in the basement cauldron and toss her remains in the pile with the rabbit bones.

But nothing happened. Josephine opened her eyes. The hallway was empty, but Elizabeth's door was now open. Josephine took a deep breath and crossed the hallway to look inside.

It was a familiar scene. Elizabeth was tossing and turning in bed. Dorcas looked down upon the girl in silence for a moment before touching her forehead and whispering something into her ear. Elizabeth stopped moving and slept like the dead.

Josephine hid in the hall again and watched as Dorcas left the room and shut the door, then floated into Mary's room.

Just a dream, Josephine reminded herself.

Mary kicked and thrashed harder than either Allison or Elizabeth had. It took a few beats longer, but Mary eventually fell still at Dorcas's touch.

This time, Josephine didn't try to hide as Dorcas passed her, and it didn't appear to matter; either the witch hadn't seen

Josephine or she didn't care that she was watching her bizarre ritual. Dorcas drifted to the far end of the hall and entered Josephine's parents' room. Both her mother and father were shaking in bed, as was Louisa in her crib. Dorcas went to them one by one, calming them into a deep sleep, but before she approached the crib, she flicked her fingers sideways in the air and Louisa's lucky rabbit's foot flew to the floor.

If you can't even try to stop Dorcas from casting her spells on Louisa, Josephine chided herself, *then you're all as good as dead.*

No. Josephine shook her head. *It's just a dream.*

And if it's just a dream, she thought with a small spark of hope, *then you can wake up.*

Wake up, she commanded herself.

Wake up.

Wake up, wake up, wake up—

"You are awake," Dorcas said. She'd materialized out of thin air directly beside Josephine.

Before Josephine could do anything—run, scream, fight, think—Dorcas thrust her palm against Josephine's forehead and whispered into her ear.

Josephine finally knew what Dorcas had said to everyone as they slept.

"Rest in peace."

The dream was still fresh in Josephine's mind when she awoke the next morning. Sunshine streamed through her windows and warmed her face, a pleasant sensation that was an odd contradiction to her nightmare.

That was dark, Josephine thought as she rubbed sleep from her eyes. *And weird. Maybe the weirdest dream I've ever had, and that's saying something.*

On second thought, maybe not as weird as my you stew dream.

But then she heard Dorcas's voice, as clear as a bell. *You are awake.* That's what she had said just before *rest in peace.*

What if Josephine hadn't been dreaming?

What if her nightmare had actually happened?

Josephine sat up quickly and wondered where her notebook was. She found it under her pillow, turned to a fresh page, and began writing as the memory of the dream—if that's what it was—fought to slip forever from her mind.

ELEVEN

By the time Josephine placed down her pen and closed her note-book, she was certain it hadn't been a dream. The nightmare had been real. And she was pretty sure she knew what Dorcas was doing. While her family slept, she was casting spells or hypnotizing or using telepathy on them, to keep them blissfully unaware of the danger they were in. And she was keeping them in the dark to prevent them from leaving the house. They weren't intruders, as Josephine had once felt. Dorcas *wanted* them there.

But why? If she wanted to harm them, why not kill them the first night they arrived? Why wait?

And how long was she planning on waiting?

I *can't wait*, Josephine thought. *I need answers* now.

She shuffled downstairs, her eyes dry and her back stiff and achy. She wasn't hungry, but her family was eating breakfast like it was their last meal.

"So good," Elizabeth said after she took a bite of bacon.

"I don't think I'll ever get tired of the food here," Mary said. She drank a sip of orange juice and sighed contentedly.

"Baba, baba, baba," Louisa said, shaking her bottle in the air.

"Eat up," their father said. "There's plenty more where that came from. Morning, Josie! Sleep well?"

"Mm-hmm," Josephine said with a nod.

"I don't know if I buy that," Mrs. Jagger said. "You look like you're coming down with something." She spooned some porridge into Louisa's mouth.

"Maybe I had a bad dream or two," Josephine admitted.

"I had the best sleep," Allison said. "Super deep. I don't think I dreamt at all."

"Lucky you," Josephine muttered under her breath.

"What?" Allison asked.

"Nothing." Josephine turned to face her father. "Can I come into town with you today?"

"What do you mean?" he asked, genuinely confused.

"When you take the van to the mechanic?" Josephine searched her father's face but found no understanding there. It was like she was speaking a different language. "To check what's wrong with the engine?" *He's forgotten the appointment he booked.*

"There's something wrong with the van?" Mrs. Jagger asked her husband.

She's forgotten too, Josephine thought. She noticed the blank looks on her sisters' faces. *They've all forgotten.*

A thought dawned on her. *I didn't write it down, but I didn't forget.*

Maybe I'm . . . remembering.

Something finally clicked in Mr. Jagger's mind, a memory no brighter than a dim flicker of light. "Oh yeah, right. I'd forgotten about that. The . . . engine light came on a couple days ago. I booked an appointment to take the van to a mechanic today." Although Josephine had helped trigger his memory, his look of confusion remained.

"So . . . can I come?" Josephine asked. "I feel like I'm starting to get a touch of cabin fever here."

"Actually, I was thinking I'd just stay here and write today, maybe do some stuff around the house. We've still got a few days before we have to drive back home, and the van's probably fine."

"But you'll lose your appointment."

"How busy can a mechanic in Canaan be? I'll call and reschedule for tomorrow. You can come with me then, okay?"

No, that's not okay. Josephine felt her temperature rise, but she told herself to remain calm. If her father wasn't interested in leaving the house, even just for a few hours, maybe she could get her sisters on board. "I saw a bowling alley when we drove through town, and a pizza place. We could play a few rounds and grab a slice for lunch."

"Why would I want to eat at some pizza joint?" Elizabeth said. "The food here in the house is off the charts."

"I'd rather paint," Allison said.

"And I'd rather practice music," Elizabeth said. "Time's ticking, and there's no way Mom and Dad will allow me to bring all of Great-Great-Aunt Mercy's instruments back home to Amherst."

"There'd only be space in the van for the instruments if we left *you* here," Mr. Jagger said.

Although it was clearly meant to be a joke, Elizabeth didn't look too upset at the prospect.

Josephine looked at Mary. "How about you? Want to go bowling with me?"

"I don't know . . . ," Mary said.

"What if we went shopping instead?"

That changed Mary's attitude. She smiled and laughed. "You haven't offered to go shopping with me in—"

"Forever. I know. That's how desperate I am to get out and do something different. Please?"

"Well, okay," Mary said.

"Thank you," Josephine said, preparing to cut to the chase. "And I was thinking, maybe, we could quickly visit the library."

"Ah-ha!" Mary said, raising a finger in the air. "An ulterior motive! Books! I should've known."

"You don't already have enough to read here?" Elizabeth asked. "You *are* a nerd."

Josephine chose to ignore that. "Dad? Now will you take us?"

He sighed. "I have this story idea—"

"Oh, for heaven's sake," Mrs. Jagger said. "I'll take the van to the mechanic's and drop you two off in town."

"Thanks, Mom." Josephine got up and gave her mother a quick hug.

She shrugged. "I could use a bit of a break too, and looking after my two oldest kids will be easier than looking after the three youngest. Sorry about your luck, dear."

"It's all good," Mr. Jagger said. He took the baby spoon out of his wife's hand and fed Louisa another bite of porridge. "You'll help me write, won't you, sweetums?"

Louisa babbled and a small stream of porridge dribbled down her chin.

"So, um, Josie?" Mary asked. "Where are all the stores?"

They were standing at the intersection of Gale Street and Christian Hill, which appeared to be one of Canaan's major intersections. There weren't any people, passing cars, or even a traffic light. They had dropped the van off at a gas station on the corner that also served as the local mechanic's shop, and their mother had opted to wait in the station while the mechanic assessed the vehicle.

Josephine took in her surroundings. Across the street from the gas station was a country restaurant, and south of that was the motel they had planned on staying in their first night.

Feels like a lifetime ago, she thought, and although her memory seemed to be improving since she began writing everything important that happened in her notebook, it was weird to remember how quickly and clearly she could recall everything that took place *before* she first set foot in the house.

There was a church and a health center to the west, and Wayne's Lanes & Jo's Grille to the east. Government roadside signs directed travelers to an American Legion north on Christian Hill and the Canaan library to the south. Josephine wanted to head straight there, but knew she had to fulfill her end of the bargain to her sister first. Which brought her back to Mary's question: *Where are all the stores?*

"There's got to be something around here somewhere," Josephine said. "People who live here have to buy stuff, right?"

A cold gust of wind howled through town, stinging Josephine's nose and ears and kicking up a streak of snow.

"I'm freezing," Mary said, pointing at the restaurant across the street. "Let's go ask someone in there. At least we'll be warm for a minute or two."

A bell chimed when they opened the door to the restaurant.

The place was empty, but an old woman wearing a hairnet and a pink apron emerged from the back. Her name tag read GRACE.

"Little late for breakfast; little early for lunch," Grace said. "Which means you can sit anywhere you like and order bacon and eggs or sandwiches and burgers. Whatever your hearts desire."

"Sorry," Mary said, "we're not here to eat. We're not from here and were wondering if there are any good shops in town?"

"Driving or walking?"

"Walking."

"Driving would be better. In Beecher Falls, there's a consignment shop, a furniture store, and Momma Bear's." Grace offered no further commentary.

Josephine and Mary exchanged a look, then Josephine said, "Thank you, um, for that, but we're walking. So what are our options?"

Grace smacked her lips, then pointed west. "Head along Gale and take the bridge over the Connecticut. In West Stewartstown, you'll find Solomon's for groceries and Pauline's for jewelry. Mind you, you'll be crossing the state line, so your dollar will be going to New Hampshire."

"Perfect! Thanks," Mary said. She'd perked up at the mention of jewelry. She put her arm over Josephine's shoulders and led her back out to the street.

"Does it bother you if our dollar goes to New Hampshire?" Josephine teased as they walked over the bridge that crossed the Connecticut River.

"No, but it bothers me that we're walking, not driving," Mary retorted. "That Beecher Falls consignment shop sounds pretty awesome."

"Not to mention Momma Bear's!"

The girls laughed and spotted Pauline's Boutique in a green building beside a laundromat. They walked inside and found the store had a wide jewelry case, wall shelves filled with decorations, and a smiling salesperson standing in the center of it all who welcomed them with a warm hello.

"Thank you," Mary whispered blissfully to Josephine, then flew to the jewelry case like an arrow.

Josephine waited patiently as Mary asked to try on an assortment of rings, necklaces, and watches. Josephine walked around the shop and looked with little interest at crystal dragons and mermaids, pewter photo frames, and candles.

Something caught her attention. It had jumped out of the fray as if desperate to be seen. It was a small statue of a tree with a window and a door, like a fairy's house. Carved into the door, so small Josephine almost missed it altogether, was a pentagram identical to the ones carved in the trees around their house.

"Can I help you find anything?" the salesperson asked from behind.

Josephine jumped, but was quick to regain her composure. "Just browsing," she said, then added, "I like this tree."

"So do I, but I can't seem to sell it. Most people don't give it a second look. Sometimes I wonder if people see it at all."

Josephine had a hard time believing that—it had practically shouted her name as she'd walked past. "Why don't you put it out on display?" Josephine asked. It was blocked from view by a few other items.

The saleswoman considered that for a moment, then said, "Maybe I don't actually want to part ways with it." She smiled. "My name's Isabelle."

"Josephine."

"Do you girls live nearby? I don't think I've ever seen you in town before."

Josephine almost answered with the truth, then decided to simplify things. "Just passing through."

Mary was nearby but oblivious to their conversation, too absorbed in a bracelet she'd tried on.

Josephine pointed at the door on the tree. "That's an interesting star," she said, feigning ignorance.

"It's a pentagram. They're said to ward off evil forces."

"Evil forces?" Josephine said. "Like . . . witches, maybe? Or ghosts?"

Isabelle nodded with a squint and a smile. "That's right. Where did you say you're from?"

"I didn't. Amherst."

"And you're just passing through."

Josephine couldn't tell if it was a statement or a question. She nodded. "Just passing through."

"Well, I don't mind telling you about a local urban legend since I live here in New Hampshire, but no one in Vermont would ever dare speak of it. At least, not with a stranger, and an outsider at that."

Josephine waited for Isabelle to continue, but when she didn't, she began to wonder if the woman had had second thoughts. "They'd never speak of what?"

Isabelle smiled conspiratorially. "I don't know . . . maybe I shouldn't be telling you any of this. It's a little . . . dark."

Ah, Josephine thought. *She's a gossip. She wants to tell me, but she wants me to tease it out of her first.* She leaned in a little and returned Isabelle's smile. "I was interested before, but now I *need* to know."

"How old are you, anyway?"

"Old enough to handle an urban legend." When Isabelle didn't continue, Josephine added, "I'm seventeen."

Isabelle's smile spread from her mouth to her eyes. "All right, Josephine. You've convinced me, so here it is. They say a Salem witch used to live just across the border, in Vermont, a long time ago. People back then carved pentagrams on trees around her house to prevent her from leaving the woods. Many carved stars on the doors and window frames of their homes, just in case. A few of the oldest houses in Canaan still have these markings. These days, of course, people think it's all a bunch of superstitious nonsense from a different time, but some believe the witch is still out there. They warn people to stay out of the woods. They think she eats anyone who wanders too close to her lair." Isabelle snapped her fingers. "And that's another likely reason why no one has bought this tree. Too close to the truth."

"Well, that's a first," Mary said as they walked back across the bridge to Vermont. "You bought something and I didn't."

"What can I say?" Josephine said. She glanced down at the bag she carried and pictured the tree within it. "I liked it, and she gave me a good deal."

"What's next? I borrow a library book, not you?"

An old-fashioned sign in front of the library read ALICE M. WARD MEMORIAL LIBRARY. It was a picturesque yellow building with plenty of windows. The library stood out warmly amid the gloom of an overcast day.

As they climbed the front steps, Josephine gave up on the

hope that she'd be able to do what she wanted to do without having to answer any questions. The library was small, and she had a feeling the librarian would have a view of each and every book from the front desk.

"Before we head in," Josephine said, stopping Mary, "I should let you know the real reason I wanted to come here today."

"Sure. What's up?"

Josephine hesitated. "You're not going to believe me."

"Try me," Mary said. "I might surprise you. And even if I don't, at least we'll get to go inside where it's warm."

She's not even going to remember this in a short while, so why not tell her the truth? "All right, here it is: I think our great-great-aunt's house is haunted."

Mary laughed. "You mean, like, by a ghost?"

"Yeah, but it's worse than that. It's haunted by the ghost of a witch."

Mary's smile faded. "I can't tell if you're joking."

"I wish I was."

After a moment of silent contemplation, Mary said, "Okay. I believe you."

"Really?" Josephine said.

"You're the most honest, reliable person I know. Of course I believe you."

"Thank you," Josephine said, wrapping her sister in a tight embrace. She instantly felt ten times lighter than she had before, like she might float away when she let go of Mary.

"What have you seen?" Mary asked.

"Hm?"

"In the house. You must have seen some freaky stuff to think it's haunted."

"I'll tell you later. For now, let's just say the house has a lot of history."

"And you came to the library hoping to read about some of that history," Mary said, connecting the dots on her own.

"Exactly." Josephine knew Mary would have forgotten what she had already told her about Dorothy. "I met a girl about the same age as me. Lives in the next house over. She found a book in the local history room that had a drawing of a woman who used to live in our house a long time ago. I want to read the book for myself. The woman . . . was accused of witchcraft."

"The plot thickens," Mary said with a raised eyebrow.

"You can say that again," Josephine said, not really sure if Mary still believed her or not.

Mary looked at the library, then back at her sister. "Let me guess: you'd prefer if the librarian didn't know what you're up to."

Josephine nodded.

"Sounds like you're going to need a distraction," Mary said. "Wait behind me and watch for my signal. I'll try to buy you ten minutes."

Josephine followed Mary inside as she approached the circulation desk, where a librarian was seated. Her badge had a Canaan library logo and the name JANE.

"Hi there," Mary said. "I'm looking for a book."

Jane looked up from her computer with a pleasant smile. "I'll be happy to help. What's the title?"

"I don't remember, but it has about this many pages." Mary held her forefinger and thumb an inch apart. "And a blue cover. Oh! And a woman's face on it."

"Oh, boy," Jane said. "This is going to put my master's degree to the test."

When Jane turned back to her computer and began to type, Mary casually knocked a stack of flyers off the desk.

"Sorry!" Mary said. "I'm such a klutz."

"Don't worry. It happens all the time."

"Really?" Mary asked.

"No," Jane replied.

Josephine used the brief distraction to quickly scan the library. To her right was a door with LOCAL HISTORY ROOM painted on the wall above it.

"Let me help pick those up," Mary said. She bent to collect the flyers and bumped against a book cart, toppling it with a loud crash. Books slid across the floor in every direction.

"How about you just wait a moment and I'll pick everything up," Jane said, clearly flustered but trying her best to remain composed. "Then I can help you find your book."

Mary smiled and laughed with awkward relief. "Thanks. That might be for the best."

Jane smiled—a little less genuinely than when they'd first approached the desk—and crouched down to tidy up the mess. Mary gave Josephine a thumbs-up and silently mouthed the word *Go*.

Josephine didn't waste any time. She entered the local history room and closed the door as silently as possible.

There was a small table with four chairs in the center of the room and a few bookshelves against one of the walls. Luckily, there weren't many books for her to search. Josephine flipped through her notebook and found the entry she was looking for.

Dorothy saw picture of Dorcas in the Canaan library, in an old book. Red leather? Local history room?

Josephine scanned the shelves. There was only one book bound in red leather. She pulled it off the shelf and looked at the cover. The title was stamped with gold-leaf foil.

Early Histories of Canaan, Vermont

Bingo, she thought with a thrill as she placed the book on the table and opened the front cover. The paper was thick and yellowed, and the text was handwritten with dark ink. She flipped through the pages quickly, scanning the writings for any mention of Dorcas.

After pages and pages devoted to the weather, local agriculture reports, and birth, marriage, and death notices, Josephine came face to face with what—or rather, whom—she was looking for.

A sketch of Dorcas stared at her. It was a younger version of Dorcas than Josephine knew—she still had both of her eyes—but there was no mistaking the witch.

Her twisted smile is a dead giveaway, Josephine thought. It was the same smile that had haunted Josephine since she'd arrived in Vermont. She turned the page and found a lot more information about Dorcas than she had expected. She sat down, suddenly feeling a little lightheaded, and read the entry.

At the age of four, Dorcas Good was the youngest person accused of witchcraft in Salem, Massachusetts, near the turn of the 17th century. Her mother, Sarah Good, was also among the accused. While locked up in jail, Sarah gave birth to Dorcas's younger sister, but the baby died before seeing the light of her second day. Sarah was hanged shortly thereafter, but it's unknown what happened to Dorcas during this time. Most likely she was acquitted and released from prison, but there are no records of this and nothing is known of her childhood.

Many years later, townsfolk in the area that would later become Canaan began reporting that they were often afflicted by maladies and illnesses that had no discernible cause. Many reported that they felt like they'd been cursed, though they had no idea how or why. Then, one day in autumn, Dorcas, now an older adult, was spotted drinking rabbit's blood in the woods near a house where she lived alone.

Josephine peeled her eyes off the book and took a deep breath, thinking of the rabbit bones she had found in the basement. The contents of her stomach roiled and she forced herself to continue reading,

It was believed that sacrificing rabbits and drinking their blood, coupled with charms and spells and other remedies, gave Dorcas an unnaturally long life. The townsfolk grew concerned that Dorcas would move on to something more powerful, from sacrificing rabbits to sacrificing humans. They formed a mob and stormed Dorcas's house to demand the truth: Was she a witch? They found their answer, and the answer was an unequivocal yes. She stepped out of her house with blood pouring out of her empty eye sockets. She raised her eyes above her head and told the mob that they had prevented her from seeing. Without eyes, she could see great distances. She could see through walls. She could see into men's souls. She could see everything.

With a sickening feeling in her gut, Josephine thought of her own habit of covering her eyes when she needed to think hard about something.

That's not the same, she comforted herself. *Covering my eyes with my hands is nothing like scooping them out of my skull.*

She looked at the next page to continue reading, but that was the end of the entry and there was no further mention of Dorcas in the rest of the book. It seemed like an odd omission. What happened next? Did the mob flee, or attack?

But then she noticed that there were some jagged bits of paper sticking out from the spine's interior.

Someone tore out a page, she realized. But who? And what were they hiding?

"Can I help you with anything?"

Josephine jumped and spun around. Jane was standing in the doorway, looking at Josephine with a mix of suspicion and disapproval. Josephine shut the book quickly and shook her head. "No. I'm good, thanks."

"That's a peculiar choice for holiday reading," Jane said, eyeing the book.

Josephine struggled to think of a reason to explain her interest in Canaan history—other than the true reason—but drew a blank.

"Ah!" Mary said, entering the room. "There you are! I got my book." She held up a small library book that was nearly falling apart and looked to be about fifty years old. "Well, it wasn't the one I was looking for, the one with the green cover, but it looks interesting."

Jane frowned. "I thought you said the book you were looking for had a blue cover."

"Right!" Mary said. "My mistake. Anyway, it's time to go. Mom will be waiting for us."

Josephine took the opening Mary had created and rushed past Jane, flashing her a quick smile. Jane continued to look at her disapprovingly. Josephine wasn't accustomed to getting that type of reaction from a librarian, and she didn't like it one bit.

"I don't think she liked me," Josephine told Mary once they were safely outside and putting the library behind them.

"Neither do I," Mary agreed. "On the other hand, she liked me a lot. She let me borrow this book without a library card—just a promise that I'd return it in a couple of days."

Josephine read the title—*The Kirkman Guide to Witchcraft*—and shot her sister a questioning look.

Mary shrugged. "I said it looked interesting. And if there really is a witch haunting the house, maybe this will be useful somehow."

Josephine laughed.

"What?" Mary asked.

"Before we went in you joked about borrowing a book from the library instead of me and, well, that's what happened."

"It's the end of the world as we know it," Mary said, and the girls shared a laugh.

It felt good to get out of the house for the morning and spend some time together, but for Josephine, the moment was bittersweet. She was afraid Mary's joke had been closer to the truth—*it's the end of the world*—than her sister could ever possibly know.

TWELVE

Shortly after lunch Josephine curled up under a blanket on the family room sofa and flipped through the library book Mary had borrowed.

Mary passed through the room, bouncing Louisa in her arms. Upon seeing *The Kirkman Guide to Witchcraft*, she frowned and said, "When did you find the time to visit the library?"

"When do I *not* find time to visit the library?" Josephine said.

When they'd returned to the house an hour before, Mary had hopped out of the van—the mechanic couldn't find anything wrong with the engine so he had simply turned off the check engine light—and left the book behind on the car seat. When Josephine had tried to hand it back to Mary, her sister had taken a quick glance at the book and said it wasn't hers. They'd only just returned to the house and Mary had already forgotten about the jewelry store, the tree statue Josephine had bought, their visit to the library, the book she'd borrowed—all of it. Mrs. Jagger's memories had turned hazy too. Josephine had taken the book inside. She'd also collected some logs from the woodpile beside the basement's cellar door and taken them to her room.

"Fair enough," Mary said, her gaze quickly moving away from *The Kirkman Guide to Witchcraft* as Louisa began to fuss and squirm in her arms. "Let's go find you something to play with," Mary said, and off they went, leaving Josephine alone in the family room once more.

Josephine sighed and rubbed her face, fighting back tears. She'd never felt so alone in her life. Being part of such a big family meant she always had someone to talk to, someone to hang out with, someone to ask for help whenever she needed it. But now she was the only person who had any idea what they were up against, and although Mary had believed her, she was doomed—like the rest of the family—to forget every detail before she could help.

At least books always helped Josephine take her mind off her troubles.

After skimming a few chapters covering topics like superstitions regarding water, the magical qualities of the number seven, and things Josephine had never heard of, like witch bottles and binding ceremonies, Josephine came to a chapter titled *Magickal Uses for Household Items* that caught her attention. Specifically, there was a short section about lavender:

Lavender is an aromatic flowering plant in the mint family and has a diverse list of applications for witchcraft. It puts people at peace by reducing stress and anxiety, and also helps encourage sleep. Lavender stored in pouches throughout the house will not only work as an insect repellant but can also open the mind and soul, making people highly susceptible to charms and other such influences.

Josephine shook her head and reread the passage. *That's why there are lavender pouches in each bedroom. Dorcas put them there to make it easier to get into our minds and control us.*

Other sections in *The Kirkman Guide to Witchcraft* also made her think of Dorcas. She learned that people around the world had carved pentagrams on trees, doors, and windows—even fireplaces—to prevent witches from entering their homes. The color purple—like the door to the basement—was a sign of a witch's power and authority. There were countless drawings of cauldrons that looked just like the one in the basement, and Josephine also read that rabbits and snakes have many connections to witchcraft. Those two animals were both on a list of "familiar spirits."

Familiar spirits (or simply familiars) are protective entities that assist witches—particularly young ones—with the practice of magick. Most often seen in their animal form, familiars might also appear as human and could be demons, fairies, or other supernatural beings.

With rabbit bones in the basement and a snakeskin in the dining room, Josephine couldn't help but wonder . . .

She shut the book in frustration. Questions were sprouting in her head like spores, and she was annoyed about the missing page in *Early Histories of Canaan, Vermont*. She had a feeling that particular page had been removed on purpose, most likely because it contained some extremely important information— information she might need to protect herself and her family.

What about Mr. Finger? she wondered. *He has spent more time here than anyone else I know, besides my family. Does he know anything about the house's history that might help us? Has he ever seen Dorcas, or felt her presence? Has he been charmed by her too? At the very least, he might be able to tell me a little more about my great-great-aunt.*

More questions, questions without answers.

She sighed in frustration and got to her feet. She needed some fresh air to clear her head, and since Mr. Finger wasn't around, she figured it wouldn't hurt to ask Dorothy if she knew anything about the missing page.

It was mid-afternoon and the sun was hanging low in the western sky, casting a golden glow on the land that turned trees into black silhouettes and made the icy ground sparkle as if coated in diamonds.

As soon as she passed the row of pentagram trees, Josephine felt a little weight lift off her shoulders. She knew she couldn't remain on the safe side forever, but it was a relief for the time being.

Dorothy's house was near. Josephine hoped Dorothy would be home, but what would she say if her parents answered the door and innocently asked why she was looking for their daughter?

Oh, I just want to ask her if she knows anything about a page missing from a library book that might help me protect my family from an evil ghost witch.

Josephine smiled and told herself, *Better to lie. Tell them you want to do "normal" teenage stuff with their daughter, like smoke some drugs or have sex with strangers. They'd be more likely to let*

Dorothy hang out with me if I said that. She was joking, of course, and she wasn't too concerned. She'd figure out something to say on the spot if she needed to.

A shadow passed between the trees to her left.

She froze and scanned the woods. There was nothing there but more trees. But the skin on the back of her neck prickled. She felt like she was being watched.

Is it Dorcas? No, it can't be—I've passed the protective barrier.

And then it hit her.

"Laurence?" she called out, unable to keep her voice from trembling. "My name's Josephine. I'm Allison's sister."

Laurence didn't answer, but Josephine heard feet crunching in the snow somewhere behind her.

"Will you come out?" Josephine asked. "Why are you hiding?"

There was a short pause before Josephine heard a young boy whispering. She couldn't be sure, but she thought the voice had said, "It's a game."

"What did you say? *It's a game?* Like, hide-and-seek?" She wanted answers and hoped she could lull Laurence into a false sense of security. "Allison's not here . . . do you want to play with me instead?"

The wind answered, soft as snow and just as cold, carrying Laurence's answer on its back. "Too late. You're already dead."

Josephine's insides turned to ice.

"What are you doing?" Dorothy called out urgently. She stood near her old fort. "He'll kill you! Get in here now!"

Josephine took off like a shot, her feet pounding and her heart pumping. She weaved through trees as branches scratched her face and snagged her hair. She felt like she was being chased—no, hunted. Dorothy stepped out of the way as Josephine stormed into the fort. Dorothy followed her in and slammed the door shut. Snow fell through the gaps in the roof.

Josephine pointed to the pentagram carved above the door as she tried to steady her nerves and catch her breath. "Are you sure that will keep Laurence out?"

Dorothy nodded. "Why were you talking to him?"

"I was coming to see you. I saw him out of the corner of my eye. I didn't think he meant me any harm . . . not until he spoke." Josephine shivered. "What would he have done? If he caught me?"

"I don't know. Maybe something bad. Maybe nothing at all. He hasn't hurt your sister, has he?"

Josephine shook her head. "Not that I know. Why would he threaten me like that?" *You're already dead.*

"Who knows why ghosts torment the living? Maybe out of jealousy, maybe for fun, maybe for power or survival or . . ."

The weight she'd carried the last few days returned and became too great a burden for Josephine to bear any longer. She leaned forward, cupped her face in her hands, and fought back tears.

"I don't know what to do," she said. "I don't know how to save myself or protect my family. I don't know what Laurence and Dorcas are up to, and I don't know what's happening in her house. I feel like I'm buckling under the weight of too many unanswered questions. I just need to *know*, you know?"

"I know," Dorothy said with a sad, slow nod. "The truth will set you free."

Josephine laughed bitterly.

"What did I say?" Dorothy asked.

"Dorcas used that same expression, only . . . only she called it ridiculous. She doesn't want me to know the truth. Withholding and obscuring the truth is one of the ways she's terrorizing us. I'm so fucking sick of her mind games."

Josephine was reminded of the missing page from the library book, the reason she'd come to see Dorothy in the first place. She asked if Dorothy knew anything about it.

"Sorry, no. I didn't even notice that a page had been torn out. But that reminds me. Remember how, after you told me my name reminded you of *The Wizard of Oz*, you said the book is really good?"

Josephine nodded.

"Well, I was curious, so I went to the library and borrowed a copy, as well as a collection of *Grimms' Fairy Tales* and, holy fucking shit, you weren't kidding! They're super violent. The Tin Woodman chops up a pack of wolves with his axe, and the Scarecrow snaps the necks of a murder of crows with his bare hands. And in *Cinderella*, the evil stepsisters cut off pieces of their own feet when trying to fit into the glass slipper. And in *Snow White*, the queen tries to eat Snow White's lungs and liver. How gross is that?" She smiled and laughed as she spoke, clearly not turned off by the gorier elements she'd found in the fairy tales she had read.

When Josephine didn't respond, Dorothy asked her if she'd read *Snow White*.

"I've been meaning to for years, and I've watched all the big adaptations countless times, but I haven't read the original fairy tale yet," Josephine said with the most disinterested tone she could muster, hoping Dorothy would stop there. Josephine didn't have the heart to think about violence and gore, not even the fictional kind. With every passing hour, it felt more and more like she was living in her own personal dark fairy tale.

"You can borrow the library copy if you'd like," Dorothy said, "once I'm done with it." Suddenly, her face brightened. "Oh, another thing. My grandma called my parents this morning. She's planning to come visit on New Year's Eve. She might know a few things we can do to protect you and your family from Dorcas."

"Yeah, maybe," Josephine said. "I'm sorry, but it's been a long day." Josephine had her doubts that Dorothy's grandmother would be of any help. "I'm going to head back."

"Okay," Dorothy said. "But be careful. If Laurence is still out there, come back here right away."

Josephine nodded and ran back to the house so quickly it felt like her feet hardly touched the ground.

"There you are," Mrs. Jagger said when Josephine entered through the front door. "Did you go for a jog?"

Josephine nodded as she swept her hair out of her face and tried to catch her breath. It was a small relief that her mother had provided the perfect explanation for how she looked; Josephine didn't have the mental energy to come up with an excuse.

"Well, you're just in time," Mrs. Jagger said. "Dinner's ready."

"Thanks," Josephine said. "I'll get changed and be down in a bit." She raced up the stairs and paused for a moment outside of Mary's room, listening. When she was pretty sure she was the only person on the second floor, she slipped inside and grabbed the pouch of lavender from Mary's mantel. She then collected the pouches from Allison's, Elizabeth's, and their parents' rooms, then shut herself in her own bedroom. She tossed all the pouches, including her own, into the fireplace, stacked two logs above a crumpled piece of paper torn from her notebook, struck a match, and lit a small fire. After her failed attempt to burn the books, she was relieved to find the pile of logs from outside didn't have the same protective spell cast over it. The lavender gave off a flowery aroma that instantly calmed Josephine. She shook her head to focus and opened the nearest window to air the room out. Before long, the lavender was nothing but ash. She left the fire burning—its flickering, orange light was comforting.

Night would fall soon, and night was Dorcas's time. Josephine had no idea what to do nor who to turn to. If her parents wouldn't believe her—and she was certain they wouldn't—would the police? Doubtful, but even if they did, what could they do? Mary believed her, but like everyone else, she couldn't maintain her memories long enough to be of any help. Josephine was thankful she'd met Dorothy, but even she could only do so much.

It's just me and you, she thought, picking up her notebook and jotting down everything that had happened that day.

When Josephine had recorded everything she could remember, she put the notebook down and rubbed her face. Something caught her attention—a book on the shelf in the closet. One she hadn't noticed before even though its bright red spine had just jumped out like a sore thumb.

A cold gust of wind howled through the open window and the closet door slammed shut. Josephine tensed and swore. She got to her feet and closed the window, then returned her attention to the closet.

Even though her mind was screaming at her to let sleeping dogs lie, she crossed the room, opened the closet door, and turned on the light.

Click-click.

She tried to slide the book off the shelf—for a moment it didn't budge, thanks to how tightly the books were packed together, but finally, it came free. After turning the book over and reading the cover, Josephine had to laugh.

Snow White and Other Fairy Tales.

I've been meaning to for years, she'd told Dorothy, *but I haven't read the original fairy tale yet.*

Well, here's your chance.

She flipped through the pages to see how long *Snow White* was, and a piece of old, yellowed paper fell out and fluttered to the floor.

Josephine had an unshakeable feeling that she knew where the piece of paper had come from.

The missing page from *Early Histories of Canaan, Vermont.*

She put *Snow White* back on the shelf and picked up the paper with a shaking hand. It wasn't rational, but she was afraid that the page might suddenly turn to dust or, worse yet, that someone might leap from the shadows and snatch it away.

Dorcas tore this page out of the library book, Josephine thought. *She hid it here years ago. What will she do if she finds out I've read it?*

It didn't matter. Josephine *needed* to read it. The potential reward—knowledge—was worth the risk. Under the light of the closet's hanging bulb, she began:

The legend of Canaan's witch doesn't end there. Many of the townsfolk who were alive the night the mob was formed believe that Dorcas's power extends beyond the grave.

Josephine stopped, confused, and reread the first two sentences. *Beyond the grave?* She thought back to what she'd read in the library's local history room. It hadn't mentioned Dorcas's death, which was a really big gap. Could there be a second missing page? As much as it frustrated her to admit it, it seemed likely. She flipped the page over, saw that the back was blank, and then continued reading.

They say that, as the flames consumed her body, Dorcas vowed with her dying breath to have her revenge on the assembled. She cast a resurrection charm on herself and her house, keeping her spirit tethered to this plane. Since that day, she has abducted people who unknowingly wander into her web. She keeps each victim trapped for seven days. At midnight on the seventh day, she is able to bind them to her house and then, over the course of many years, she slowly drains their life force. Before that person dies, she abducts a new victim and the process begins anew.

Worse yet, it's believed that, should Dorcas be able to bind a family of seven to her property at the same time, she might be able to generate enough power to perform a resurrection and walk the earth as an immortal.

The moment Josephine finished reading the last word, the paper caught fire. The flame burned a hole at the heart of the page that spread so quickly it singed her fingertips before she could let go. The smell of sulfur filled Josephine's nose and tickled the back of her throat.

Someone laughed, a sound that seemed both near and far . . . or was the sound only in her head?

Josephine resisted the childish urge to bury her face under a pillow and press it against her ears. Instead, she clenched her fists, stood as straight as she could, and said, "Show yourself, Dorcas."

Dorcas didn't appear, but her laughter continued to drift through the shadows.

"I know it's you," Josephine said.

The disembodied laughter slowly faded away.

Silence.

Had Dorcas been in the room? Had she left? Or was she watching Josephine with her gouged-out eyes? It didn't matter. Josephine felt more empowered than she had since they'd arrived. She couldn't run—she had to stand her ground. She finally knew precisely what Dorcas was trying to do.

At midnight on New Year's Eve, my family and I will take the stone man's place, fused into the cellar's walls—a lifetime of pain and misery. And Dorcas, more powerful than ever, will be resurrected.

As terrifying a thought as that was, Josephine was grateful to know the truth. The truth could—*would*—save her family. The truth was the key to defeating the witch.

The truth will set you free, Josephine thought. She began to laugh, softly at first, but she laughed harder and louder until the sound reached a pitch that was nearly impossible to tell apart from Dorcas's laughter. She felt altogether assured, delirious, and mad.

We're all mad here.

Josephine smiled. It felt good to laugh.

PART THREE

THIRTEEN

Early morning sunlight filled the kitchen when Josephine entered. Other than Louisa, who was drinking from a bottle in the family room with her father, her sisters were still upstairs.

"Quick, someone call Guinness," Mrs. Jagger said. She looked at her watch. "It's a new world record."

"It's, like, eight o'clock," Josephine said.

"Well, it's a world record for you."

Josephine poured herself a glass of orange juice and joined her mother at the table without comment.

"Couldn't sleep?" Mrs. Jagger asked.

"No, I had a great sleep." It wasn't a lie. It had been one of the best sleeps she'd ever had without wearing her headphones, and easily the deepest since they'd arrived in Canaan. Her eyes had closed as soon as her head had hit the pillow, and she didn't think she'd had a single dream all night.

But in a way, that scared her more than any of the nightmares she'd had. Ignorance is bliss, but at what cost? Wasn't it better to know what Dorcas was up to throughout the night?

Mrs. Jagger smiled. "I'm glad to hear that. You've looked tired the past few days. Is everything okay?"

Even though Josephine knew everyone else's memories were continually resetting, her mother's innocent question still upset her. She didn't want to deal with everything on her own. She wanted her mom and her dad to be able to help her—no, more than that; she wanted her parents to take over. She wanted her parents to be, well, parents. She shouldn't have to be responsible for their safety, and for her sisters', and yet . . . here she was.

Josephine briefly considered lying, smiling, saying everything was fine and nothing was troubling her and she didn't know what her mother was talking about.

Instead, she lowered her gaze and her voice, and said, "It's this house, Mom. We're not welcome here."

"What?" Mrs. Jagger said with a shocked laugh. "What are you talking about?"

"What am I talking about?" Josephine had to laugh too. "*What am I talking about?* Well, let's see. I'm talking about a witch who used to live here, who built this house. Shit, she was *killed* in this house."

Mrs. Jagger reeled as if she'd been slapped, her mouth wide open in shock. Josephine never spoke like that in front of her parents, let alone *to* them.

Josephine continued without pause. "I'm talking about a witch who still haunts this fucking house, a witch only I can see."

"Josephine!" her mother said, but Josephine didn't stop.

"And she's awful, Mom, like nothing you've ever seen, not even in your worst nightmares. Skin like wax, hair like stringy tar, a monstrous smile and empty eye sockets that still look at you, that still *see* you. But it's what she wants to do to us that makes her truly awful."

"Stop it, Josephine."

"She's keeping us here on purpose, Mom. She's keeping us here long enough to kill us or eat us or trap us in the basement walls or turn us all against each other or who knows what else, all in the hope that doing so will resurrect her. And there's nothing you or Dad or any of us can do about it because none of you have a fucking clue what's going on!"

Mrs. Jagger stood up abruptly, knocking her chair over, her mind a tangle of jumbled, repeating thoughts that berated Josephine: *Crazy, crazy, crazy, my daughter has lost her mind, crazy, crazy, what can we do, crazy, she's dangerous, crazy, crazy, she's gone CRAZY!*

Put on your net, Josephine screamed at herself through the uproar, relieved by the internal silence that followed as soon as she had.

Her mother pointed to the kitchen door, where Mr. Jagger had appeared with Louisa; the baby was beginning to wail. "Go to your room," she said.

Josephine laughed loudly and pointedly. "I'm seventeen. You can't send me to my goddamn room!" She stood up and clenched her fists, feeling like she'd been yanked to her feet by invisible strings. She was vaguely aware that she was losing control, but she didn't care. She clenched her jaw to stop herself from yelling any more—and that's when she caught sight of the knife.

It had been left out on the kitchen counter, within reaching distance from where she stood. It gleamed in the sunlight, calling to her.

Pick me up.

She picked up the knife.

"Josie—" her mother said.

"What are you doing?" her father said.

Louisa's wails turned to full-blown cries.

Josephine pointed the knife at her mother. Tears sprang free from her eyes and ran down her cheeks, but she didn't feel sad or angry or scared. She only felt a hint of confusion encased in a resolution as thick and cold as ice.

What are *you doing?* she asked herself.

I'm doing what needs to be done, she answered.

"I'm doing what needs to be done," she told her father, her voice much shakier and far less sure than the voice in her head had sounded.

"Josie, put the knife down," her father said urgently.

Louisa's entire head was beet red. She was crying so hard that she'd gone hoarse and she sounded more like she was choking.

"Put the knife down!" her mother screamed.

"No!" Josephine screamed back. She turned and ran past her father, into the foyer, up the stairs, and into her bedroom. She slammed the door behind her and leaned against it for a moment, covering her face with her forearms. What had just happened? What had she done?

What needs to be done.

But what did that mean? How was threatening her parents with a knife what needed to be done? She looked at the knife, a little unsure how it had gotten into her hand, then threw it across the room in disgust. It skittered across the floor and came to a stop in the corner nearest the closet.

Footsteps pounded up the stairs, snapping Josephine out of her thoughts. If she could just avoid her parents for an hour or two—maybe even just a few minutes—they'd forget all about her mental break and everything would be okay.

Will anything ever be okay again?

"Shut up," Josephine mumbled. She rolled her desk chair to the door and jammed it under the handle. If her parents wanted in bad enough, they'd have to break the door down.

A shadow passed in the hall. The handle turned. The door shook. But the chair held.

"Josie, open the door." It was her father.

She didn't answer.

"I'm alone," he said. "I'm not mad. I just want to talk. I need to make sure you're okay."

"I don't want to talk to anyone right now," Josephine said, her voice weak. "I just want to be left alone."

"I'm afraid I can't do that. I love you too much."

"Go away."

"I'm not going anywhere until you let me in."

No, no, not by the hair of my chinny chin chin.

Mr. Jagger sighed loudly. "Look, Josie, if you let me in, we can work this out together."

"Why should I believe you?" Josephine asked.

"Because I believe *you*," he replied.

Josephine held her breath. She was afraid that if she moved a muscle, she'd wake up back in the real world, the world where no one believed her and even if they did—like Mary had and her father was now claiming—they didn't believe her for long. But he had come to her. Could it be that her father knew what was happening? Had something happened to him that had somehow embedded itself in his memory?

"Please open the door," he said.

Josephine hesitated a moment longer, then moved the chair and unlocked the door. She turned the handle and opened the door.

Dorcas walked in. "Little pig," she said.

"No," Josephine said, shaking her head in shock and taking a few steps backward.

Dorcas followed her. "Little pig," she repeated.

"Stay back!"

Dorcas raised her hands and smiled. Her nails were long and her knuckles were knobby. "I don't want to hurt you. I want to talk."

"I have nothing to say to you," Josephine said, trying to sound confident and strong, but her trembling voice gave her away. She wished she hadn't thrown the knife across the room.

Little good it would do against her.

"Fine with me," Dorcas said. "I'm not interested in anything you have to say. I only want you to listen to me, and listen well."

"Did you hurt my dad?" Josephine asked, sudden panic flowing through her veins. "Did you do anything to my mom?"

"My, my, my. For a girl who has nothing to say to me, you certainly are full of questions." Dorcas waved a hand in the air and the bedroom door closed behind her. "Your parents are fine. Both still downstairs. Talking, eating, already forgetting all about you. See? You have nothing to worry about, Josephine. You're all alone."

Josephine felt a little bit of her fear evaporate as anger took its place. Dorcas was taunting her, teasing her.

"I might be alone," she said, her voice a low growl, "but I still won't let any harm come to my family."

Being angry, Josephine decided, felt much better than being afraid.

"I don't doubt you'll try to protect them," Dorcas said, wringing her hands together. "But you will fail. This is my house. Not yours. And I'm far more powerful than you. You can burn my lavender"—She pointed at the fireplace mantel. There was another pouch there . . . or was it the same one Josephine had burned the night before?—"and you can conspire against me with that loathsome girl in the woods, but for what? Like I said, this is my house. You can't get rid of me and you certainly can't keep me out."

The early morning sun, shining brightly through her window, suddenly shot to its peak in the sky and then set on the western horizon, and the room was plunged into darkness. It became so cold that Josephine's breath clouded in front of her face. Dorcas dissolved into thin black tendrils of smoke that swirled in the air before vanishing. The sun quickly rose in the east and stopped where it had been before, and the room's temperature returned to normal.

Josephine stood alone, her head spinning. It seemed like Dorcas had sped up time, skipping an entire day. Time had done that at least once before, back when . . . back when Josephine had first set foot in the house. She hadn't written it down, so the memory was foggier than most, but Josephine thought she could remember time speeding up a little after her father had slipped and hurt his head.

As helpless as Josephine felt, she still had her anger. She decided she'd hang onto it for as long as possible. She didn't think that would be a difficult thing to do.

But everything Dorcas had said was discouraging. Josephine knew Dorcas was more powerful than her, and her ability to alter time was further proof of that. She couldn't think of any way to get rid of her, or any way to keep her out. How could you prevent a ghost from entering a house when the ghost could pass through walls?

I might not be able to stop a ghost, Josephine thought. *But a witch . . .*

She thought of the trees with pentagrams carved into their trunks that prevented Dorcas from leaving her property.

She thought of the ceramic tree she'd bought with a similar pentagram.

She thought of the knife she'd thrown to the floor, its blade reflecting sunlight that caught her eye.

And then she thought up a plan. She'd trick Dorcas into leaving the house, and while the witch was outside, she'd carve pentagrams near all of the house's entry points—every door and window, even the fireplaces—preventing Dorcas from ever entering the house again. Simple.

Yeah, simple, she thought sarcastically.

Maybe not, but it was the only plan she had, and she'd make it work. She had to.

Josephine crossed the room and picked up the knife, then paused. She'd heard something—a rustling sound from within the closet. She tightened her grip on the knife's handle and allowed her anger to rekindle, to spread through her limbs, heating her from within.

"I know you're in there, Dorcas."

The rustling was joined by something that sounded like a whimper, or perhaps soft laughter.

Josephine reached out but hesitated, her fingers a few inches from the handle.

"Come out," she said. "Now."

"No, no, not by the hair of my chinny chin chin," someone inside the closet whispered.

Josephine grabbed the handle and opened the door. She dropped the knife in surprise.

It wasn't Dorcas. It was Helen. Or rather, a vision of Helen. Because Josephine knew it couldn't have been the real Helen who had suddenly appeared and disappeared in the house, so far from her home, a couple of days before. If Josephine believed that, she'd be—*crazy, crazy CRAZY*—concerned for her mental well-being, or at least more so than she already was. No, Helen must be a vision.

Visions can't lock people in closets, Josephine thought. Did that mean Helen had died? Was she a ghost?

Helen was sitting on the floor, her back leaned against the bookcase, hugging her knees tight to her chest. Her eyes were red and her cheeks were wet.

"What are you doing in here?" Josephine asked. "What are you doing *here*?" She spread her arms out, indicating the room, the house, the entire state of Vermont.

Helen sniffled and rubbed the heels of her palms across the bags under each of her eyes, wiping away tears. "I came here to apologize, Josephine. I'm so, so sorry."

The answer took Josephine by surprise. A voice in the back of her head told her it should be the other way around, considering what Josephine had done to Helen years ago, but she said nothing.

Left to fill in the silence, Helen continued. "I was such a jerk. What I did was awful."

Josephine tried to speak, but wasn't sure how to respond.

"I'm sorry I tricked you into the closet," Helen said. "I'm so sorry I trapped you in there."

Josephine knew Helen wasn't referring to the incident from a couple of nights ago. She was referring to the time she had locked Josephine in the closet in Helen's mom's boyfriend's house, nine years ago. Since that time, Josephine had tried her best not to think about that day, but the memory came rushing back so quickly and vividly that she couldn't stop it.

They had been best friends. Helen had never done anything mean to Josephine before.

They were eight years old and playing with the Mickey Mouse Clubhouse toy set Helen's mom had bought her daughter during their family trip to Disney World. Helen asked Josephine to get Pluto—he was in the back of her closet—and then slammed the door and held it shut.

Josephine fought to free herself. She pushed against the door, pounded it with her fists, yelled and screamed and cried, all to no avail. Helen had hit a growth spurt that summer and was much taller than Josephine, and easily overpowered her. Josephine was only trapped in the cramped, hot, pitch-black space for three or four minutes, but it felt like three or four days.

When Helen finally opened the door Josephine stared at her in shock, frozen with fear. She could think of no reason why Helen had done that. She didn't see any regret or shame in Helen's expression, nor any joy or mean-spiritedness or anything else. Her face was blank, void of emotion. Josephine pushed past Helen and ran out of the house, all the way home. She threw herself on her bed and pulled her blanket over her head, shutting out the world.

"I still don't know why I did it," Helen said, as if she could read Josephine's mind and see the memories playing there like a movie. Maybe she could. Josephine still wasn't sure if any of this was real, or if it was another one of Dorcas's tricks. But it seemed real. It *felt* real.

Helen continued. "All I can say is I wish I hadn't done it. I wish I hadn't hurt you. I wish that every day. But of course, wishes can't change the past."

The day following the incident, Josephine didn't see Helen after school. Nor the day after that, or the day after that. Her mom didn't return Josephine's mother's calls. Josephine didn't see Helen in her yard or even looking out through her bedroom window. It was as if she'd disappeared off the face of the planet.

But she hadn't disappeared. She took a new route home to avoid passing Josephine's house and rarely left her bedroom in the evenings or on weekends. Josephine saw her again for the first time two years later—sitting alone on a park bench, looking like the years had not been kind to her.

"Wishes aren't real," Helen said from within Josephine's closet. "I used to believe in magic and fairy tales, but that's ridiculous. I know that now. The only thing I know for sure is that I did what I did and I regret what I did and the only thing I can do to begin to make up for what I did is apologize. That's why I'm here, Josephine. To apologize to you."

Josephine opened her mouth to say *it's okay*, to say it wasn't that big of a deal—it was just a few minutes, after all—and that she forgave her. But those words didn't come out. They lodged in her throat and refused to be voiced. It would have been easier to say those things, but it wouldn't have been completely honest either. Instead, she said, "It's not your fault."

Josephine was a little shocked she'd said that. Not because it wasn't true, but because she'd vowed to never tell anyone what had really happened.

Helen frowned. "Of course it was my fault."

"No, it wasn't," Josephine said. "It was mine."

When Josephine had seen Helen sitting on a park bench, picking bits of Wonder Bread off her peanut butter sandwich and throwing them to a flock of birds hopping at her feet, she almost turned around and left before Helen saw her. But she hesitated, and watched, and was filled with a dull ache.

The birds pecked eagerly at the bread without getting too close to Helen. Josephine felt a little like the birds. On a deep level, she missed her friend and wanted to know what had happened to her the past two years, but on another level— one much closer to the surface—she was still afraid of her. But Josephine also felt something else: guilt. That feeling helped her fight through her desire to turn around and run. Her guilt compelled her to approach the park bench. The birds scattered.

"Hello, Helen," Josephine said.

Helen looked up slowly. Her skin was pale, almost yellow, and she had dark bags under her eyes. It took her a few beats to recognize Josephine, and when she did, her eyes widened and she smiled a little. But then her face suddenly fell. "Josephine," she said, in a hushed tone.

Josephine nodded. "How are you, um, doing?"

Helen sighed and said, "Not good." She clearly didn't have the energy to lie. She didn't look like she had the energy to walk back home. "I shouldn't have done it." She looked at Josephine with pleading, tear-filled eyes. "Will you forgive me?" She got to her feet.

Josephine took a step back.

Helen grabbed Josephine's hand before she could retreat any farther.

Josephine winced and tried to free herself but couldn't. Helen's grip was strong. She smelled like mildew. Her nails were long and dirty.

"I shouldn't have done it," Helen repeated. "Will you forgive me?"

Josephine nodded, but Helen wasn't settled or calmed. She leaned in close to Josephine and shouted in her face. "*I shouldn't have done it! Will you forgive me?*"

Josephine didn't forgive her, nor did she tell Helen the truth. She yanked her hand free and ran all the way home, just like the day Helen had locked her in her closet.

The vision of Helen (*you don't still believe that's all she is—a vision—do you?*) not only looked older than that day in the park seven years before . . . she looked worse, both physically and mentally.

"What do you mean, it wasn't my fault?" Helen asked. "What do you mean, it was yours?"

Josephine briefly regretted admitting as much as she had, but there was no stopping now. And besides, telling Helen the truth was long overdue. "It was my fault. Not locking me in your closet—that was you—but what happened to you after. The isolation, the doubt, the guilt, the fear, the anxiety. Everything you felt. Everything that dragged you down."

"I never told you . . . how do you know what I went through?" Helen tapped a forefinger against her temple. "How do you know how I *felt*?"

"Because . . ." Josephine paused, swallowed, and felt a tear slip down her cheek. "Because I put those feelings there."

Helen frowned. "You . . . put those feelings . . . ?"

"In your head," Josephine said.

"How?"

"I don't know." Josephine sat down in the doorway to the closet. "I don't understand how it works. All I know is, from a young age, I could . . . sometimes . . . influence people. That's the best word I can think of to describe it—influence. The headaches that follow, sometimes lasting for days, are horrendous, so I try not to do it, but if I get really upset, or really mad, or really scared . . ."

"You *influence* them?"

Josephine nodded and chewed at her thumbnail. "I can make them feel things. I can change their emotions. And I can hear thoughts." *I think I can do more than that too*—she briefly recalled passing her father on the stairs and him being knocked back a step as if she had pushed him, and Louisa somehow appearing at the top of the basement stairs moments after she had pictured her there, but then cast those thoughts aside. "I can sometimes control my influence by imagining a net surrounding my brain, keeping my thoughts in and other people's out. Wearing noise-canceling headphones used to help too, but I accidentally broke them when we got here."

Helen shook her head and held up her hand to stop Josephine. "Wait. You're telling me you made me feel all those *awful* things?" Helen asked.

Josephine nodded.

Neither girl spoke for a beat. Josephine's heart pounded in the quiet. *Thump-thump. Thump-thump. Thump-thump.* She'd never told anyone about her ability before, not even her sisters. She didn't even like thinking about it. And now that she'd told Helen, she couldn't decide if she felt better or worse. Maybe a bit of both.

"Say something, Helen," Josephine said, breaking the silence. "I can forgive you, but . . . can you forgive me?"

"Forgive you?" Helen said. "I can't even *look* at you."

Helen picked up the knife.

Josephine didn't have time to react, didn't have time to protect herself.

But Helen didn't mean to attack her.

Instead, she pointed the tip of the knife at her own eye. *I can't even* look *at you.*

Time stopped. The hollow absence of sound was the only thing Josephine could hear. And then Helen thrust the knife into her eye with a wet *squelch.*

Clear liquid squirted out and ran down her cheek.

With a flick of her wrist, Helen popped her eyeball out of her skull. It was still impaled on the tip of the knife.

Helen flicked her wrist again and her eyeball slid off the knife. Still attached to her brain by the optic nerve, it dangled and bounced against her chin like a large, juicy grape.

"What the fuck?" Josephine screamed as she slammed the closet door shut and skittered backward like a crab. She stopped and covered her eyes—*she carved her eye out of her own fucking head*—with her hands as she tried to collect her thoughts and come to grips with what had just happened.

Once she had steadied her nerves—*her optic nerve . . . it looked like a bloody tangle of thin cables and wires*—she opened the door.

Helen was gone. The closet was empty. Other than the knife—it sat in the middle of the floor.

The closet light turned off on its own.

Click-click.

FOURTEEN

Silence. Josephine couldn't take the silence any longer.

"Show yourself," she said. Not loudly, but assertively.

Helen didn't reappear and Josephine didn't sense Dorcas's presence, so who had turned off the closet light? She was the only person in the room, and unless she had developed the ability to move objects with her mind, it hadn't been her. One more mystery to add to her growing list.

She looked at the knife on the floor. It was an inanimate object. It couldn't hurt her, not on its own, but she watched it as closely as she would have watched a venomous spider crawling up her leg.

She rubbed her face and took three deep breaths. Her confrontation with Helen—whether she'd been a vision or a ghost or Dorcas in disguise—had left Josephine shaken and disturbed. She decided she would carry out her plan and carve pentagrams in the house once she had calmed down a little more. It was still morning, after all, and she couldn't exactly go carve up the walls with her parents around. She'd need a lookout, and not just to keep an eye on her parents. She needed someone who could see Dorcas, to make sure the witch didn't catch Josephine in the act. And the only person who could see Dorcas, other than Josephine, was Dorothy.

There were so many problems with the plan that was developing in her head. Dorothy had offered to help, but when push came to shove, would she still be willing? Was it fair to put her in harm's way?

Josephine sighed. She couldn't just leave the knife in the closet and do nothing. Her face was reflected on the blade, and Josephine got a good look at how tired and unraveled she looked. She grabbed the knife and stepped out of the closet, then emptied the contents of her backpack onto her bed. She put her notebook, a pencil, and *The Kirkman Guide to Witchcraft* in the bag, followed by the knife so no one would see it.

Josephine laughed.

Nothing but the essentials, she thought.

"Are you going somewhere?" Allison asked when Josephine entered the kitchen and sat down at the table.

"I wish," Josephine said. She looked up quickly, realizing she'd spoken out loud when she hadn't meant to. Her sisters and parents were staring at her. "I mean, no. Why?"

"Your backpack," Allison answered.

"Oh, right. It's just my notebook. I got tired of carrying it around everywhere. Figured this would be better." Josephine slid her backpack off her shoulder and placed it on the floor beside her chair. The knife within clunked loudly on the floor.

"I'm not an expert," Elizabeth said, "but that didn't sound like a notebook hitting the ground."

"Yeah, it sounded a lot heavier," Mary said. "Are you conceal-ing a weapon in there, Josie?"

"What?" Josephine asked. *How does she know?*

"I'm kidding!" Mary said with a smile and a laugh. She turned to Elizabeth and swatted her arm. "Knowing Josephine, it's gotta be a book or two. Or ten."

Elizabeth rolled her eyes as if Mary had just said the most obvious thing in the world. "You think?"

Josephine sighed in relief.

"As I was saying before Sleeping Beauty waltzed in," Elizabeth said, turning her attention back to Allison, "what were you doing in my room in the middle of the night?"

"What?" Allison stopped chewing and shook her head. "I slept through the night."

"I could've sworn I heard a chiming sound like your harmony bell sometime after midnight."

"Maybe you were sleepwalking?" Mary suggested.

"I take it off—" Allison said.

"What?" Elizabeth interrupted. "You told me when I gave it to you for your birthday that you'd *never* take it off."

"You didn't let me finish," Allison said. "I take it off to sleep, and that's the *only* time I ever take it off. I promise. I love it."

Elizabeth smiled and blushed. "Okay, cool. Sorry. It seemed real, but it must've just been a dream."

The conversation reminded Josephine that she had likely lost a day and a night. *If I'm right about that, if I did lose a day, it would now be Thursday.* "What day is it?" she asked her parents.

"You don't know?" Mrs. Jagger asked with a laugh.

"Well, I just want to make sure," Josephine said. "Time here has a funny way of . . . slipping by."

Mrs. Jagger nodded. "I suppose you're right. It's . . . huh. What day *is* it?"

"It's . . ." Mr. Jagger checked his watch. "Thursday. The thirtieth of December."

Unreal, Josephine thought. No one had asked her where she'd been for the past twenty-four hours. They'd all probably lost a day too—they just didn't know it.

Mr. Jagger placed a plate of toast and fresh-cut fruit in front of Josephine with a smile.

Josephine's stomach rumbled as she took a big bite of the bread. It was thick and buttery and tasted like it had been baked fresh that morning.

"Eat up," Mr. Jagger said. "Mr. Finger is coming over with some paperwork this morning. Should be here any minute."

There was a pause as the girls looked at one another, their eyes eventually settling back on their parents.

Mrs. Jagger nodded with a smile. "We're signing to take ownership of the house. We've officially decided to move here, but not until summer so Mary and Josephine don't have to transfer during the school year."

The girls cheered, all except Josephine. She knew they weren't going to be moving into the house in the summer. She knew none of them would survive that long, not if she didn't stop Dorcas. She also knew that whatever paperwork Mr. Finger was bringing over would likely be fake. There probably wasn't even a Great-Great-Aunt Mercy. It seemed painfully obvious that the whole story was one big lie, but Josephine needed to know for sure.

"Hey, Dad?"

"Yes, Josie?"

"Where's your iPad?"

"It's . . ." He put his hand to his chin and looked around the kitchen. "I'm not really sure."

"Did you bring it into the house?" Mrs. Jagger asked. "I haven't seen it all week."

"You know something," he said. "I don't think I did." He frowned deeply and tapped the side of his head, like a stage actor overperforming for the people in the back row to see. "I think—I think I used the landline to call . . . who did I call? A mechanic? And Mr. Finger. Right?" He shook his head and looked to his wife for support, but she only shrugged. "My memory's a bit foggy, but I don't recall using my cellphone once since we arrived either."

"Me too," Mrs. Jagger said. "It's been nice disconnecting for a few days, hasn't it?"

Mr. Jagger nodded.

"If I find it, can I use it for a bit?" Josephine asked.

"Sure," Mr. Jagger said, innocently adding, "Why?"

Josephine shrugged and thought up a lie. "I need to do a bit of research, you know, for my story." She shoved the rest of her breakfast into her mouth, cleared her plate, and walked outside, hoping to find the iPad before Mr. Finger arrived.

Mr. Finger was standing on the front porch, his hands clasped in front of his body and a thin smile on his lips.

"Morning, Josephine," he said in his reedy, quiet voice.

"Oh, hi," Josephine said awkwardly. She stepped around the lawyer. "My parents are in the kitchen."

"I came to see the whole family. Baby, girls, parents, and all." His eyes were hidden behind the reflective surfaces of his glasses.

"What do you want with my sisters?" Josephine's insides curdled. "What do you want with *Louisa*?"

Mr. Finger ignored the question. "I trust everything here is to your satisfaction?"

"What do you care?"

"I've been charged with making sure your transition to this house is as smooth as possible. I only want what's best for you, Josephine."

"You don't even know me," she said. It felt like her breakfast was threatening to make a reappearance. *If I'm going to puke,* she thought, *at least let it be all over his shiny shoes.*

"Oh, but I do," he said, his smile stretching even thinner than before. "I know that you're an avid reader and that you've been searching books for clues. I know that you want to be an author and you've been doing a lot of writing here in this house, but you're not writing what your family thinks you're writing. I know you've become friends with that nosy girl who lives eastward. I know you're haunted by your past, and your past has followed you here, *literally* speaking. I know you think you can save everyone, but I also know this simple, irrefutable fact: *you can't,* Josephine. You're all going to die. And then my master will walk this earth, flesh and bone once more."

As he'd talked, Josephine had stood rooted to the ground. Her hands had formed fists and her jaw had clenched. Hot tears—not of sadness or fear but of anger—had run down her cheeks.

But she didn't retreat. Instead, she took a step forward.

Mr. Finger's smile faltered.

Thoughts swirled inside her head like a tornado. They screamed and yelled, raged and snarled, each word fighting to be heard over the others. *Hurt. Stop. Kick. Push. Finish. Punch. Burn. End. Kill.*

She took another step toward the lawyer and he took a timid step back.

Suddenly, Josephine's mad thoughts fell silent . . . all but one. Two words. In the new silence of her head, they were powerfully loud:

Fear me.

The left lens of Mr. Finger's glasses cracked in half. He gasped, covered his eye, and took a few more steps away from Josephine. A trickle of blood ran down his left cheek.

Holy shit. Josephine covered her mouth. *Did I do that?*

"Mr. Finger? Josephine?" It was her mother, standing in the open doorway. "What's happened?"

Josephine forced her body to relax and her head slowly cleared.

"Oh, God," Mrs. Jagger said, looking at Mr. Finger's face. "You're bleeding."

"I'm fine, I'm fine," he said with a forced laugh. "My glasses cracked. Must be the cold."

"Are you sure you're okay?"

"Of course. But might I trouble you for a small bandage, and some tape for my glasses? I'm afraid I won't be able to see a thing without them."

"Yes, no problem. Please, come in." She helped Mr. Finger into the house.

He took one last look at Josephine over his shoulder. She saw a hint of anger and a healthy dose of fear before the door closed.

But she'd also seen something else. His left eye, no longer hidden by the reflection of his glasses. Even after everything she'd been through, everything she'd seen in the house, it was still hard to believe her *own* eyes, but his eye had looked . . .

It looked like a snake's eye, she thought.

A chill crept up her spine and she shivered as if someone had just walked over her future grave.

She walked along the snowy driveway and got into the van, sitting in the front passenger seat. It was still cold, but at least she was sheltered from the wind. From where she sat, she could see through the family room window. Her parents were sitting side by side on the couch and were reading over some papers. Mr. Finger was seated in a chair beside the couch, facing the window. He wasn't looking at Mr. and Mrs. Jagger. He was intently staring straight ahead, through the window, into the van, directly at Josephine.

Another chill crept up her spine. She shook it off, locked the doors, and began searching the van, trying to not think of the lawyer. Easier said than done, but after a few minutes, she found her father's iPad in the pocket behind the driver's seat. She pressed the power button and was relieved when it turned on, but her relief was short-lived. The iPad's battery only had 6 percent power remaining, and the charging cord wasn't anywhere to be found. Had her father left it in Amherst?

She entered his password and then glanced up. Mr. Finger was still staring at her. He hadn't moved a muscle.

"Go ahead," Josephine said. "Watch me all you want. See if I give a shit."

It was a lie, but saying it out loud made her feel a little better.

There was no way Mr. Finger could've heard her, but he smiled again for the first time since his lens had cracked.

Josephine hated that smile. How had he even gotten to the house from wherever the hell he lived? There wasn't another vehicle in the driveway—there never had been any time he'd visited. She turned her attention back to the iPad. The battery was now at 5 percent.

"Damn it," she said under her breath, then got to work. It took a little longer than usual for the iPad's data to connect to the internet, but once it did, she immediately launched a web browser and searched for *Mercy Jagger Canaan*. There was nothing of any relevance, so she tried *Mercy Jagger Vermont*. There were a few websites that mentioned both Mick Jagger, lead singer of the Rolling Stones, and the state of Vermont, but nothing about anyone named Mercy Jagger living in the area.

Everyone who'd been alive during the last ten or twenty years had some sort of online record. Social media accounts, telephone listings, small-town news, membership or volunteering databases . . . either Great-Great-Aunt Mercy lived completely off the grid, or she didn't exist at all.

Inside the house, Mr. Finger still stared, still smiled.

What about you? Josephine thought. *Surely a lawyer will get plenty of online hits.*

And yet, a search for the words *Finger* and *lawyer* and *Canaan* and *Vermont* in a variety of combinations turned up nothing. No website, no listings, no news articles, no case histories. Nothing.

Josephine had to laugh. "You're a ghost," she said, not meaning to imply that Mr. Finger, like Dorcas and Laurence, was a spirit; his snake eye made her think otherwise.

She looked up.

Her parents were still visible within the family room.

But Mr. Finger was gone.

FIFTEEN

Someone *tap-tap-tapped* their fingernails on one of the van windows.

Josephine tensed and the iPad slipped from her hands. The screen went black as it landed in her lap, the battery fully drained. She looked for who had tapped, expecting to see Mr. Finger standing outside in the snow, smiling in at her. Instead, her eyes met Dorothy's.

The girl was pale and shaking, with her hands squeezed into her armpits for warmth. She waved and then quickly stuck her hand back under her arm. "Are you going to let me in before I freeze to death?"

Josephine reached across the van and unlocked and opened the door. Dorothy sat down in the driver's seat. She rubbed her hands together and blew on them.

"I hate the cold," she said. "So much."

"I'm counting down the days to spring. Hey," Josephine said, a sudden thought striking her. "Did the past day seem to, I don't know, go by really fast?"

Dorothy shook her head. "No faster than normal. Why?"

"Never mind. So what brings you out into the cold and past the safety of the pentagram trees?" Josephine asked.

"I wanted to make sure you're okay. After what happened last time I saw you, with Laurence and everything, I was afraid . . ." Dorothy's words trailed off for a moment, then she blinked. "So I came over to check on you and saw you sitting here."

"Aw," Josephine said in a slightly mocking tone. "You like me."

"Shut up," Dorothy said with a droll smile, whacking Josephine's arm with the back of her hand.

A chill ran up Josephine's arm, into her shoulder and the base of her neck. It felt cold and hot and electric all at the same time. Her heart pounded out an extra beat. She felt a little dizzy as an unanticipated thought entered her head.

Do I like Dorothy . . . more than just friends?

She had never felt that way about a girl before, but she had also never really felt that way about boys either. She hadn't given it much thought, but she had figured she was probably ace—not sexually attracted to anyone.

Dorothy was looking at her as if trying to figure out what Josephine was thinking. With every passing second of silence, things became slightly more awkward. *Say something. Say anything. Just stop sitting here silently.*

"Anyway, what's up?" Dorothy asked, breaking the silence before Josephine.

Tell her why you're in the van. Josephine tapped her father's dead iPad. "Um, I did some googling and it's obvious that Dorcas invented the whole Great-Great-Aunt Mercy story to trick my family into coming here. And I'm certain this fake lawyer, a man who calls himself Mr. Finger, helped her."

A glimpse of Mr. Finger's serpentine eye flashed in Josephine's memory. She decided she should write a few notes before things started to fade. She grabbed her backpack and pulled out the knife to get at her notebook.

Dorothy's eyes went wide at the sight of the blade. "Whoa! What the hell are you planning on doing with that?"

"Oh." Josephine looked from Dorothy to the knife and back to Dorothy again, then blushed. "Sorry. I didn't mean to freak you out. It's, um, for protection." She put the knife back in the bag and took out her notebook.

"I don't think you can stab a ghost to death."

"That's not what I meant. I'm going to carve pentagrams near every entrance in the house so that Dorcas can't enter it."

Dorothy smiled. "That could work. Just like the stars on the trees and my old fort. But you're going to need to wait for Dorcas to leave, and she rarely does."

"Yeah, I know," Josephine said, trying not to sound defeated. "I have a plan to get my family out of the house for an hour or two, but I have no idea how to lure Dorcas out."

Dorothy gave it some thought, then nodded. "You take care of your family and I'll take care of Dorcas."

"How?"

"I'll give her something she wants." Dorothy slipped her necklace over her head and squeezed the wooden pentagram pendant in her fist. "Me."

"You?" Josephine asked, trying to ignore the slight thrill she felt that Dorothy would do that for her. "What would Dorcas want with you?"

"Ouch," Dorothy said.

"That's not what I meant and you know it."

Dorothy laughed. "I know, I know." Her smile faded and her face hardened. "I used to be friends with someone . . ." Dorothy sighed, more a sorrowful sound than a tired one. "Someone Dorcas took from me. I've vowed to not let her take anyone else"—she looked at Josephine with sad eyes and quickly looked away—"and she's aware of that."

Josephine's heart ached for Dorothy and the pain she had clearly gone through. "You can't, it's too dangerous," Josephine protested, but she had a feeling Dorothy had made up her mind.

Dorothy handed Josephine the necklace. Josephine tried to push it back but she insisted.

"I have to," Dorothy said. "It's the only way to get her out of your house. She'll sense that I'm not wearing my necklace and she'll come for me. Once she gives chase, I'll run as fast as I can back to the safe side of the trees, then double back, careful to stay out of her sight, so I can help you carve pentagrams. We won't have much time. As soon as she discovers that you've sealed her out of her own house, well, she'll be fucking furious. But as long as we've carved all the pentagrams in time, we'll be safe."

Josephine took the necklace. "Thank you." It felt insufficient for what Dorothy was willing to do for her, but Josephine didn't know what else she could say. Not for the first time, Dorothy had left Josephine at a loss for words.

"Don't mention it," Dorothy said. "The problem with the plan is, even if we're successful, she'll still be out in the woods, thinking up ways to get back at you. What will you do then?"

"I'll figure that out when I get there."

"How can you be sure?"

"Because I have no other option."

Josephine entered the front foyer and closed the door as slowly and quietly as possible. Despite her best efforts to enter the house undetected, her mother appeared in the doorway to the family room.

"There you are," she said.

"Yep, here I am," Josephine agreed. "What's up?"

"Mr. Finger said . . ." Mrs. Jagger frowned. "He said . . . something about you." She chuckled. "Isn't that odd? I can't recall exactly, but I think—I think he was concerned about you." She gave her daughter a surprised, questioning look, the type of look that begged for some comfort, some sense that things weren't as bad as they seemed.

Josephine shrugged and shook her head. "I have no idea why. Is he still here?"

Mrs. Jagger shook her head. "No, he left a couple of minutes ago. I'm surprised you didn't see him."

I'm not, Josephine thought. "Where's Allison?"

"Upstairs, I think. Why?"

"Top secret sister stuff," Josephine said with forced good humor and a fake smile. She turned and walked up the stairs without waiting for her mother to answer. The sooner she put her plan into motion, the better.

The bedroom door was open a crack, but Josephine knocked anyway.

"Come in," Allison said from within. She was sitting behind her canvas, stroking a paintbrush across its surface with a determined look in her eyes. "I'm just putting the final touches on this."

"The painting of the house?" Josephine asked.

Allison nodded, put her brush down, and leaned back to observe her work. "All done," she said.

"Can I see?"

Allison nodded again and stood up, then crossed the room and drank some water from a glass on her bedside table. She had an odd, slightly disconnected look about her that made Josephine feel a little uneasy.

Allison sat on the edge of her bed as Josephine approached the painting. Her curiosity—largely morbid—propelled her forward like a strong wind at her back.

At first glance, Josephine wasn't sure what she was looking at. It wasn't a painting of the house, but a plume of mist rising in the woods. But after staring at the painting for a moment, hidden details began to jump out, like an optical illusion.

The mist wasn't mist—it was smoke. Translucent, phantom smoke rising from a pile of ash where the foundation of the house should have been. The smoke drifted up from the ground and swirled near the tips of the trees. No, that wasn't quite right either. The smoke, Josephine realized, swirled into the shape of the house. The longer she stared, the clearer she could see the wooden walls, the three triangular points of the roof—even the front door with its snake handle.

And then she saw the windows. Or rather, the windows saw *her*. They were like eyes peering out from the canvas. Josephine felt naked under their gaze, like they were stripping parts of her away, revealing the core of her soul. All her regrets, all her joys, all her shortcomings, and all her secrets—all were on display, wilting under the gaze of the smoky house.

Staring out from one of the windows was Dorcas.

"What do you think?" Allison asked, suddenly standing behind Josephine.

Josephine jumped and took a deep breath to steady her nerves. "It's . . . interesting."

"Thanks," Allison said with a wide smile. If she knew how creepy her painting was, she didn't show it. It was like with the story Josephine had written about herself as a cannibalistic witch; Josephine was certain Allison hadn't created her painting alone.

"I don't know what to paint next," Allison said with a sigh.

"I'm sure you'll think of something," Josephine said. *I'm sure Dorcas will think of something.*

Remembering why she'd come to Allison's room, Josephine added, "I saw Laurence just now."

"Oh, really? Where?"

"In the woods. West of here, past that abandoned house you mentioned. Far past it. He was looking for you."

Allison perked up. "Did he say why?"

Josephine shrugged, feigning indifference. "Hide-and-seek, I think? He said something about hiding deeper in the forest than ever before. Wanting to give you a 'real challenge' this time."

With a laugh, Allison said, "I know these woods pretty well by now. If he's out there waiting to be found, I'll find him. He won't even see me coming!" She walked toward the door, but Josephine stopped her.

"But he might *hear* you coming, especially if you're wearing your harmony ball."

Allison instinctively clutched her necklace with a downcast look in her eyes. "It's so quiet, especially under my jacket. You don't really think he'd be able to hear it, do you?"

I have a feeling the dead hear very, very well, Josephine thought. "He might. **Is it** worth the risk? If you really, truly want to sneak up on him, it might be best to leave it. Don't worry—I'll watch it for you."

Allison shook her head but then, after hesitating a moment longer, slipped the necklace over her head and handed it to her sister. The look of pain on her face nearly broke Josephine's heart.

She'll be fine, Josephine reminded herself. But *would* Allison be fine? Josephine couldn't say for sure. She was sending her younger sister out into the deep, dark woods, and the forest was filled with fangs.

If I do this, Josephine thought, *if I'm actually able to trick Dorcas . . . yes, Allison will be fine.*

It's my only hope. Our *only hope.*

Josephine took the necklace and added it to her backpack where it rattled against Dorothy's.

Enacting the rest of her plan was easy.

After Allison left the house, Josephine waited fifteen minutes to give her sister a head start. She would've preferred to wait a little longer to allow Allison to get farther away, but she was also afraid Allison might forget what she was doing and head back home. If that happened, the plan would be ruined before it had gotten under way.

Josephine snuck outside, counted to ten, and returned inside. She slammed the front door behind her. The bang echoed in the foyer and, Josephine hoped, throughout the house.

"Mom! Dad! Everyone! Anyone! Come quick!"

Josephine didn't need to wait long. Her mother was the first to appear, a concerned look on her face, followed soon by her father holding Louisa, and finally, Mary and Elizabeth.

"What? What is it? What's wrong?" Mrs. Jagger asked in a panic.

"Allison's in trouble," Josephine said, wishing she was a better actor. At least she now had plenty of experience lying, which would help her sell her story. "She's gone!"

"Gone?" Mr. Jagger said. "Where? Is she playing outside with that boy, or painting, or . . . ?"

"No," Josephine said, cutting her father off. "All of her art supplies are upstairs in her room, and I saw Laurence a few minutes ago—he hasn't seen her all day."

"How do you know she hasn't just gone for a walk?" Mary asked.

"I found this outside in the snow." Josephine held out her fist and dangled the necklace so everyone could see it. The harmony ball chimed as it swayed side to side.

The effect of producing Allison's necklace was immediate and more successful than Josephine had hoped.

"Oh, dear God," her mother said.

Mr. Jagger put Louisa down and hurriedly put on his boots and coat without a word, his face pinched and red.

Mrs. Jagger followed suit.

"I'm coming with you," Mary said.

"Me too!" Elizabeth added, sounding like she was choking back tears.

Louisa started to cry. Perfect timing. Josephine lifted her into her arms and said, "I'll stay here and watch the baby. Hurry back as soon as you've found Allison. I feel like I'm going to be sick . . ."

Mr. Jagger nodded gravely and the four of them rushed through the door without another word.

Louisa began to settle down as Josephine bounced her in her arms and counted aloud to one hundred. Then, she flicked the front porch light switch on and off three times, just as she and Dorothy had discussed.

After a moment, the door creaked open. Dorothy peered inside. "Are they gone?"

"They're gone."

Dorothy nodded. There was no fear in her eyes, only grim determination, and Josephine's appreciation and respect for her rose to new heights. Without another word, Dorothy closed the door.

Josephine moved to one of the living room's windows to watch what happened next.

Dorothy ran about twenty or thirty yards from the house and then turned to face it.

"Hey, you dumb witch!" Dorothy yelled. "You want me? I don't have my pendant, so come and fucking get me!" She didn't wait to see what—if anything—happened next. She turned and ran east toward her own house. Within a few seconds, she passed out of Josephine's sight, the forest swallowing her up.

Josephine scanned the woods, watching for movement. Nothing happened. The seconds ticked by, the longest of her life. She didn't breathe. Louisa asked for her baba, but Josephine ignored her.

Maybe it wouldn't work. Of course it wouldn't work—it was a stupid plan. Dorcas wouldn't be foolish enough to fall for it. She'd know something was up. She'd never leave the house.

"Baba," Louisa said. "Baba."

And then, Josephine heard something faint—

Crunch, crunch, crunch.

Footsteps, outside, in the snow. Slow, tentative, and barely audible, but there.

"Baba!"

Dorcas came into view, leaving the safety of her home with hesitant steps. She whipped her head around to take one last look at her house—

Josephine dropped to the ground beneath the window and squeezed Louisa to her chest. Her heartbeat pounded with so much force that she pictured her ears leaking blood.

"She didn't see me, she didn't see me, she didn't see me," she whispered on repeat. But did she truly believe that? Not completely. She felt like any minute now she'd hear a *tap-tap-tap* on the window, and she'd look up to see Dorcas staring down at her from outside.

Louisa began to cry louder for her baba.

"Shh," Josephine said, bouncing her sister on her lap, trying to make her settle. When that didn't work, Josephine said, "Okay, okay, I'll get you your baba."

Josephine put Louisa down and peered over the bottom of the window frame.

Dorcas was nowhere to be seen. That meant she could be anywhere.

The front door creaked open.

It was Dorcas, Josephine was certain of it.

From where Josephine was crouched in the living room, she could see late afternoon sunlight brighten the front foyer, but she couldn't see anyone there. Maybe Dorcas wouldn't see her. Maybe Louisa wouldn't cry and they could run, escape. Maybe—

Dorothy stepped into view.

"Josephine?" she called.

Josephine was too relieved to answer. She picked up Louisa and rushed to Dorothy's side. She wrapped her free arm around Dorothy's shoulders.

"Did it work?" Josephine asked when they separated. She gave Dorothy her necklace back.

"It worked," Dorothy said. "She followed me, but I ducked behind a bush and watched her pass. She continued on, so I waited a moment and rushed straight back here."

Josephine's sense of foreboding felt like a tangible thing, something she could see and touch and taste. "Then we don't have any time to waste."

They worked as quickly as possible, carving pentagrams in the wood above every door and window in the house. When their hands cramped, they took turns handling the knife. While carving a pentagram above the basement door, Josephine heard murmurs from the wall behind the mirror but Dorothy didn't mention it, so Josephine was happy to let that sleeping dog lie. Josephine nicked the tip of her thumb with the blade. As they moved upstairs, she stuck her thumb in her mouth to stop the flow of blood instead of looking for a bandage.

There was no time. And yet, miraculously, they finished the job before either girl saw or heard or sensed Dorcas within the house. They even remembered to carve a pentagram near the mouth of each fireplace and on the hatch leading to the attic— Josephine had been tempted to peer inside, but her nerves had gotten the better of her.

"Is that every entrance?" Dorothy asked. She still clutched the knife tight in her hand.

They sat down on the family room couch, their cheeks flushed.

Josephine handed Louisa her third bottle since they'd started.

"I think so, yes," Josephine said. "My parents are going to kill me."

"Even if they realize you just saved their lives?"

Josephine nodded.

"The carvings are small," Dorothy said without much hope. "Maybe they won't notice them?"

Josephine shrugged. It didn't matter. All that mattered was that she'd bested Dorcas and protected her family, and she couldn't have done it without Dorothy's help. "Thank you."

"You're welcome." Dorothy looked at Josephine and frowned. "I know you probably don't want to live here after all this shit, but it wouldn't be the worst thing in the world."

The tips of Josephine's ears burned. She looked away quickly, knowing her entire face must be flushed. "What do you mean?"

"I mean . . ." Dorothy paused and gathered the courage to say what came next. "Most of the kids here are only interested in hockey and hunting and shit like that. You're different. I like it. I, uh . . ." Dorothy cleared her throat and rubbed her forearms. "I like you."

Josephine felt like the world had shifted slightly. She took the knife back from Dorothy. "I like you too."

Dorothy had been right. Josephine's parents didn't notice the pentagrams when they returned.

They're distracted, Josephine thought. *It can't be long before someone sees one of the carvings, and then I'll have to come up with an explanation.*

They had found Allison in the woods. Allison said she had gone out to play with Larry but hadn't found him (*thank goodness for that*, Josephine thought), and she couldn't quite recall how she'd lost her harmony ball necklace. It must have accidentally slipped off when she'd put on her scarf . . . or something like that.

Everyone was tired from the afternoon's events and went to bed shortly after dinner. That was fine with Josephine.

She wrote a few notes in her journal before turning out the light and laying her head down. The air was cool, but her blankets were heavy and warm. She closed her eyes and breathed deep with contentment. She felt good. Better than that—she felt great. She'd overcome her fears, shut out the bad, bested the evil, all while making a fast friend—maybe one day more than a friend. The best feeling of all was knowing Dorcas could no longer enter the house.

But then, a sound silenced her thoughts. A sound from within the closet.

Click-click.

SIXTEEN

Light bled out from beneath the closet door. Someone had pulled the string and turned on the bulb.

Josephine wanted to pull the blankets over her head, like she used to do when she was four or five years old and thought that bad things lived under her bed and in her closet. Her parents had said that it was all in her head, that there was no such thing as monsters, that nothing hid in the shadows; but despite everything her parents had told her when she was younger, monsters *were* real, and now one *was* in her closet.

No, she thought. *You don't know that. It could be one of your sisters, playing a joke.*

"Allison?" she asked, her voice trembling. "Elizabeth?" It couldn't be Mary, could it? Just to be safe, she called her older sister's name too.

No one answered.

Because it's Dorcas. Dorcas is in your closet. She's come for you and your family and she's going to eat you first. Or maybe she will eat everyone else first while you watch helplessly.

Stop it, she told herself. *Stop it right now. It can't be Dorcas. It can't. Dorothy led her outside. We carved pentagrams at every entrance. She has no way to get back in.*

Click-click.

The light turned off.

Time seemed to slow down and speed up all at once, as if reality couldn't decide whether to torment Josephine and draw the night out or take pity on her and get through to the morning as quickly as possible.

As she was trying to decide what, if anything, she should do, the closet door opened a crack. Five long fingers emerged from the darkness within and gripped the edge of the door, guiding it open.

Dorcas stepped into the moonlight. She was smiling, but Josephine could tell that she wasn't happy.

"You've defaced my house," Dorcas said.

Josephine's eyes and mouth went wide with fright. A tear slipped down her cheek. "How . . . ?"

"How what?"

"Did you . . . ?"

"Get in?" Dorcas asked. "With your pentagrams carved near every door, every window?" She waved a hand at the open closet behind her. "This is the only entrance I'll ever need. I can come and go as I please, leaving and returning through here."

I'll carve another pentagram the moment you leave, Josephine thought. *One near each of the closets in the house, trapping you wherever the hell you dwell in the walls.*

Dorcas shook her head as if reading Josephine's mind. "Think you can stop me? You can't." She pointed her forefinger at

Josephine and then dug her nail into the closet's doorframe. She dragged her nail across the wood—*scriiiiiiiiitch*—scratching a pentagram deep into the surface. As soon as she'd connected the final line, the pentagram began to smoke.

Once the smoke cleared, the pentagram was gone without a trace, as if it had never been there at all.

Dorcas blew a small sliver of wood off her finger. It drifted lazily like a dead leaf falling to the forest floor. "You see? Long ago, I cast a powerful charm on this closet. The others too. You can't stop me from getting in or out. This is my house. We're connected. And we'll never be apart."

"What do you want from me?" Josephine asked, not truly expecting an answer.

"I don't want anything *from* you," Dorcas said. She pointed at Josephine again. "I just want *you*."

"You want to kill me," Josephine said. She saw no reason in beating around the bush, no reason to pretend she didn't know what Dorcas was planning.

"Kill you? No, I need you alive." Dorcas thought about this for a moment, then added, "In a manner of speaking."

"You need me alive to keep *you* alive."

Dorcas clasped her hands together and laughed. "Oh, my dear girl, I need you alive for so much more. I need you alive to keep *everything* alive. For if you die . . ."

The witch cupped her hand around her mouth.

"All will be lost."

She blew out a puff of breath through her hand as if blowing out a candle. She disappeared immediately, and it was suddenly early morning. Sunlight had replaced the moonlight, and a bird chirped outside.

Dorcas had done it again. Time had jumped ahead several hours—it was now the morning of New Year's Eve. Josephine was still in her bed, both relieved to be alone and frightened by what had just happened. The beginnings of a headache spread through her skull. She studied the fireplace and windows and could see from where she lay that the pentagrams were gone.

I'm not safe here, she thought, panic coursing through her veins. *I need to get out. I need to get out now.*

She dressed hurriedly, threw a few things into her backpack, and ran from the house before anyone else in her family woke up.

Three hours later, Dorothy opened the door to her fort and said, "Josephine? Are you in here?"

"Yes," Josephine whispered from the corner where she'd been hiding since fleeing from the house.

"Is everything okay?"

"No."

Understanding dawned on Dorothy's face, a look that was quickly replaced by one of despair. "How'd she get in?"

Josephine told her what had happened, leaving out no detail. When Josephine had finished, feeling like she'd been forced to live through the terrifying experience all over again, Dorothy sat down beside her and sighed.

"You should run away," Dorothy said. "Far, far away. It's the only thing left to do."

Josephine shook her head. "I can't leave my family."

"But she'll kill you—"

"I can't leave my family," Josephine repeated. "How would I live with myself?"

Dorothy nodded. "Yeah, I know."

With a defeated shrug, Josephine said, "So that's it. We tried, but there's nothing else I can do. I appreciate everything you've done for me, Dorothy. If I hadn't met you, I think this would've been a bit of a shitty week."

Dorothy looked at Josephine in confusion, but then Josephine smiled to show she was kidding around, and Dorothy smiled back. Both girls even managed to laugh a little.

"I might as well tell you this," Josephine said. She had already told Helen about her abilities, and she figured, since the end was near, why keep it from Dorothy? "I can . . . kind of . . . *influence* people."

Dorothy didn't say anything. She probably didn't understand. How could she? Josephine didn't fully understand it herself, and she'd lived with it all her life.

"Like, with my mind. I can get into people's thoughts and make them feel certain ways."

Dorothy's eyes went wide with excitement. "No fucking way! Can you read minds?"

"Not exactly—"

"Are you reading my mind right now? What number am I thinking of?"

"No, no, no," Josephine said, waving her hands and shaking her head. At least Dorothy hadn't laughed her out of the fort. "I can't read minds. Well, sort of, but not really. I can't do it on command. It's hard to explain. And the way I influence people? It's like . . . ." Josephine thought for a moment, trying to come up with a way to put it into words. "Have you ever been hit by an emotion out of the blue? Like, you're just sitting there watching TV or reading a book or something, and then, all of a sudden—BAM! You're sad. Or nervous. Or giddy, but, like, for no reason?"

"Sure," Dorothy said. "When I was younger, I used to have this really bad recurring dream. In it, I had a sister, a baby sister. And . . . I never really remembered all the details—they had always mostly disappeared by the time I woke up—but she was unhealthy and always died. I must've had that dream one hundred times and my sister died one hundred deaths, but each and every time I had it, it haunted me for days. Like you said, I'd be eating breakfast or reading in the library or playing with friends at school, when suddenly I'd start crying. I hated whoever killed her and wanted to do something bad to them, but of course there wasn't anyone to blame. I'd remind myself it was just a dream and I didn't even have a sister, and I'd be okay for a while, but then, after some time had passed, the same feelings—sadness and anger—would come creeping back up on me out of the blue and I'd be filled with rage all over again." Dorothy brushed at her cheek and laughed bitterly. "I bet that all sounds pretty stupid."

Josephine shook her head. "Not at all. My ability to influence people is a lot like that. But instead of those emotions being caused by a dream . . . they're caused by me."

Dorothy didn't look convinced. Or maybe, Josephine thought, she looked a little concerned. "Have you ever influenced my emotions at all?"

"Absolutely not," Josephine said with an emphatic shake of her head. "And I never would. The last time I did it was nine years ago." After a few false starts, Josephine told Dorothy what had happened with Helen. "I didn't know the full range of my abilities before that. I didn't know how bad it would be. I acted out of anger and it nearly killed my friend. She dropped out of school, closed in on herself, and experienced a lifetime of pain, all because of me. I haven't influenced anyone's emotions since then, and I'll never do anything like that again."

"Is it easy to control?" Dorothy asked. "How do you know you won't accidentally influence anyone if you're, like, really angry or something?"

"I can control influencing people a lot easier than I can control the voices," Josephine said. It took her a moment to realize what she'd said.

"Voices?"

I've come this far, Josephine thought. *Might as well carry on.*

"Yeah. I hear other people's voices," she said.

"I knew it! I knew you could read minds!"

"I can't! At least, not like in the movies. Other people's thoughts just pop into my head. I can't read people's minds at will. Envisioning a net around my brain sometimes helps stop the thoughts from entering when it gets out of control, but that's only a temporary fix, at best."

"C'mon," Dorothy said with a wry smile. "What number am I thinking of?"

Josephine shrugged. "Sorry to keep disappointing you, but I have no idea."

Dorothy looked a little disappointed. "Fine, fine. Can you at least tell me what it's like?"

When Josephine didn't answer right away, Dorothy continued. "Like, do the thoughts in your head sound like other people's voices? How can you tell them apart from your own thoughts?"

"No, the thoughts are in my own voice, or my internal voice. It's hard to explain, but it's like someone's speaking directly inside my head, using my own voice, telling me things I should have no way of knowing." Josephine looked at Dorothy and almost laughed at the nearly unreadable expression on her face. "Look, I get it. This all sounds ridiculous. That's why I've never told anyone before." *Before Helen*, Josephine thought, *and now you.* "I get it if you don't believe me."

Dorothy shook her head. "No, I believe you. Just don't do anything inside my head without my knowledge, okay?"

Josephine raised her hands. "Of course not."

Inside Dorcas's head.

The thought entered Josephine's head like a needle—precision-sharp. She covered her eyes. "It just . . . it just happened."

"What happened? Did you . . . ?"

"Yes," Josephine said. "I heard your thoughts." She netted her brain.

Dorothy smiled widely. "Cool! It worked."

"What worked?"

"You didn't get into my head—I got into yours. Kind of. I think. What did you hear?"

"'Inside Dorcas's head.'"

Dorothy laughed. "Right! See? It worked! You heard my thoughts! I *wanted* you to, so I tried to, I don't know . . . *send* it to you. Sort of like a test."

"What does that mean, inside Dorcas's head?"

"Do you think you could get inside Dorcas's head?" Dorothy asked. "Influence her into doing, I don't know, something? Even if it's just leaving you and your family alone?"

Josephine considered it, and she couldn't believe she hadn't thought of it before. Would it work? Dorcas was not only a witch, but she was also a ghost. Could Josephine get into her mind?

It's worth a shot, Josephine thought. *Get inside Dorcas's head . . .*

Dorcas had clearly been in *her* head. All of the random thoughts that had popped into her mind, making her threaten her parents with a knife, making her think burning the house down with everyone inside was a good idea, making her think and do things that she never would have otherwise done . . . it would feel good to give Dorcas a taste of her own medicine.

"Yeah," Josephine said. "I think it might work."

"Then I've got another idea," Dorothy said. "And not just a way to keep Dorcas out of her house temporarily, like with the pentagrams. Better than that. I think we might be able to get rid of her. Forever."

It sounded too good to be true, but although Josephine had already been hit by several setbacks, she still had enough hope remaining to believe Dorothy.

After all, she couldn't help thinking, *what do I have to lose?*

"What is it?" she asked.

"You're not going to like it," Dorothy said.

"Try me."

"Well, you're going to need to collect some things that Dorcas has handled or, better yet, put a charm on. Charms forge a powerful bond between the object and the witch. You also need something that represents the source of Dorcas's power, and some items that are known to ensnare witches, and you need to put everything in a bottle. Then, you need to bury the bottle somewhere near the house, or better yet, *in* the house. And if we're lucky—which is a big *if*—Dorcas's soul will be trapped forever within the bottle at midnight."

Josephine laughed in disbelief. "That's a ridiculously detailed plan. How do you know so much about this shit?"

"I'm smart! I know things!" Dorothy smiled and shrugged. "And, you know, I asked my grandmother. Who also knows things. Especially things like this."

Josephine didn't love the idea of sneaking around the house collecting Dorcas's things, but given her options—namely, do this or die—she didn't see what the problem might be. "And why, pray tell, don't you think I'd like this plan?"

"Well, it can't just be any bottle. It has to be charmed by . . ." Dorothy's words trailed off.

"Tell me," Josephine said.

"It has to be charmed by a good witch."

"Your grandmother," Josephine said. "She doesn't just know a lot about witches—she *is* a witch, isn't she? A *good* witch?"

Dorothy nodded. "I've never told anyone that before. It feels good. It's how she and I both know so much stuff about this."

"Are you . . . ?" Josephine stopped speaking before finishing. Was it too personal to ask someone such a question?

But Dorothy didn't seem to mind. She shook her head and said, "Nah. I can't even figure out how to use my mom's slow cooker, let alone cast spells and shit."

"When is your grandmother due to arrive?"

"Later this afternoon," Dorothy said. "Which doesn't leave us a lot of time to get everything right."

Midnight will be the start of the seventh day we've been here. The day Dorcas will be able to bind my family to her house. Her resurrection day.

"You're right," Josephine said, "I *don't* like it."

But her options were few and far between. In a way, that was somewhat liberating, but it was also anxiety-inducing.

Josephine took a deep breath and said, "All right. Tell me more about what needs to go in this bottle."

SEVENTEEN

As she walked through the woods, Josephine wondered if her parents would be concerned. She had left the house before anyone was awake, and it was now a little past noon. Would anyone have checked on her when she didn't show up for breakfast?

She needn't have worried. No one seemed to have noticed her absence.

"Hey, Josie," her father said as she entered the kitchen. "You're just in time for lunch."

By the looks of the empty plates and bowls spread across the table in front of her sisters and mother, she was actually a little *late* for lunch. But she happily accepted a grilled cheese sandwich and a bowl of tomato soup. Her stomach felt like it might start eating itself.

"Are you feeling okay?" her mother asked, giving her an inquisitive look from across the table. "You look a little tired."

"I'm fine," Josephine said with a nod. *We've had a variation of this conversation before.* She dunked the corner of her sandwich in the soup, which was thick and creamy, and took a big bite. The food was once again, predictably, delicious.

"Have you been to the grocery store yet?" Josephine asked her parents.

"We haven't had to," Mrs. Jagger said. "Mr. Finger has brought a few bags of food each time he's visited."

"Which is fortunate, because the van's engine light came on, so I had to take it to the mechanic's this morning," Mr. Jagger said. "They're keeping it overnight—they drove me back here."

"The light came on again?" Josephine asked.

Mr. Jagger looked confused. "No, it just came on for the first time. But that's weird . . . they said the same thing. Said my wife brought it in earlier in the week with the same problem. I told them it must have been someone with the same make and model since we haven't been into town since we got here."

Josephine brushed her hair back with her hand and shook her head with a smile. "Oh, yeah, right. I don't know why I said 'again.'"

Dorcas let him go, she thought as the smile faded from her face. *With the van being in town, she's eliminated our best chance at escape. We're trapped here.*

"Anyway," Mr. Jagger said, "as I was saying, no trips into town for now—we'll have to make do with what we have."

"That's probably a good thing," Mrs. Jagger said. "I heard on the radio there's a big storm coming that's expected to last through the night. They're advising people to stay home instead of going out for New Year's Eve celebrations."

"Wait," Josephine said. "The lawyer has been delivering food this entire week?"

Mr. Jagger nodded. "Nice of him, don't you think?"

"Yeah, I do," Josephine said. A little *too* nice of him. She put her half-eaten sandwich down and pushed her plate and bowl a few inches away.

"Something wrong?" Mrs. Jagger asked.

"No, just full." She excused herself and left the kitchen before anyone asked her any more questions that could only be answered with a lie.

The food's enchanted, Josephine realized with a sickening feeling in her gut. *Not dangerous or poisoned—we all would've been dead days ago if that was the case—but made to taste better than it should.*

Another way to trick my family into loving the house. There's probably something in it to pacify us. All part of Dorcas's plan to keep us here seven days.

But food wasn't enough to seal the deal and make her family stay for the week.

Dorcas had put other charms on the house.

Josephine thought back, retracing her steps through the house, going through each day since they'd arrived like a ghost floating through her own memories. And then she thought of her closet—of all their closets—and a lightbulb turned on in her head.

Click-click.

Shortly after we arrived, we each found something in our closets—something near and dear to our hearts.

Josephine made a mental list in her head as she walked upstairs.

Rare books in my closet.

Art supplies in Allison's.

Musical instruments in Elizabeth's.

Clothing and jewelry in Mary's.

A typewriter in Dad's.

And dolls that resemble our family in Mom's.

Josephine still didn't know why there wasn't a doll resembling her mother, but she had a feeling Dorcas had given the Josephine doll *X*s for eyes to taunt her, knowing she'd probably find it.

The connections were so obvious she felt a little foolish for not putting two and two together sooner.

Better late than never.

On second thought, better now than ever.

Josephine smiled. Dorothy had told her she should collect items that Dorcas had handled or, better yet, put a charm on. Everything in their closets had been charmed—Josephine was certain of it.

I'll take a small paintbrush from Allison, a guitar pick from Elizabeth, a ring from Mary, one of the keys from Dad's typewriter, one of the dolls from Mom, and . . .

She opened her closet door and took *Through the Looking-Glass, and What Alice Found There* off the shelf.

. . . a single page from my book.

Last week, she never would've considered damaging any book, let alone one so valuable, but things had changed. Without hesitation, she tore the title page clean out of the book with the speed and savagery of a small child plucking the legs off a wriggling spider. She placed the damaged book back on the shelf, reminded of *Early Histories of Canaan, Vermont* and its ripped-out pages.

Hopefully this works, she thought. *Hopefully Dorothy is right.*

She is, Josephine thought in response. *Dorothy's the only person right now who you can trust.* She looked at the torn page in her hand. *This will work. It has to.*

Josephine rolled up the page like a pirate's map, placed it in the side pocket of her backpack, and set out to collect everything else.

Taking something from each of the closets was simple, but Josephine worried that the next task would be much more challenging.

I need something that represents the source of Dorcas's power.

The stone face in the basement. The man entombed in the wall.

Josephine was certain he was Dorcas's last sacrifice, and he seemed to be keeping Dorcas alive—in a manner of speaking.

She stood in front of the purple door and hesitated. She didn't like the thought of what she needed to do. Not one bit. She reached into her backpack, pulled out her knife, sighed heavily, and opened the door.

The flashlight had been returned to the top step. Josephine thought back to the time her family had entered the basement. She'd dropped the flashlight when she had seen the face in the wall, and her dad had picked it up shortly before finding the spider's nest. Louisa had nearly fallen down the stairs, Josephine had caught her, and everyone left the basement. She shrugged, wondering why she was making a big deal of it.

Because your father dropped the flashlight when Louisa fell, a voice in her head said. *Because the flashlight should still be at the bottom of the stairs, not the top.*

Josephine didn't recall seeing the flashlight at all when she had rushed down and hurriedly carved a pentagram above the cellar door either. Her instincts were screaming at her that something was wrong, but she ignored her hesitance, turned on the flashlight, and made her way down. The steps groaned loudly underfoot as she descended.

The air was as humid as the first time she had gone down. The odd smell of smoke and meat was back too, and it burned the back of her throat with every breath. She felt like she might be sick.

All of this is déjà vu, she thought in despair.

Thump-thump. Thump-thump. Thump-thump.

It was her heart, once again beating so loudly in her chest that she could hear it like a drum. But then she put her fingertips on the wall . . . and she was no longer quite so sure it *was* her own heartbeat. The walls seemed to pulse with every *thump*.

Thump-thump. Thump-thump. Thump-thump.

It was subtle—nearly imperceptible. She pulled her fingers away with a mild sense of revulsion, then carried on.

The mirror commanded her attention as soon as her feet touched the dirt floor. Knowing what was trapped in the wall behind it made her freeze. Her reflection looked back at her, regarding her with curiosity. And then it spoke.

"Hello, Josie."

"What?" Josephine asked.

Thump-thump! Thump-thump! Thump-thump!

Her heartbeat—or the house's—doubled in intensity.

You're seeing things, Josie, she told herself. *Your reflection didn't just speak. No way.*

But her reflection looked at her with a crooked grin. "I said hello."

The reality sank in—or began to sink in, at least. Josephine had a feeling that, of everything she'd witnessed in Dorcas's house, this might go down as the most fucked up. She took a step backward.

Her reflection raised her hands. "You have nothing to fear from me, Josie."

Josephine didn't believe that.

"I'm you, after all," her reflection said, her smile widening. "I'm not going to hurt you. I want to help you. I need to warn you."

Josephine remained tense, ready to fight or flee. "Warn me about what?"

"About things you already know, but won't let yourself believe," the reflection said cryptically.

You're either dreaming, hallucinating, or that's Dorcas in the mirror. She was willing to bet the third option was the closest to the truth.

"You're not dreaming," her reflection said, "you're not hallucinating, and I am certainly *not* Dorcas."

How can you hear my thoughts?

"I already told you: I'm you." *How else could I get into your head?* the reflection said.

Dorcas has entered my head, Josephine thought. *If you're her—*

Her reflection shook her head. "I'm *not* her. I need to warn you about this house. Would Dorcas do that? This house isn't what it seems, Josephine. Not by a country mile. You know what I'm talking about."

You don't need to get into my head to figure out I already know this house is messed up. It's haunted. It's cursed. The ghost is controlling my family and planning to trap us all here forever, and here I am talking to myself in a mirror.

"I'm not talking about any of that," her reflection said in a serious tone. She leaned forward and lowered her voice an octave or two as if afraid someone else might be listening in. "Those are all things that Dorcas is responsible for, things she's done."

I thought—

"I know what you thought, but once again, I'm not warning you about Dorcas. I'm warning you about the house." The reflection spread her hands apart and looked around. "The rooms, the doors, the windows, the walls, the stones, the wood—*especially* the wood. It's not what it seems. It's alive. It's dead. It's a house like no other. It's not really a house at all."

Josephine shook her head in confusion. She didn't know what to believe.

The reflection laughed as if something she'd plucked out of Josephine's mind was the funniest thing she'd ever heard. "Don't believe me? I don't blame you. I wouldn't believe me either if I were in your shoes, which I guess I am." She laughed some more. "Ask your girlfriend. Ask Dorothy. She'll know what I'm talking about. Go on and ask her."

If she already knew anything—

"She'd have told you? Maybe. Maybe not. She doesn't want to scare you any more than you already are. She likes you. She wants you to stay. She wants you to stay forever." Josephine's reflection smiled. "She knows more than she's told you. Oh, yes, she does. Ask her the truth about this house. Ask her to pull back the curtain. You won't like what you see, but it's better to know the truth than to remain in the dark like a mushroom." The reflection reached out through the surface of the mirror, plucked one of the brown mushroom caps off the wooden frame, brought it back into the mirror, regarded it with a smile, and then popped it in her mouth and chewed.

Josephine didn't want to spend any more time in the basement, but she still needed something from the face in the wall behind the mirror.

Her reflection sighed. "All right. Fine. You won't leave? I'll *make* you leave."

Josephine didn't like the sound of that. She swallowed and felt a weight settle in her gut. She wanted to run away more than ever, but she still couldn't.

She saw a blur out of the corner of her eye. Something had moved, but there was nothing in that part of the basement other than dirt and bones.

The bones. The bones had moved. The bones were *moving*. One of the rabbit skeletons pulled itself across the floor, digging its front paws into the dirt and dragging its hind legs behind it, as if its back half had been run over by a car. As if it wasn't *dead*. And then it suddenly got up on all four feet and hopped one, two, three times.

Josephine heard a choking, mumbled sound. It took her a moment to realize the sound had come from her.

A second rabbit skeleton slowly got to its feet, then a third, a fourth, and a fifth. Within moments, all the rabbits—fifty or sixty, if not more—had risen. The basement was filled with the *click-clack-crack* sound of bare bones grinding against one another.

Whether from the ridiculousness of the sight or the madness of it, Josephine laughed. She sounded exactly like her reflection.

She looked at the mirror in time to see her reflection raise her hands and bend her fingers like claws. She was no longer smiling but looked angry, and her anger was focused on Josephine.

The rabbits stopped hopping in random directions and turned to face Josephine. They had no eyes, only empty eye sockets, like Dorcas. And then the rabbits began to hop toward her.

Click-clack-crack! Click-clack-crack! Click-clack-crack!

The sound was as awful as nails screeching across a chalk-board. Josephine turned to run, but not before she caught sight of her reflection again.

Her hands don't look like claws, she thought. *Her fingers are spread apart and twitching as if strings are attached to the end of each, like a puppet master. She's controlling the skeletons.*

Her reflection continued to jerk her hands up and down and the rabbits continued to hop.

Click-clack-crack! Click-clack-crack! Click-clack-crack!

Acting on impulse, Josephine threw her flashlight at the mirror. The glass shattered into hundreds of tiny shards that rained to the ground. The rabbits immediately collapsed into small piles of unconnected bones.

Josephine retrieved the flashlight—luckily, it still worked—and picked up the largest piece of mirror she could find. She looked at the reflective surface, and her eyes looked back at her. But they were *her* eyes, not whatever she'd talked to before. She tossed the piece to the ground.

Mirror, mirror, not-on-the-wall, Josephine thought darkly, *can you be put back together after such a big fall?*

I certainly hope not.

Josephine had the sudden feeling that she was being watched.

The mirror had been bumped back when the flashlight had hit it. The section of wall that had previously been hidden was now exposed. And the stone man was staring at her.

The sight of his face made her feel nauseous, but she also felt a twinge of relief. He wasn't a spider's nest. He wasn't in her imagination. He was real. She'd be able to get what she needed for the witch bottle.

His wide eyes looked at Josephine with a mix of hope and sadness. His mouth opened and closed like a fish trying to breathe out of water. *Or like he's trying to say something.*

Josephine took a step toward him and leaned in close to listen.

His mouth opened and closed, opened and closed, opened and closed.

There was a noxious whiff of something unpleasant in the air, a mix of swamp gas and burnt hair.

"Are you . . . ?" Josephine asked. "Are you trying to say something?"

Open, closed. Open, closed. Open, closed.

Josephine reached out a trembling hand and pinched one strand of curly, gray hair that protruded from the wall above the man's forehead.

"I'm sorry, but I need to take this. It might save my life."

Open.

She plucked the hair. It came free with very little effort.

Closed.

She placed the hair in the side pocket of her backpack.

Open.

"Help," the stone man whispered.

Josephine screamed and fell backward.

"End . . ."

Something poked out of his mouth.

"My . . ."

Something thin. Something black.

"Suffering."

A spider's leg. The spider crawled over the man's tongue, between his lips, and out of his mouth.

A second spider joined the first, but it didn't come out of the man's mouth. It came out of his left eye, squeezing its way out from between his lower lid and his eyeball. A third one forced its way out of his right eye. A pair of smaller spiders poked through his nostrils.

More spiders came, pouring through every opening in his face. Together they formed thin, black streams that looked like diseased veins spreading rapidly across the wall.

A cluster of spiders had already reached the stairs to the main floor, so Josephine ran toward the cellar door as quickly as she could. Her heart beat faster and harder and louder than ever before—*THUMPTHUMPTHUMPTHUMPTHUMP!*—but then she realized that no, that wasn't her heartbeat; it was the stone man's heartbeat, pulsating through the walls, the vibrations pumping through her body, pounding in her head. She took the stairs two at a time and thrust the cellar door open. Daylight enveloped her like water as she ran outside, temporarily blinding her, but she didn't slow down—she didn't *dare* slow down. She ran as fast as she could, ran as fast from the house as possible, as bushes clawed at her legs and branches scratched at her face. When a branch slashed her cheek deep enough to draw blood, she still didn't slow down. She ran for three or four minutes at full speed before coming to a halt to catch her breath. Her nerves were still shot and she was about to start running again when she saw someone lingering a short distance away.

Watching her.

Laurence.

EIGHTEEN

Josephine had been so focused on running away from the house that she hadn't mentally prepared herself for the possibility of coming face-to-face with the other ghost that haunted the woods. She tried to stop on a dime, but her left foot slipped on an ice-slicked rock and she fell to one knee. Pain shot up through her thigh. She winced and gritted her teeth. Her knee throbbed, but she managed to get back to her feet. She didn't know where she'd run next—Laurence was blocking her path to Dorothy's house. She turned to run back in the opposite direction.

"Wait," Laurence said.

Not a chance, Josephine thought. She started to run.

"Wait!" Laurence shouted again, sounding increasingly desperate.

Josephine picked up her pace.

"Allison's in danger!"

That got her to stop.

"Tell me something I don't know," she yelled over her shoulder.

"What?"

Josephine turned and faced Laurence. "We're all in danger, my whole family. But if you've done anything to her, if you've hurt her—"

Laurence waved his hands in the air, looking confused. "What are you talking about? I'd never do anything to hurt Allison. She's my friend."

Josephine felt her cheeks flush. She'd been intimidated before, but now she was irate. She approached Laurence and raised a finger at him, thinking that he must be helping Dorcas. "I know you're working with her, I just don't know how."

Laurence took a step away from Josephine. He looked scared.

Good. Josephine's anger fueled her confidence.

"But I'm going to figure it out," she said. She felt like she was having an out-of-body experience, like she was watching a character on a screen. It felt good to surrender control, to allow her adrenaline to take over. "And as soon as I do, I'm going to make you suffer, even if I don't make it out of this alive."

Laurence's face contorted into a look of pure panic. He lost his footing and fell backward. He remained on the ground and did something that completely shocked Josephine. He cried.

Please don't hurt me. It was his panicked thought, piped directly into her head on repeat. *Please don't hurt me, please don't hurt me, please don't hurt me . . .*

She would never have imagined she could make a ghost cry.

Unless, of course, he wasn't a ghost.

Just a boy. A scared little boy. Scared of you.

Her anger evaporated as she wrapped her brain in her mental net. She was left feeling foolish, embarrassed, and ashamed. Josephine exhaled a long stream of pent-up air. The next breath she took hitched in her throat, as if she was about to begin crying too.

"I'm sorry," she said. "This whole week has been so, so much. I don't know what's right, what's wrong, who to trust, or what to do. I feel like I'm on the verge of a complete breakdown."

Laurence wiped his tears away and rubbed his jacket sleeve across his runny nose. Josephine held out her hand. He flinched and looked at her suspiciously.

Josephine sighed and felt the cold for the first time since she'd left the house. It was freezing and the sky was filling with flurries, the prelude of a coming storm. "C'mon, it's too cold to be sitting in the snow. Let me help you up."

After a moment's hesitation, Laurence took Josephine up on her offer. She half expected her hand to pass through his, and she was a little relieved when she felt solid flesh and bone inside his mitten. He got to his feet and brushed snow off his legs, never taking his eyes off Josephine.

"I can tell you don't trust me," she said.

He said nothing.

"And I don't blame you," Josephine added. "I don't trust me either. I feel like I'm starting to forget who I am. Do you want to hear something ridiculous?"

Laurence just looked at her.

"I thought you were a ghost. I was convinced of it. Just because you live somewhere in these woods, and because my sisters—not Allison—had never seen you, and . . ."

And because of something else, but what that something else was, Josephine couldn't quite remember. But she knew exactly who to blame for that.

"Because of Dorcas," she said. She searched Laurence's face for recognition, but his expression was too hard to read. "Do you know Dorcas, Laurence?"

He shook his head, but he also said, "I . . ."

"You what?"

"I've never seen her, but my neighbor . . . he told me stories."

"What stories?"

"Stories about a witch who lives in the woods. A witch who can't die. And he warned me to never cross beyond the star trees, because that's where she lives, and she can't get me as long as I stay on my side. And . . ." His voice faltered and his face screwed up tight as if he was about to begin crying again.

"And what?" Josephine asked gently.

"And if I ever crossed the line she'd catch me, and she'd kill me, and she'd eat me, and she'd pick her teeth with my bones." Laurence broke down and began sobbing again.

Damn, Josephine thought. *His neighbor sounds like quite the guy. Not wrong, but fucking dark.*

"That's what happened to *him*," Laurence said as tears ran freely down his red cheeks. "That's what happened to Mr. Lavoie. He crossed the line. He got killed. He got eaten, and it's all my fault!"

All of the boy's pent-up grief broke free and he cried hard and loud. Josephine put her arms awkwardly around him and let him cry it out. She didn't know what else to do. But as she held him and let him sob, she started to draw some new conclusions.

Once the worst of his outpouring had passed, she let go of Laurence and asked him a question. "Did your neighbor— Mr. Lavoie?"

Laurence nodded miserably.

"Did Mr. Lavoie live in the house over there?" She pointed west, back the way she had come. "The abandoned place?"

Laurence nodded. "Yeah, the second abandoned house that way."

Allison had only mentioned one, but Josephine wasn't surprised there were two. There were probably plenty of abandoned houses in these woods.

"What did he look like?" Josephine asked.

Laurence was silent for a moment, then removed one of his mittens and reached into his pants pocket.

"I keep this with me all the time, to remember." He pulled out a tattered photograph, smoothed it against his thigh, and handed it to Josephine.

"That's me," he said, pointing at himself. "And that's Mr. Lavoie."

Laurence looked a few years younger in the picture. They were sitting on the wooden steps of a front porch, smiling, holding glasses that were beaded with condensation. In the distant background, Josephine could see Dorcas's house.

And then her eyes landed on Mr. Lavoie's face . . .

"He made lemonade the way I liked it—more sour than sweet—and he'd invite me and my parents over to tell stories as we watched the sunset. My parents loved his stories, but Mr. Lavoie never told them about Dorcas. That story he'd only share with me when we were alone. He said my parents weren't the types to buy into that sort of tale, which is why he had to be the one to warn me."

Josephine heard everything Laurence had said, but she'd been more engrossed in his photograph. She knew Mr. Lavoie—she simply hadn't known his name.

He was the stone man, the face in her basement wall. He was Dorcas's battery. "Help," he had pleaded. "End my suffering."

Josephine kept that to herself. Laurence was already plenty upset.

"I was scared, but not scared enough," Laurence continued. "I was also curious, so one day after school, a few years ago, I took a step past the trees. It was scary and exciting, like playing with a Ouija board or chanting 'Bloody Mary' to a mirror, and when Dorcas didn't appear, I guess I started to doubt Mr. Lavoie's story. To be honest, I never really believed it at all—it sounded more like a fairy tale than real life. So I ignored his warning and walked farther, deeper into the woods than I'd ever gone. When I reached Dorcas's territory, a weird feeling came over me and I was the happiest I'd been in my life. I wanted to stay there forever, but then I heard Mr. Lavoie screaming at my back. He was running toward me faster than I'd ever seen him move, yelling at me to get away, to run back home, and then . . ." He shook his head. "And then he suddenly flew through the air. It didn't make any sense. One second he's running, and the next he's sailing into the sky, like an invisible, giant hand had pinched the back of his shirt and cast him aside. He landed hard and hit his head and started bleeding, but he locked eyes with me and told me once more to run. And then that same invisible hand grabbed a hold of him and dragged him to Dorcas's house. I ran. I ran so fast that my lungs burned and my heart felt like it was trying to beat its way up through my throat and out of my mouth, but I didn't stop until I reached my home. I never saw her—I never saw anyone other than Mr. Lavoie—but do you think that was Dorcas? That she somehow threw him through the air?"

"I have no doubt," Josephine said. "Did you tell anyone what had happened?"

"I told my parents, and although they didn't seem to believe me, they checked Mr. Lavoie's house to make sure he was okay. He wasn't there, but they said he was probably out shopping or something and I was imagining things. When he didn't return home the next day, they finally called the police. The officers asked me a bunch of questions and searched the woods, including all the abandoned houses, but they never found him. He's still considered missing, but I know what really happened. Dorcas caught him, killed him, and ate him."

"Dorcas caught him, but she didn't kill him."

Laurence looked hopeful.

"Don't get too excited, Laurence. She's kept him alive, but he wishes he was dead."

"How do you know?"

"He's in my basement—Dorcas's basement. Trapped in the walls." *And she's eating him, but slowly.*

"Can we save him?" he asked.

Not likely. "Maybe. I don't know."

"I want to help," Laurence said. "I told you your family is in danger, and I don't want anything bad to happen to you, especially Allison. I've tried to warn her a bunch of times, but she never remembers."

"That's Dorcas's doing, messing around in our heads." Josephine considered what Laurence could do to help. She admired his willingness to do something, but she couldn't put him in harm's way. "I've got an old bottle, and I've filled it with items Dorcas has charmed. If a good witch buries it, it will trap Dorcas's soul within the bottle forever."

"A good witch?"

"Don't worry," Josephine said with a nod. "I know someone who knows someone. But the bottle also needs a few things that are believed to ensnare witches, and I haven't had time to collect them yet."

"I can collect them for you," Laurence said eagerly. "What are they?"

"I don't know."

Dorothy hadn't been specific about that aspect of the bottle, so Josephine had assumed that meant she'd bring them, but what if she was wrong? What if Dorothy assumed Josephine would collect them? Laurence wanted to help, so Josephine might as well let him. But how could he if she didn't even know what they needed?

And then she remembered *The Kirkman Guide to Witchcraft*. It had an entry about witch bottles.

"Wait," Josephine said. She pulled the book out of her backpack and flipped through the pages.

"Here," she said when she found the right page. "It says to include salt and pepper because they are known to burn witches' skin, seven bent nails to hold power over them, and some sort of spiky plant so the spell will cling to them."

Laurence smiled. "That will be easy. I'll get some salt and pepper from home, and my dad's tool shed is filled with old nails."

"What about the plant?"

Laurence crouched and plucked a burr free from Josephine's bootlace. "Burdock burrs. This forest is full of them. I'll only need to walk through the woods for fifteen minutes and my clothes will collect them for me."

"Thank you, Laurence. I see why Allison likes you so much."

Laurence blushed.

Josephine laughed. "There's no salt and pepper in my house, and I don't recall seeing any tools either. I bet Dorcas has made sure of that herself. It's a good thing I met you—" She was about to add, "and Dorothy," but Laurence interrupted her.

"Of course there's no salt and pepper or tools. I don't even know how you've lived there so long."

"With Dorcas dwelling in the shadows, it hasn't been easy."

"What?" Laurence couldn't have looked any more confused if he had tried. "You and your family should have frozen to death the first night you arrived at the ruins of Dorcas's house."

"Excuse me?" Josephine asked. It was her turn to look as confused as possible.

"Sorry," Laurence said. "That came out kind of mean. I didn't mean to imply that I wanted you to have frozen—"

"No, not that," Josephine interrupted. "What do you mean, *ruins*?"

"Yeah, ruins," Laurence repeated. "The house burned down, like, ages ago. All that's left is the stone cellar and a dozen or so charred logs."

Josephine shook her head. "No, that's not right. No, you're wrong. The house is *there*. We've literally been staying in it all week."

Laurence just shook his head.

"You're wrong." Josephine laughed.

Laurence didn't join her.

She stopped laughing. "You're wrong," she repeated, her tone much more serious. "I don't know what you're trying to prove. That I'm stupid? Gullible? But I'm not falling for it, and it's not funny."

"I'm not trying to prove anything," he said.

"I saw Dorcas's house in the background of your photo," Josephine said, trying to keep an even tone. "It was fine. It looked just like it does now."

Laurence retrieved the photo and handed it to Josephine. He wiped a melting snowflake off its surface and tapped the house with his finger. "How can you say that looks fine?"

Josephine's eyes quickly passed over Mr. Lavoie and Laurence and their lemonades and their smiles and settled on Dorcas's house.

"Because it does!" she yelled, finally losing her calm. Laurence had gotten under her skin. The house looked exactly like it had all week. It looked . . .

It looked . . .

It looked translucent. It hadn't before, but now its exterior walls shimmered as she tilted the photo left to right as if by some trick of the light, an optical illusion. It no longer appeared so solid. It no longer appeared so *there*.

It faded. As Josephine stared at the photograph, the house disappeared.

Less than ten seconds after she'd taken the photo from Laurence, Dorcas's house was gone. All that was left of its walls were a few burned support beams, just like Laurence had said.

"What is this, some kind of joke?" Josephine said of the photo. "Expose it to sunlight and part of the image fades away?"

Laurence just stared at her, clearly uncomfortable and unsure what else to say.

That irritated Josephine almost more than anything else.

"This is ridiculous," she said, turning abruptly and marching with purpose toward the house. "And I can prove it."

She didn't wait to see if he'd follow, but he kept up behind her, weaving around trees and ducking under branches. Before long, they'd reached the ring of pentagrams.

And there, in the distance, was Dorcas's house. Just as she'd known it would be.

"See," Josephine said, mad with relief and delirious with indignation. "What did I say? The house is fine."

Laurence looked from her to the house and back to her again.

"Why won't you say anything?" Josephine demanded. She pointed at the house. "Why can't you admit that you were wrong?"

She stopped speaking and stared. It looked like a row of translucent trees had materialized between her and the house, but that wasn't right, and Josephine knew it. The truth didn't make sense, but that didn't make it any less true.

A row of trees in the distance was visible *through* the house.

Josephine felt like her eyes were open for the first time since they'd arrived, and the truth was taking shape before her.

The house shimmered. It faded.

It was gone.

Left behind in its wake was some burnt wood and the stone cellar dug deep into the ground, quickly filling with snow.

"I don't . . . I don't understand."

"It burned down years ago," Laurence said, his voice jumping out of the silence. "It must be, I don't know . . . it must be cursed or something. By Dorcas. So you and your family can see it."

"We've done more than see it," Josephine said. "We've walked its halls. Sat on its furniture. Slept in its beds. Used its phone. We've eaten in its kitchen and been sheltered by its roof and been kept warm by its furnace. Laurence, I could feel everything in the house with my own hands. What kind of curse is that?"

His answer was simple and direct.

"A powerful one," he said.

Josephine's head swam and her vision spun. She placed her hands on her knees, afraid she might faint. If she did, maybe she'd wake up, see the house, and know it had all been a bad dream. Or better yet, maybe she'd wake up back in her own bed in Amherst. But when she looked up again, the house was still a burnt ruin.

The house wasn't merely haunted. It itself was a haunt. A ghost of its former self. An illusion made real through dark magic. A testament to Dorcas's power.

Something hit Josephine's cheek, stinging her skin. She looked to the gray sky and held out her hand. Sleet ricocheted off her palm.

The storm had begun.

PART FOUR

NINETEEN

Laurence left with a promise of returning to the safe edge of the pentagram trees in two or three hours. He'd bring the last few items they needed for the witch bottle, even if he caught hypothermia while collecting burrs in the woods.

Josephine thanked him half-heartedly. Not because she wasn't thankful for his help—she was, incredibly so—but because all she could think about was the house. The house that wasn't there.

Alone, she slowly approached the front door—well, the spot where the front door had previously been. Now that her mind had been opened, there was nothing but a stone step leading to open space and the rubble-filled cellar.

How does the spell work? she wondered. *How is it possible that a house can be seen one minute and gone the next? How can some people—like my family and Dorothy and Mr. Finger— enter the house while others—like Laurence—cannot? How did I stand on a second floor—or a first floor for that matter—that's not real? How is all the furniture inside invisible? How is my family inside invisible?*

She thought that, maybe, the house would slowly reappear the closer she got to it. She thought that, perhaps, she would hear her family's voices trickle out even if she couldn't see them. Neither of those things happened. Josephine stood on the front step and slowly reached her hand out. She thought she might feel the door even if she couldn't see it, but she felt nothing. She waved her hand side to side. Still nothing.

How can I protect my family if I can't get back inside?

She envisioned the door's brass snake handle and held her hand in the spot where it should have been. She closed her eyes and pictured it in her mind. She concentrated, focusing everything on that handle, thinking about what it looked like, what it felt like. She lifted the mental net off her brain—every single imaginary knot and strand of rope—and opened her mind more fully, more completely, than she had in a long time. She felt a headache immediately blossom, but she pushed past it, ignored it, *embraced* it.

And then, as if the door had been there all along, it suddenly was.

With her eyes still closed tight, too afraid that the handle would disappear if she opened them, she pressed the snake's head down with her thumb and pushed. She felt a little resistance and heard the door groan as it swung open.

"Josephine! There you are!"

Josephine made a sound halfway between a laugh and a gasp and finally opened her eyes. It was Mary. Josephine leapt forward and squeezed her sister in a tight hug.

Mary laughed. "What's this about?"

"I thought I might never see you again," Josephine said honestly.

"Well, there's a simple solution for that: don't disappear in the woods for hours on end."

When Josephine finally let her sister go, she looked over Mary's shoulder at the house in awe. It was all there, just as she'd last seen it. Hallway, stairs, family room on the left, dining room on the right, electricity, warmth, smells of food cooking in the kitchen, sounds of her family moving about and talking in other rooms . . . all as if it had never *not* been there. Which, in a way, Josephine supposed was true. She'd briefly unseen it and was thankful she had been able to trick her mind into seeing it once again.

Mary noticed the way Josephine was looking at the foyer, then glanced over her own shoulder in confusion. "Josie, are you all right?"

Josephine's first instinct was to lie, to say yes, everything was a-okay, but she couldn't bring herself to keep on pretending, not after everything she'd seen.

"No," she said. "Can we talk?"

Mary's face was full of concern.

Josephine continued. "I need to tell you something again for the first time."

Mary stared at Josephine for a long time. She opened her mouth to speak a few times but didn't say a word. They had moved from the foyer to Mary's bedroom, and Josephine had shared everything from the first day they'd arrived to Laurence's revelation that the house had burned down years ago.

Finally, Mary managed to speak.

"So you're telling me this bed"—she pushed down on the mattress for emphasis—"isn't really here?"

"Yes," Josephine said.

"But I've been sleeping on it all week. We're sitting on it right now."

"Well, it's complicated. Maybe it actually *is* here. I'm not really sure." Josephine looked at Mary. Although she'd taken the news rather well, Mary looked a little pale. "Are you feeling okay?"

"Oh, sure," Mary said sarcastically. She reclined back. "I just need to lie down for a moment on my imaginary bed."

"But you believe me? About, well, everything?"

"I do. You're the most honest, reliable person I know."

Josephine smiled. "That's the second time you've said that."

"Of course it is." Mary sat upright suddenly. "I have an idea." She stood up and searched her bedside table's surface, then the drawer. She moved on to the desk and searched there, then checked the top of her dresser.

"What are you looking for?" Josephine asked.

Mary kept searching. "Pen and paper."

Josephine reached into her backpack and pulled out her notebook. "How about this?"

Mary turned around and smiled. "Why didn't I think to ask you first?"

"No one's been thinking clearly since we arrived." Josephine had a thought. "Is your idea—"

"To write myself a note?" Mary crossed the room and sat back down on the bed beside her sister. "Yes, it is."

Josephine handed Mary her pen and a piece of paper from her notebook. Mary scribbled a quick note.

> The ghost of a witch named Dorcas is wiping your memory
> and about to kill you and the rest of the family. Only
> Josephine can stop her but she'll need help. Do whatever
> she says.

She read what she had written and tapped the pen against her lips.

"No, that's no good," Mary said. She crumpled the paper into a ball and asked for another sheet.

Josephine tore another page free and handed it over. "Why not? I thought it summed things up rather well, and I liked the bit about doing *whatever* I say."

"Within reason," Mary cautioned. "But no, it was too much. If I forget this entire conversation like you say I will, I'd read that note and think it was some sort of joke."

She wrote on the second page.

> Do whatever Josephine says, even if it sounds absurd.

Mary considered this for a moment, then added, ESPECIALLY if it sounds absurd.

"What do you think?" Mary asked.

Josephine nodded. "It's good. Once you've forgotten this conversation and read that note, I'm going to get you to make me a sandwich whenever I want one, even in the middle of the night."

Mary laughed. "This note is all powerful. Don't you dare abuse it!"

"I won't," Josephine said. She hugged Mary. "Thank you."

"What are sisters for?"

"Making sandwiches in the middle of the night?"

"No way." Mary folded the note and slipped it into her jeans pocket, then wrote herself one last note, this one on the back of her hand, before giving the pen back.

Check your jeans pocket!

They talked a little longer, enjoying each other's company, even though Josephine couldn't shake the feeling that they were living in the calm before the storm. The actual storm outside continued to get worse. The wind howled against the windowpanes and snow piled up around the house—how the snow didn't blow straight through the walls, Josephine couldn't say.

As Mary spoke, her words suddenly trailed off in the middle of her sentence and she stared at the wall with a glassy look in her eyes.

Josephine was about to ask if she was all right when Mary blinked and shook her head, then smiled awkwardly. "I'm sorry. I think I spaced out. What was I saying?"

She's forgotten, Josephine realized. *Forgotten everything.*

"You were about to tell me how much you love me," Josephine said.

"Really?" Mary said with a shake of her head. "I thought I was talking about . . . something else. I was going to tell you I love you?"

"I love you too." Josephine hugged Mary, stood up, and quickly crossed the room. She hadn't yet witnessed anyone in her family *forgetting*, and it broke her heart. She was afraid she might start crying if she stayed in the room a moment longer.

She stepped into the hall and swung the door behind her. Before it shut, she saw Mary reaching into her jeans pocket with a frown. She'd clearly read the back of her hand.

Clever sister, Josephine thought as she walked down the stairs.

Each step through the woods was harder than the last. The snow was getting deeper by the minute and Josephine's boots sank nearly to her knees in places where the wind had blown a dune into existence. The screeching wind stung her ears and made her eyes leak a steady flow of tears. She pulled her scarf a little higher, pushed her toque a little lower, and trudged onward.

In a way, the storm was a relief. It distracted Josephine from the melancholy she'd felt when she had left Mary. It was pain, the storm—a raw and immediate physical pain that made her emotional pain a little less pervasive, a little less prominent. Her emotional pain was still there, she knew, but she preferred those feelings to be buried.

She passed the pentagram trees and carried on through the woods. To the birds looking down from their sheltered nests in the treetops high above the forest floor, Josephine was a small dark blur in a swirling sea of white snow. Her singular goal, to find Dorothy so they could finalize the plan, propelled her forward.

Finally, after what felt like forever, she reached the fort. She opened the door and looked inside. It was empty.

"Damn it," she said. She'd have to go to Dorothy's house and ask for her. She hadn't met Dorothy's parents yet and the timing wasn't ideal, but that couldn't be avoided. She approached the house.

"Josephine!" Dorothy called from behind, her voice blending with the high-pitched wind. She was standing near her fort. "I'm over here!" Dorothy waved Josephine over.

As soon as they had entered the fort, Josephine said, "Where were you? I just looked in here, like, ten seconds ago."

"I was nearby, looking for you," Dorothy said.

"I must have missed you," Josephine said. "I'm distracted, I guess. Things are worse than they first appeared, and nothing is truly as it seems. Laurence isn't a ghost—he's just a boy—and the house . . ." She laughed a little, still finding it hard to believe. "It's not really there. It's keeping Dorcas alive, and it can be seen and felt because of a charm Dorcas cast on it before she died, but it burned down years ago."

"What? Are you serious?"

"As a heart attack."

"But I—I was in it. How could I have been in something that's not there?"

Josephine could only sigh, shake her head, and shrug.

Dorothy exhaled loudly. "She's even more powerful than we thought."

The girls were silent for a moment. The wind blew snow through the thin gaps in the fort's log walls.

"I've got more bad news," Dorothy said with a tremble in her voice. "My grandmother's flight was canceled because of the storm."

Josephine sighed and shook her head, but she wasn't surprised. *If it weren't for bad luck, I'd have no luck at all.* "What do we do now?"

"We fill the witch bottle, just like we planned. We fill it, bury it, and hope for the best."

When Josephine didn't answer, Dorothy added, "What else can we do?"

She's right, Josephine thought. What else could they do? Nothing. But that didn't mean they should stop trying. There was no way Josephine was going to give up, not after everything she'd already been through. She nodded and echoed what Dorothy had said. "Okay. We fill the bottle, bury it, and hope for the best."

Dorothy looked a little relieved. She moved aside one of the logs she used as a stool and dug her fingers into the dirt. It should have been frozen solid, but the ground there was loose. With a little tugging, Dorothy freed an old glass bottle, brushed off the dirt, and handed it to Josephine. It looked like a wine bottle from long ago, and had a wide mouth stopped with a thick cork.

"Did you collect everything you need?" Dorothy asked.

"Most of it." Josephine reached into her backpack and began pulling out the things she'd taken from each of her family's closets, as well as the stone man's hair, which she'd placed in a small clear bag. "This is from the man in the basement wall. His name is Mr. Lavoie. He used to live on the other side of Dorcas's house. Did you ever meet him?"

Dorothy eyed the hair intently, then cast her stare aside. "I did. He was . . . the person I knew that Dorcas took."

"I'm sorry," Josephine said. She opened the baggie, pinched the hair firmly, afraid it might blow away in the wind, and dropped it into the bottle. The torn page, paintbrush, guitar pick, ring, and typewriter key all fit in easily enough, but the doll she had grabbed—Mary—was slightly too large. Josephine tried twisting Mary this way and that, feetfirst and headfirst, but nothing worked.

"Just break her already," Dorothy said after watching Josephine struggle for nearly a minute.

Josephine looked at the doll in her hand and sighed. She knew Dorothy was right—she needed to break it to make it fit—but it pained her all the same.

You're being childish, she told herself. *It's just a doll, not your sister.* She took a shallow breath, held it, and broke off one of Mary's arms. It snapped easily with a soft crack, like a wishbone. Josephine winced, then broke off Mary's other arm, both of her legs, and finally, her head. One by one, Mary's torso, amputated limbs, and decapitated head dropped into the bottle. Her wax eyes stared lifelessly through the glass, accusatorily.

You killed me, Josie, Josephine thought in Mary's voice. *You tore me apart and threw away the pieces, like yesterday's spoiled leftovers.*

Josephine corked the bottle and shoved it in her bag, silencing the dark thoughts infecting her mind.

"What about the other items?" Dorothy asked. "The ones that are supposed to bind Dorcas within the bottle. Did you get those?"

"Laurence offered to collect them for me. He's a good person. Shy, but good. He knew Mr. Lavoie and wants to stop Dorcas as much as we do."

"Then it's lucky you met him, and even luckier I was wrong about him." Dorothy smiled. "You should bury the bottle close to the stone man, right under the feet of the old mirror where you talked to your reflection."

Something about that didn't sit quite right, but Josephine couldn't put her finger on why. Dorothy's suggestion seemed as good a place to bury the bottle as any. She brushed the concern away and focused again on what had to be done. "I saw a shovel in the basement the first time I went down there. I can use it to dig the hole." Josephine looked down and studied her hands. "Even if none of this works, I just wanted to say thanks. Everything you've done for me . . . well, I don't know what I would have done without you."

They hugged, and Josephine felt as warm and comfortable as if she were hugging one of her own sisters. *Maybe the way I thought I felt about her before was a little premature*, Josephine thought. *Maybe Dorothy feels more like family than anything else.* If that was the way things went, she'd be perfectly happy. *Friends and partners come and go, but family is forever.*

"Promise me you'll stop her," Dorothy said when they separated. "Not just for you and your family, but for me too."

"I promise," Josephine said.

You can't promise that, she thought. *You probably won't ever see Dorothy again. You probably won't survive the night.*

Maybe, she thought in response, *but if not for Dorothy, I wouldn't have stood a chance.*

On her way home, Josephine found Laurence where she'd last seen him, standing on the safe side of one of the pentagram trees. With snow covering his boots and toque, he looked like he'd been there a while, waiting for her to pass by, but his mood was remarkably upbeat.

He gave her a baggie filled with salt and pepper, another with seven nails he'd bent with his father's pliers, and a handful of burdock burrs.

"I could've easily collected more, but I figured that would be enough."

With thanks, Josephine added Laurence's items into the bottle one by one, ending with the burrs.

Josephine held her breath, but nothing happened. She realized she'd expected a bang or a flash of light or some other dramatic signifier that the magic had worked.

This isn't a fairy tale, Josie, she reminded herself, but then, upon further reflection, she realized her life *was* closer to a fairy tale than anything else.

She tried not to dwell on the fact that a good witch hadn't charmed the bottle, and everything she and Dorothy and Laurence had done might have been a pointless waste of time.

"So, what now?" Laurence asked.

"Now I bury this in the basement, wait for midnight, and hope it works."

"What can I do?"

"Stay away."

Laurence looked a little taken aback by Josephine's directness.

"I'm serious," she said. "Stay away. It's too dangerous, and you've done plenty for me, Allison, and the rest of my family. Thank you, Laurence."

"People I don't know well call me Laurence," he said. "My friends call me Larry."

Josephine smiled. "Thank you, Larry."

"If this works, will you ask Allison to come see me before you leave? I'd like to say goodbye to her."

"Of course." Josephine brushed some snow off the top of Larry's head. "It's late and cold. Head on home."

With a nod, Larry said, "Good luck," and turned to leave. He began to walk east.

Josephine frowned. "I thought you lived that way." She pointed west, the direction of Mr. Lavoie's abandoned house.

He shook his head. "No, my house is this way."

"You must live near Dorothy, then."

The name didn't get a reaction out of Larry.

"She's the girl who gave me this," Josephine said as she rattled the bottle.

Larry just shrugged.

It's a big forest, Josephine thought. A shiver racked her body. As she'd said, it was late and cold, and she still had work to do, so she said goodbye to Larry and returned to Dorcas's house for the final time.

TWENTY

Standing in the front foyer as the snow melted off her shoulders, Josephine knew the heat from the furnace wasn't real—nor was the furnace itself—but she didn't care. It felt warm, it felt good, and after spending the afternoon outside during a frigid winter storm, it didn't matter to her whether it was real or not.

Careful, she cautioned herself. *That's Dorcas's plan. Like the witch in* Hansel and Gretel, *she's giving us all exactly what we want and preparing to . . .*

Oh, shit . . .

The truth poured over Josephine like a tidal wave.

Dorcas is the witch from Hansel and Gretel, *or as close to her as anything could possibly be in the real world.*

Both witches—the fairy tale one and the real one—lured innocent people into their homes and devoured them.

The story I wrote, Josephine suddenly thought, recalling the first night they'd spent in Dorcas's home. *It was a retelling of* Hansel and Gretel *but with me as the witch. Dorcas got into my mind and wrote it with my hand. Why would she do that?*

The answer was obvious.

She was toying with me.

Josephine clutched the bottle to her chest. She couldn't let it out of her sight.

"Hi, sweetheart," her mother said. She had suddenly appeared in the doorway to the kitchen. "Our New Year's Eve dinner is ready."

"Thanks, Mom." The thought of skipping dinner and sneaking down to the basement to bury the bottle breezed through her head like a blast of Arctic wind, but she couldn't bring herself to do that. The meal might be the last one she and her family would enjoy together. Josephine wouldn't miss it for the world.

"What's that?" her mother asked, noticing the witch bottle.

"Oh, this? Nothing, really. Just an old bottle I've filled with some things from around the house. A decoration for my bedroom."

"You've always been so creative," Mrs. Jagger said. "I'm proud to be the mother of so many talented girls." She put her right hand in her jeans pocket, and Josephine caught sight of the same small, odd bulge that she'd noticed there before.

"What do you have in there?" Josephine asked, pointing at her mother's pocket.

Mrs. Jagger laughed a little. "Oh, nothing really. It's just— it's just something I like."

"What?"

"Well . . . this is silly, but I found some dolls in my closet the morning we arrived, and they—they remind me of the family. I've kept one with me at all times. Like I said, silly."

"That doesn't sound silly at all," Josephine said. *They resemble the family because they* are *the family.* "Which one have you kept with you?"

Mrs. Jagger was still smiling, but she also looked like she might start crying. "The one that looks like me."

"Can I see it?"

After hesitating a moment, she said, "Okay." She slowly took the wax doll out of her pocket and handed it to Josephine.

Josephine gasped.

"See?" Mrs. Jagger said. "It looks just like me, right?"

It didn't look like her mother, because it *wasn't* her mother. The doll was a spitting image of Dorcas.

Josephine nodded—she didn't want to tell her mother the truth and she couldn't find the words to outright lie to her—and handed the doll back.

Mrs. Jagger quickly slipped it back into her pocket. "Are you okay?"

"Yeah, I'm fine." Josephine tried to smile.

"You look tired, or distracted. Like you've got a lot on your mind."

Josephine shrugged and tried to smile a little wider. "I always have a lot on my mind; stories competing for my attention, begging to be written."

Mrs. Jagger shook her head and frowned. "This is different somehow. When you're working on a new story idea, you seem so excited it's as if your feet might lift off the ground. This is the opposite. It's like something is weighing you down, tethering you to the floor."

"Thanks, but I'm fine. Really. I am."

"Okay, well, if you want to talk about anything—"

More than you can know, Josephine thought.

"—just let me know, okay? I love you."

"I love you too, Mom."

Her parents had pulled out all the stops, as if they knew it would likely be their last supper. Grilled lamb chops with garlic, bean stew, roasted carrots and parsnips, and freshly baked bread dipped in olive oil.

They sat around the table and ate and talked and laughed in the flickering light of half a dozen candles. The storm raged on in the coldness outside, but that only made the dining room feel even warmer and cozier. The girls took turns feeding Louisa and holding her in their laps. Mr. Jagger read a short piece from his work in progress, which was met with applause. Elizabeth played "Auld Lang Syne" on violin while Mary and Allison sang. Mrs. Jagger served rice pudding for dessert and although everyone said they were too full to swallow another bite, they all finished their bowls clean.

It was as close to a perfect evening as Josephine could have ever hoped for—except, of course, that it wasn't. It was far from perfect. Her mind was filled with terrible thoughts, images of things that had already happened and fears of what was yet to come. Try as she might to ignore it, her gaze was regularly drawn to the discarded snakeskin still hidden beneath the dining room table. And the witch bottle, squeezed between her thighs through the entire meal for safekeeping, was a hard and cold reminder of what she needed to do. The night was growing old, but there was work to be done before she'd be able to rest.

She laughed bitterly, knowing she wouldn't find any sleep that night.

When Louisa accidentally spilled some milk and her family jumped up to help clean the mess, Josephine seized the opportunity created by the distraction to leave the dining room. She grabbed her backpack from the hallway, then opened the purple door slowly, quietly, and slipped into the basement stairwell.

She picked up the flashlight from the top step and made her way down. The stairs groaned as loudly as ever, but there was nothing Josephine could do about that. She reached the ground and paused, listening. She didn't hear footsteps or scurrying in the dirt or bones going *click-clack-crack* in the darkness. She also didn't have the sensation that someone or something was hiding in the shadows.

"C'mon, Josie," she muttered to herself. "Get digging and get out of here."

She found the shovel where she'd last seen it, leaning against the wall in a corner of the basement. She picked it up and wiped a strand of tangled cobwebs off the handle, then walked to the broken mirror. Only it was no longer broken. The reflective glass had either been replaced or magically reassembled. Josephine knew which was the more likely explanation. She placed the bottle and her backpack on the ground and pushed the mirror to the side, then placed the flashlight down as well.

The flashlight that had once again somehow made its way back to the top of the stairs, she realized. *All along, Dorcas has wanted me to come down here. She wanted me to see my own, twisted reflection. She wanted me to see the rabbit bones. She wanted me to discover Mr. Lavoie.*

As if on cue, the stone man opened one eye. It rolled around in his dirty socket before closing. He uttered a low, throaty moan, then fell silent.

He doesn't have much time remaining, Josephine thought. *And neither do I.*

She cast all thoughts aside and thrust the shovel into the ground. Its blade lifted the dirt easier than she had anticipated. Before long, there was a tiny hole in front of her and a small mound of dirt to the side. A few more shovelfuls and the hole would be deep enough to bury the bottle.

Dig. Dig. Dig.

Thud.

It was a hollow sound. She'd struck something. Wood.

Josephine dropped to her knees and shined the light into the hole. There was something buried underground, but she couldn't tell what. She brushed some loose dirt aside. It was a lid.

She sat up straight and cast a nervous glance over each shoulder to make sure she was still alone, and then frantically dug with her hands. Before long, she had freed a wooden box. It was the size of a hardcover book and covered in intricate carvings. The small lock that sealed the lid was rusted and brittle. The desire to break the lock and open the box was overwhelming.

No, Josephine thought. *Bury the bottle first, then open the box.*

She listened to her rational side, buried the bottle, and filled the hole with dirt. She used the shovel to pat it down and dragged the mirror back into place. With that task done, she turned her attention back to the box and picked it up.

The cellar door rattled, then creaked open.

Josephine nearly dropped the box in fright, grabbed her backpack, and jumped behind the mirror. It wasn't the best hiding place—not even close—but she didn't have time to find a better one. She remembered to turn off the flashlight at the last possible second.

Two pairs of feet walked down the cellar steps.

"This is always the hardest part," Mr. Finger said.

"Yes, but anticipation is good," Dorcas replied. "Anticipation is great. It creates excitement. It builds hunger. It makes the reward taste . . . sweeter."

"I hate waiting. And I'm already plenty hungry."

"It won't be long now. Only a few hours. The witching hour is nigh. It's almost time for the binding ceremony. Until then, we wait."

They stepped off the bottom stair and crossed the basement. Neither had bothered to close the cellar door; soft blue moonlight bathed them in a cold glow. Josephine, luckily, remained cloaked in complete darkness. But then Dorcas paused a few feet from Josephine's hiding place.

"What is it?" Mr. Finger asked.

Dorcas didn't answer. She scanned the basement.

Josephine placed her hand over her mouth to hold back a scream. She held her breath and wished there was some way to stop her heart from beating.

Thump-thump. Thump-thump. Thump-thump.

"Dorcas? What is it?"

"I'm not sure," she said. "I sense something. Smell something." She looked suddenly in Josephine's direction.

Josephine closed her eyes. She couldn't bear to watch. Dorcas would see her, catch her, and then . . .

The wall coughed and wheezed, a feeble sound that was filled with pain.

Dorcas laughed. "It's only Lavoie."

Josephine opened her eyes to peek as Dorcas and Mr. Finger walked up the stairs to the main floor.

"Still alive, but only just," Dorcas said. "He's turning rancid in his old age." She laughed some more as they neared the purple door, still open a crack.

Mr. Finger joined in her laughter, but Dorcas silenced him with a harsh shush.

Mary walked along the main floor hall, past the open door, singing "Twinkle, Twinkle, Little Star" to Louisa as she bounced the baby in her arms.

Dorcas was in plain view of Mary, but she didn't bother trying to hide—she had nothing to worry about, since Josephine was the only member of the family who could see her. But Mr. Finger could be seen by everyone, and his presence in the basement at that time of night would've raised difficult questions to answer.

Instead of trying to run back down the stairs, or hide behind the basement door, or do anything a normal person would do to avoid being seen, Mr. Finger transformed into a snake. Not a large snake, but a small one only seven inches long, with red, black, and white stripes along his back.

It happened in a flash. Louisa squealed with interest and pointed at the snake, but Mary walked past, none the wiser.

"That was too close," Dorcas whispered to the snake. "Don't change back into your human form. We can't afford a single misstep, not this close to the binding ceremony. We both know what to do. No mistakes. Go."

The snake nodded its head once as its forked tongue tested the air, and then it slithered off along the hall's baseboards. Dorcas left the basement and headed in the opposite direction.

Josephine sighed in relief that she hadn't been caught, but her head spun with what she'd seen. She should have put it together sooner. The snake she thought she'd seen a few times slithering throughout the house. The snakeskin she'd found in the dining room. Mr. Finger's reflective glasses, obscuring his eyes. The glimpse of his pupil, a vertical line, when his lens had cracked.

He's a shapeshifter, Josephine thought. *Mr. Finger is Dorcas's familiar, bound to serve her for eternity.*

Things were looking bleaker by the minute. Josephine was torn between the desire to hide in the basement until the witch bottle trapped Dorcas at midnight, and the desire to charge upstairs, force her family into the van, and drive as far away as possible.

The van is in town at the mechanic's, she reminded herself.

Suddenly, she felt something in her hands, something cold and smooth. She looked down and was surprised to see the box she'd dug up clutched tightly in her fingers. It felt like she'd found it hours ago and forgotten she still held it. She set it down and struck the lock with the shovel. It cracked in half with the first blow. Josephine opened the lid and peered inside. The box held a single folded piece of paper, and she knew at once where it had come from.

Early Histories of Canaan, Vermont, she thought as she unfolded the paper. *I knew a second page had been torn out of the book*. Dorcas must have torn both pages out and hidden them in her house to bury the truth.

Josephine read quickly.

The mob grew incredibly agitated. Some were angry. All were scared. The men began shouting calls to action to bolster their courage, and threats were hurled at Dorcas.

The witch cut through the din with a wave of her hand. The forest became unnaturally quiet. The men fell silent, as did the birds and the insects and even the wind in the trees. It was as if the witch controlled everything from the ground beneath her feet to the sky above her head.

Although they had never met, she addressed the men by name, one by one, as if they were old friends. And then, with her mind, she reached into their bodies—nay, into their souls—and plucked out personal details, secrets and lies, that no one could have possibly known.

Past crimes, shady business deals, cheats, scams, infidelity . . . Dorcas revealed it all as the men stood by helplessly, shocked into silence, and listened to the salacious details. But the witch had one more trick up her sleeve.

She then told the assembled mob that she knew what they craved, what they desired, what they needed more than anything else in the world. Knowing these things, she said, gave her power. True power.

"Absalom Yates craves respect and wants to be mayor of Canaan. Isaac Sanders loves his daughters but wants a son. Jethro Collins wishes his crops produced a greater yield. Sampson Lewis wishes his crops produced a greater yield than Jethro's, and he's considered extreme measures to make that happen."

On and on Dorcas went, reciting the men's secret desires as effortlessly as if she were reading them from a book. One might think these revelations would have tipped the men over the edge and compelled them into action, but instead it had the opposite effect. The truth cut deep. It disarmed them, weakened them, paralyzed them.

The witch would have triumphed that day if not for the actions of Zebulon Bell, one of the youngest members of the group. Although Dorcas had also addressed him directly and revealed that he was madly in love with Absalom's eldest daughter, Zebulon managed to break free from the spell that had ensnared the others. He managed to overpower Dorcas, tie her to a chair, and set fire to the room. When asked later how he managed to resist the witch's charms when the other men, older and stronger, could not, Zebulon admitted that his grandmother was experienced in the magical arts and had taught him many of her superstitious ways. No one probed any further—he was the hero who had saved Canaan, and the townsfolk were content to let things be.

After Zebulon set fire to Dorcas's house, the rest of the men snapped out of their collective trance. They watched as the fire consumed the house like a pyre. Dorcas's screams could be heard over the roaring flames for nearly thirty minutes. By then, the house was little more than ash, and Dorcas should have been nothing more than bone.

She was still alive, but only for a moment longer. With her dying breath she shouted, "I curse you! I curse your families! I curse this land! In the name of William, my late father, Sarah, my late mother, and Mercy, my sister, I curse Canaan!"

Josephine had reached the bottom of the page. She sat still and silent for a minute or two. She waited for the paper to magically set on fire, but it didn't. The words written in old, faded ink screamed at her from the page as she continued to stare at them.

In the name of William, my late father, Sarah, my late mother, and Mercy, my sister, I curse Canaan!

Mercy, my sister.

Mercy.

Not late *sister, like William, my late father, or Sarah, my late mother. Just sister.*

Josephine's mind raced as her brain struggled to keep up.

Mercy. As in Great-Great-Aunt Mercy. As in the name Mr. Finger used to trick my parents into coming to Canaan for the week. Josephine had assumed that Mercy was a made-up name, but what if—what if it hadn't been?

What if her dad *did* have a relative named Mercy? Maybe not a great-aunt, but someone further back in his family tree?

The local history book said that Dorcas's younger sister had died in jail shortly after birth, but what if the baby had survived, been taken away from Salem, grew up, and had a family of her own, children, a lineage?

What if that lineage led to Josephine?

What if I'm related to a witch?

Josephine folded the page methodically. She placed it back in the box. She set the box down not too far from where she had dug it up. She'd thought she had already figured everything out, but it was clear she was very, very wrong. And yet, nothing shocked her. She had a feeling nothing *would* shock her anymore. And regardless of anything she'd read, nothing changed what she had to do. She had to get her family out of the house. She had to get them to safety.

And then—whether she was related to Dorcas or not—the witch would pay.

TWENTY-ONE

Josephine gripped the shovel's shaft and held it high like a base-ball bat. She didn't pause to wonder whether or not what she was about to do would work—she knew it would. It didn't make sense if she thought about it too long, but that didn't matter.

That was the thing about Dorcas's house. None of it made sense, not in traditional terms, but Josephine's gut instincts had so far mostly proven to be true. And now, her gut instincts were telling her that if she broke the furnace—an imaginary furnace in an imaginary basement—the house would no longer be heated, it would quickly grow cold, too cold to spend the night, and her family would be forced to find warmth elsewhere.

She prepared to swing the shovel full force, but then hesitated. Smashing the furnace to bits with a shovel would make a lot of noise. Her family would come running to see what had happened. So would Dorcas and her pet snake. But if Josephine broke the furnace quietly, no one would know until the temperature began to drop, and she could use all the spare time she could possibly get.

The furnace was a mass of pipes and metal boxes and valves and dials. Josephine knew nothing about furnaces and wondered what the best way would be to break it without electrocuting herself.

There was a rubber belt spinning in a loop, connected to what appeared to be a small motor, and a larger box that Josephine guessed contained a fan.

If I cut that rubber belt, I don't think heat will make it out of the basement, Josephine thought.

She stuck the handle of the shovel through the spokes of the pulley system, halting the spinning belt.

So far, so good.

Next, she took the knife out of her backpack and sawed at the belt. The rubber was thick, but once she had created a groove in its surface, the work sped up and she cut clean through the belt. She pulled the shovel free and the pulley began spinning again, but without the belt in place, the air around her quickly grew warmer.

It worked! The hot air was still pumping out from the furnace, but it wasn't being blown into the vents and up into the rest of the house.

But Josephine's sense of victory quickly evaporated. She looked at the door at the top of the stairs. The heat would still rise. Even if the temperature dropped a little, would it drop fast enough to prompt her family to leave in the middle of the night, during a storm? Probably not.

She sighed, dropped the shovel in the dirt, leaned against the furnace, and closed her eyes.

It immediately stopped working. All of its moving parts slowed down until the furnace didn't make a sound. Nothing moved. No heat—absolutely none—was produced.

She stood up straight and laughed. "I did it!"

Josephine considered her choice of words, then repeated them one more time with different emphasis. "*I* did it." She looked at her hands, half expecting to see tiny bolts of lightning dancing between her fingertips, but they didn't look any different than they had before.

Without the humming white noise of the furnace, the basement was intensely quiet. The silence was oppressive and made her feel more exposed than before.

I've got to get out of here, she thought as a shiver tickled her spine. It was amazing how fast the temperature was dropping, but then again, it was fake heat from a fake furnace. *Kill the source, kill everything else.*

That gave Josephine an idea.

"Mary, wake up."

Mary rolled over onto her side, her back to Josephine, and grumbled something completely indecipherable. She pulled her blanket tight to her chin.

"Mary!" Josephine repeated, a little louder. "Wake up!"

"What?" Mary said without turning to face her sister. "What is it?"

"The furnace is broken."

"So?"

"So . . . the storm is getting worse and it's colder than ever outside. Without a working furnace, we'll all freeze in our sleep. Don't you feel how cold it is in here?"

Josephine's words were punctuated by a wisp of breath from her mouth.

Mary's lips were beginning to turn a light shade of purple. She rolled over and rubbed her eyes. She looked at Josephine with mild confusion, then looked around the room and said, "*Brr*. It's cold."

"I know!" Josephine said.

Mary sat up in her bed and wrapped her blanket around her shoulders. "Why didn't you say so?"

"I did!"

"Oh." Mary's body was racked by a shiver. "We should tell Mom and Dad." She started to get out of bed, but Josephine stopped her.

"What's that on your hand?"

"My hand?" Mary asked. "What are you . . ." She frowned. "*Check your jeans pocket?*" She looked at Josephine accusatorily. "Did you—?"

Josephine shook her head. "It's your handwriting."

With a frown, Mary pointed at a pile of clothes on a chair beside the bed, not too far from Josephine. "Pass me my jeans."

"So bossy," Josephine said, trying to keep the tone light in the hope her sister wouldn't begin to suspect she was being set up.

Mary dug a hand into her pants and pulled out the note she'd written earlier. As she unfolded the paper she said, "Are you sure you're not tricking me somehow?"

"No!" Josephine said with a smile. "I swear!"

After a quick glance at the note, Mary said, "It's my handwriting too." Her smile disappeared as she read. She looked up at Josephine, more confused than ever. "I don't understand."

"I know," Josephine said, "and there's no time to explain. The furnace can't be fixed, and it's getting too cold to spend the night, especially for Louisa. You have to wake everyone up, convince them to leave, and lead them to my friend Dorothy's house. She lives east of here, about a fifteen-minute walk through the woods. It's a big white country house. You'll see a wooden fort before you reach it. Tell Dorothy's parents our furnace broke and ask to spend the night."

"This is absurd . . ."

"Isn't that what the note says?"

Mary didn't answer that directly. She didn't need to. Instead, she said, "I don't know Dorothy's parents. Why would they take us in in the middle of the night?"

"Because they're good people," Josephine said. *They have to be to have raised such a kind daughter.*

"Wait a minute," Mary said as realization dawned on her face. "You're not coming with us, are you?"

Josephine shook her head.

"Mom and Dad won't agree to that. They won't let you stay here."

"Tell them I went ahead to talk to Dorothy's parents to make sure it's okay."

Mary exhaled loudly, the air whistling through her teeth.

"Will you do it?" Josephine asked.

After one last look at the note, Mary nodded. "Of course."

"Thank you." Relief poured over Josephine, as soothing as a warm shower. "And Mary?"

"Yes?"

"Whatever else happens, don't come back here. Don't ever come back to this house."

"Ever?"

"*Ever.*"

Mary nodded.

As soon as she heard the front door click closed, knowing her family had left, Josephine stacked some logs in her bedroom fireplace, balled a piece of paper from her notebook, and lit a fire. The temperature was dropping quickly.

She had a theory, but needed to test it before she'd have any confidence that it might work, so she scanned the room, looking for the right place to start. Her eyes fell on her closet door. She crossed the room and reached out to turn the doorknob, but paused before she touched it.

What if Dorcas was waiting on the other side, hiding in the darkness, smiling her gash of a smile?

It was a creepy thought, but instead of making her afraid or anxious, it gave her mind clarity. She grew calm. She took a deep breath and listened to her instincts.

Josephine didn't know where Dorcas was, but she knew without a shadow of a doubt that the witch wasn't hiding on the other side of her closet door.

She opened the door slowly. The closet was, as she had known in her heart, empty of witches, ghosts, and snakes.

Click-click. The light turned on without her assistance.

Did I do that? Can I move things with my mind? There was one way to find out.

She grabbed a book off the shelf at random and looked at the cover.

Josephine laughed.

She'd picked an old printing of *Hansel and Gretel.*

Of course.

She didn't consider switching it. Like so much else that had happened to her since her family had arrived in Vermont, she had a feeling the book choice wasn't a coincidence. It was meant to be.

Josephine held the book flat on her palms in front of her body. She took one final look at the cover, then closed her eyes. She relaxed her shoulders, slowed her breathing, and concentrated on the book. She pictured it—no, *saw* it—opening.

The front cover trembled.

"Whoa!" Josephine exclaimed. She kept her eyes open and continued to concentrate on the book. In her head, she saw the cover open.

The cover sprang open.

In her head, she saw the pages turning.

The pages flipped from front to back as if by an invisible hand.

In her head, she saw the book levitate in the air.

The book quivered, but didn't rise. She shrugged, not fully convinced she'd be able to go that far, but then . . .

Then the book lifted out of her hands and hovered in the air in front of her face.

"Holy shit," she said, and the book fell back to her hands. "It's true . . .

"I'm a witch."

It made sense, and not just because she believed she might be a distant relative of Dorcas and Mercy. It explained how she'd broken the furnace with nothing more than a thought and a touch. It explained how she'd cracked Mr. Finger's lens in a fit of rage. It explained how she had knocked her father back on the stairs and summoned Louisa. It explained how she was able to hear people's thoughts. It explained how she was able to influence them.

"Good," she said with a nod. "That's good." She put the book back on the shelf, looked at the light—*click-click*—and stepped out of the darkened closet. She thought of the door closing and it did. Josephine looked at her hands again and laughed.

Now for something a little more challenging, she thought as she walked to the nearest window and looked outside. The glass was frosted with ice. Outside, snow was swirling through the air around the house. She felt a little like a small, porcelain figure trapped inside a snow globe. The trees, visible in the moonlight, bent and thrashed and creaked in the wind.

She picked one of the closest trees and focused on it.

She saw it. Its trunk and branches and bark and the forty-seven rings within it, each one marking a year of life. She could see it all, like peering into someone's soul. Like seeing without using her eyes.

She saw the tree straighten and then bend against the powerful force of the wind, the way she'd wanted it to bend.

So far, so good, Josephine thought.

She saw it snap in half and crash to the forest floor, but . . .

The tree didn't break—not in reality, just in her mind. Instead of doing what she had willed it to do, it sprang back up and then moved with the wind again.

"Damn," Josephine said. She sighed and took a step back from the window, wondering if she should try again. But she was tired and felt a headache coming on. A really bad one, worse than any she'd had before.

She sat down on the edge of her bed and massaged her temples. The throbbing began to slow down and her forehead felt instantly better.

"Am I making my headache go away?" she asked herself.

"You are," a voice behind her answered.

Josephine twisted around. Someone was sitting on the opposite side of the bed, her back to Josephine.

"Helen," Josephine said. "When did you get here?"

"Just now," Helen said. She turned to face Josephine. Her eyeball jiggled and swayed from her socket.

"Can I . . . help you with that?" Josephine said, pointing at Helen's face.

Helen nodded, her eyeball bouncing like a tetherball. Josephine held her hand palm out and thought of Helen's eye moving back where it should be. And then, as if the optic nerve was a retractable cord, Helen's eyeball slid up her cheek and into her socket with a soft *squelch*.

The eye still looked damaged beyond repair from being punctured. Josephine doubted Helen would be able to see out of it, but at least it didn't look as disgusting.

"Thank you," Helen said.

"You're welcome," Josephine said. "Why did you come?"

"Same as before—you summoned me."

"I did?"

Helen nodded.

Josephine was surprised to learn she had been able to do that without even knowing it. "So, you're not a vision, or a ghost? You're actually here, like, in the flesh?"

Helen shook her head. "No, not exactly. I'm not a vision or a ghost, but I'm not here either. The real me doesn't even *know*

I'm here. I'm back in Amherst, blissfully unaware of everything that's been happening in Canaan."

"I don't understand." Josephine's headache was returning. She covered her eyes to think, but it didn't help.

"I'm sort of like a crisis apparition, a telepathic version of myself, an astral projection, a copy of my soul that's able to cross space and exist at the same time as my permanent soul."

Josephine sighed. Her headache was back. "Now you've fully lost me."

"It's not important," Helen said. "What *is* important is that you brought me here. The question you should be asking yourself is *why*."

"I don't know." Josephine rubbed her temples again. "I wasn't even aware I'd summoned you, so how am I supposed to know why? And tonight? Tonight, I'm focused on trying to stop Dorcas. That's what I was doing before you showed up, before I 'summoned' you. I was trying to break a tree, and . . ." A thought ran through Josephine's head; she latched onto it before it could slip away. "That's it."

Helen nodded.

"That must be why I brought you here," Josephine said. "To help me."

"How?"

Josephine shrugged. "Honestly, I don't know. Not yet. But I need to stop Dorcas and I could use all the help I can get." Mary had helped her, and Dorothy and Larry, so why not Helen?

Or Helen's crisis apparition, Josephine corrected herself. "Will you help me?"

"Yes," Helen said.

"Thank you. I'm the one who fucked up your life, so I should be the one helping you."

"It's okay," Helen said with a smile. "After all, I'm not really me, remember?"

Josephine laughed. "Right. Of course. Still, I'm sorry for what I did."

"I forgive you."

"Even though you're not really you?"

"Well, I know. The real me, back in Amherst. I know you're sorry. And I'm sorry too."

Josephine slid across the bed and the girls hugged.

"Such a sweet reunion," Dorcas said. She had appeared in the middle of the room, her hands clasped to her heart in mock sincerity.

Josephine and Helen split apart in a panic.

"No, no, no," Dorcas said, waving her hands in the air. "Please don't stop your make-sweet on my account. I'm happy to wait." She smiled, toothy and wet.

Helen disappeared in thin air.

"Helen!" Josephine yelled.

"Do you think I scared her off?" Dorcas asked, slowly approaching the bed. "I didn't mean to."

"Stay back," Josephine commanded.

"Or what? You'll drop a book on my head? Or maybe a tree? How did that work out for you?"

"You—"

"Know?" Dorcas said, getting closer and closer. "Of course I know. I told you already. I know everything that happens in my house. You should understand that better than anyone by now. We're really not so different, you and I. Two of a kind, you could say. Kith and kin. Birds of a feather, now and forever!"

"We're nothing alike, even if we *are* related."

"I'm not so sure. We're very much alike. You could help me, you know. We could live together. We could live *forever* together. And I could help *you*. I could give you powers you couldn't possibly imagine. I could make sure you never die."

Josephine rose to her feet. Dorcas was nearly within reaching distance, and if this was where Josephine met her end, she wasn't going down without a fight. She formed fists and felt power surge between her fingers. "I don't want your help," she said, spitting the words out. "I just want you dead."

Dorcas stopped and looked affronted, another act. "Are you sure you don't want my help?"

"Yes." Josephine raised her fists.

"How about mine?" Dorcas said, but not with her own voice. She sounded different. Younger. Much younger.

Dorcas transformed before Josephine's wide, shocked, uncomprehending eyes.

The witch no longer stood before her.

Dorothy did.

"You haven't rejected *my* help," Dorothy said. "In fact, I'd say you've been downright *needy* all week long."

"No," Josephine said. She shook her head and felt a tear slip down her cheek. "No . . ."

"Yes," Dorothy said. "I'm Dorcas. And Dorcas is me. One and the same." She smiled, both with her mouth and with her eyes. "And we have you right where we want you."

TWENTY-TWO

"Are you okay, Josephine?" Dorothy said. "You don't look so good. In fact, you look like absolute shit."

Josephine shook her head. She couldn't believe that Dorothy was Dorcas. And yet, the transformed witch stood before her, and the pieces of the puzzle in her head began lining up, snapping together snugly, making sense in an odd, logic-defying way . . .

"Here, take a seat." Dorothy exhaled directly into Josephine's face—her breath was ice-cold and smelled of sour berries and bitter almonds—and guided her back to the bed.

Josephine couldn't resist or struggle. All tension had been flushed out of her body. But not out of her mind. It worried and riled and panicked and raged and needed answers as desperately as lungs need oxygen. She tried to turn her head to look at Dorothy, seated beside her, but discovered she couldn't move her neck. She tried to lift her hands but failed. She tried to get back to her feet but couldn't move a muscle.

All she could move were her eyes and her mouth. *I'll have to make do with that for now.*

"What have you done to me?" she demanded.

"Oh, nothing much," Dorothy said with a twinkle in her eye. "It was just a little charm from deep within. A way to get you to calm down and not do anything you'd regret. You're a bit of a firecracker, Josephine." Dorothy *booped* Josephine's nose.

"You've paralyzed me."

"Only temporarily. You'll be right as rain before long. You come from strong stock, after all, and you're no good to me dead."

"I know what you want."

"Do you now?"

Josephine tried to nod before remembering she couldn't. "Yes. You and your house live on thanks to Mr. Lavoie and who knows how many souls before him. I used to think you drank your victims' blood, but you let your house do that for you, don't you? And like with all the others who came before Mr. Lavoie, you've almost completely drained him. You need me and my family—*your* family—not only to keep you alive, but to bring you back from the dead."

"Clever girl," Dorothy said. "I'm proud to call you a Good, even if you're Mercy's direct descendent, not mine."

Clever girl. Josephine had heard Dorcas say that before, back when she'd lit her notebook on fire and nearly burned down the house, but at the time, she had thought it was her own thought. "Why did you want me to burn down your house?"

Dorothy smiled. "I didn't. You couldn't have. What I wanted was for you to feel the pain of nearly losing your family."

Josephine fought back tears. "Like you nearly lost Mercy. I know she survived infancy."

"Cleverer and cleverer. She was born in the Salem jailhouse shortly after my mother was arrested for witchcraft. People thought malnourishment killed her, but that wasn't true. She didn't die at all."

Although she still couldn't move, Josephine's mind raced ahead. "Your mother charmed her."

"Quite right," Dorothy said with an appreciative smile, like a teacher praising her star pupil. "Like the charm I've currently placed on you, only a little stronger. It slowed Mercy's breathing and heart rate enough to make her appear dead. The jailer removed her from the prison and took her to the morgue. When her body went missing that night, everyone took the disappearance as proof that Mercy must have also been a witch, but in truth, my mother had gotten word to my father, and he'd rescued Mercy and spirited her away. Far, far away. Far from Salem and the trials and everyone who wanted to harm my family."

"He brought her to Canaan," Josephine said.

"And returned for me when I was released from jail, after my mother was . . ." Dorothy fell silent for a moment. "Do you know what my mother yelled at the judge who sentenced her to death, moments before she was hanged? 'I'm no more a witch than you are a wizard, and if you take away my life, God will give you blood to drink!'" Dorothy smiled. Her eyes were wet and glassy. "She was a remarkable woman. She'd lied when she testified that she wasn't a witch, of course, but she hadn't lied about the judge's fate. He died. Choked on his own blood."

The snake slithered into the room and wound a figure eight pattern around Dorothy's feet.

"Ah!" she said, picking the snake up and holding his beady eyes close to her own. "Speaking of blood, it's time for you to feed." She held out her right forefinger and the snake bit into the flesh of her lowest joint. Upon seeing the look of revulsion on Josephine's face, Dorothy said, "Just as people have kept the house alive and the house has kept me alive, my blood has kept my familiar alive."

Josephine recalled seeing two circular scars and an angry red spot on Dorothy's forefinger the first time they'd met.

"We've been through a lot together, haven't we?" Dorothy said to Mr. Finger. "That's enough for now." She set him back on the ground and he slithered out of the room.

Josephine's heartbeat was heavy in her chest. If she could feel her heartbeat again, perhaps the charm was beginning to wear off. She looked down at her hands lying limply on her lap. She stared hard at her fingers and concentrated.

Her left thumb twitched.

Dorothy didn't seem to notice. She was too swept up in her memories. "Before the day she was sentenced to die, my mother hadn't done anything to hurt anyone. Her only crimes were using her abilities and charms to help the townsfolk of Salem, and she charged such a pittance for her work that my parents were nearly destitute. And those same people who she'd healed and soothed turned against her. That's when I first learned the truth of human nature and the meaning of the word *evil*. After my mother's neck snapped—once the shock had worn off— I vowed to only look after myself, no matter the cost."

"So why bother stringing me along all this time?" Josephine asked. "Why did you pretend to help me? Why pretend to be my friend?"

"Because—and I mean this as the highest of praise— you're special, Josephine. I picked up on that shortly after I first laid eyes on you." Dorothy laughed and Dorcas's eyeless face flashed across the young girl's for a moment. "Sorry. Poor choice of words."

With a great deal of effort, Josephine managed to wiggle her left forefinger.

"Simply put," Dorothy said, "I knew you were a witch. With my family's blood flowing through your veins, I thought one of you *might* be, but until you arrived, I couldn't be sure. And since you were the only witch in your immediate family, you were the only one who could see me. The only one who might figure things out. The only one who could ruin everything."

"Ruin everything?" Josephine spat. "Me? *You've* ruined everything. You've ruined my life. My family's lives. How did you even find us?"

"Mr. Finger might not be a lawyer, but he is very clever. And, unlike me, he can come and go as he pleases. And it pleased him to travel to Amherst, and to hide, and to watch. He's a very skilled observer, our Mr. Finger is. Always in the shadows, always watching. I bet you didn't even know he'd been watching you for weeks, long before you came to Canaan."

Josephine fought down the bile that was rising in her throat. "But why continue to terrorize me as Dorcas? Why not just pretend everything was fine?"

"You'd already seen me, and you would've continued seeing me as I lulled the rest of your family into a false sense of security. They're weak and needed little more than the items I conjured in their closets—your father's typewriter, your mother's poppets, your sisters' clothes and instruments and art supplies. But you're not weak. You would've found a way to make them leave Canaan. But!" Dorothy raised a finger in the air. "Fed a steady diet of hope from your new neighbor, a girl your own age who always helped you precisely when you needed help the most, I knew you'd stay. And here we are. The plan worked. But I didn't suspect you'd grow feelings for me. I couldn't tell if you wanted to date me or welcome me into your family. How fucked up is that?"

Dorothy's laughter cut Josephine to the bone. She closed her eyes and sighed. Dorothy had controlled her the entire time. She'd led Josephine to the library, sent her on a wild goose chase to fill the witch bottle, and made her believe—for as long as possible—that Larry was a ghost. She'd set her up to find both of the local history book's missing pages, first by enticing Josephine to read *Snow White* and second by telling her to bury the witch bottle near Mr. Lavoie. And she had been only too happy to explain the significance of the pentagrams surrounding the house. She had lied out of one side of her mouth while telling the truth out of the other, building trust and, as she'd said, giving Josephine hope. And Josephine had fallen for it.

But something in that didn't line up.

"The pentagrams," Josephine said. "I guess they're phony too. Part of your elaborate lie, your plan to deceive me."

"No, the pentagrams' power is real, as the townsfolk who carved them on the trees and in their homes discovered. As Dorcas, I can't walk past them any more than your family can walk on water."

"But I talked to you—" Josephine almost pointed at Dorothy but stopped herself in the nick of time; she didn't want Dorothy to know she was beginning to regain muscle control. "Not Dorcas, but still, *you*—beyond the circle of pentagram trees. In your fort with a pentagram carved above the entrance."

"Not my fort. Laurence's. I needed a place for you to find me, and it fit the bill. He hasn't used it in two years."

"So the house beside the fort is where Larry lives?"

Dorothy nodded. "I couldn't have you knocking on the front door and meeting his parents, could I? That would have ruined everything."

It made sense, but Josephine still found it difficult to wrap her head around. It felt a little like her memories were an optical illusion, or like she was waking up from a dream. "The day we met, I heard your mom call you."

"Did you?" Dorothy asked with the look and tone of a teacher trying to explain something to a student who can't quite grasp a simple concept. "Or did you hear Laurence's mom call him?"

Of course. Dorothy told me it was her mom and, like her other lies, I bought it.

Dorothy smiled. "You're quite gullible, aren't you?"

Josephine felt a little foolish. But at least there was a silver lining. *I've sent my family to Larry's house, not Dorothy's.*

"But if you can't walk past the pentagrams . . . ?" Josephine realized Dorothy had said she couldn't pass the pentagrams *as Dorcas.* But as Dorothy?

Dorothy confirmed what Josephine was thinking. "They hold power over *witches*, not teenage girls destined to be witches. Oh, that reminds me." She pulled her necklace over her head and tossed it aside. The wooden pendant with the pentagram set on fire and quickly burned to a small pile of ash. Dorothy eyed Josephine up and down and smiled. "Give it time and you won't be able to pass pentagrams, either."

Josephine resisted the urge to ball her hands into fists. She would never be like Dorcas.

No more waiting, she thought. *It's time to make a stand.*

She saw the storm outside. She saw snow continuing to get deeper and ice continuing to coat every surface. She saw the forest trees sagging under the weight, ready to snap at any moment. All they needed was a little push.

She fought through the lingering effects of Dorothy's charm and raised her hands in the air as she managed to rise to her feet. In her mind, she saw the seven trees closest to the house snap in half. A second later, she heard a deafening *crack* from outside that sounded like the world splitting in half. And that crack told her it had worked—she had managed to achieve what she hadn't been able to do before.

Dorothy sprang to her feet, transforming back into Dorcas as she rose. She lifted her hands above her head, palms out and fingers spread apart, as the trees crashed through the roof above their heads.

And Josephine saw that the trees didn't actually crash through the roof, but rather, they passed clean through it. Because the roof was gone. Dorcas wasn't trying to stop the trees from falling; instead, she was giving them a clear path to pass without leaving a scratch on a single surface of her house.

In addition to the roof, portions of the wall and floor disappeared and the trees fell all the way down to the basement. The gaps and holes resealed themselves and the entire house was whole again.

"Nice try," Dorcas hissed. "You're not strong enough. Not as strong as me. You never will be. What little strength you do have is about to be mine."

Josephine heard the distant sound of the front door opening and closing and she had a vision of Laurence and—*oh no oh no oh no*—Mary running up the stairs. She tried to get into their minds to influence them, to tell them it wasn't safe, to prevent them from coming any closer, to send them back to safety—but they didn't slow down.

Dorcas laughed. "Nice of the local boy and your dear sister to join us."

A random thought popped into Josephine's head despite it being the least of her worries. "But he can't see the house."

Dorcas spread her hands out and smiled magnanimously. "I let him."

The bedroom door flew open and Mary entered first, followed closely by Laurence. They stopped and stared at Dorcas in shock and fear, seeing her for the first time.

Dorcas opened a hole in the ceiling and lifted Mary and Laurence up into the attic, holding them in the air like a couple of helium balloons tethered to invisible strings. She then opened holes in the floor of Josephine's bedroom and the family room beneath, creating a four-story tunnel that led straight down to the basement floor.

Straight down to their deaths.

"No," Josephine pleaded. "Let them go—take me. Drop me instead. *Kill me* instead. Just, please, let them go."

"That's not a choice you get to make," Dorcas said. She turned her left hand and Laurence spun in the air. With a turn of Dorcas's right hand, Mary twisted and writhed in pain. Dorcas was either trying to prove that she was in charge—not Josephine—or she was simply enjoying tormenting Laurence and Mary.

"But although you can't choose to take their place, you're not powerless," Dorcas said. "No, not by a long shot. You have a choice to make. A big choice. Life and death. Who will live, and who will die. You don't have time to save both. Only one. That's the choice you have. So . . . *choose*."

Dorcas stopped twisting her hands and pointed them both at the ground.

Mary and Laurence plummeted. Through Josephine's bedroom—

"No!" Josephine screamed. Mary and Laurence screamed too; awful, throaty sounds that drowned out the world.

—through the family room—

Josephine thought of the trees she'd felled.

—and into the basement.

Josephine made one of the trees lift into the air.

Dorcas had been right. There wasn't time to save both Mary and Laurence. There was only time to save one. That was the choice she had to make, and she knew who she had to save.

The tree rose and caught Laurence.

Josephine's choice.

TWENTY-THREE

Laurence yelled in pain as his body smashed through the upper-most branches. But the tree broke his fall and stopped him from crashing to the ground in a crumpled, broken heap. He stopped screaming when he realized his life had been saved.

Mary also fell silent, but for a distinctly different reason.

Although Josephine had chosen to save Laurence, Mary hadn't hit the ground. She was levitating facedown a few inches above it, sweat and tears dripping off her chin.

Josephine hadn't saved Mary—Dorcas had. The witch yelled in anger and raised her hands above her head. All of them—not just Mary and Laurence, but Josephine too—flew up into the attic. Dorcas followed them and, with a flick of her fingers, lined up three wicker chairs and dropped Laurence and the sisters onto them. Before they could escape, strips of wicker from the armrests lashed around each of their wrists and the chair legs dug into the attic's wooden floorboards. The hole Dorcas had opened in the floor resealed and, for a moment, the only sound was the clatter of hail on the roof.

"You chose *him*," Mary said to Josephine, "over *me?*" She looked at Laurence. "No offense."

"None taken," he said.

Josephine tried breaking free of her bonds, but she wasn't strong enough. She tried using her mind but, likewise, found she lacked the mental strength. Frustrated, she gave up and fell still.

"I knew she'd save you," she said. "I also knew she wouldn't save him."

"How? Why?" Mary said.

"She needs us, Mary. She needs our whole family alive to bring her back to life. If one of us dies before she can perform her binding ceremony and fuse us to this house, she misses out on her chance to live—truly live—forever."

Mary considered what her sister had said and then frowned and shook her head. "But how did you know for certain that she'd save me?"

"It was a calculated risk, one I had to make in, like, less than three seconds. Besides, if she really wanted to kill us, she could do it with a snap of her fingers."

Dorcas, who had been watching the interaction with a twisted grin, raised her hand and snapped her fingers. The sound was like brittle bone breaking. Her grin widened.

"Why did you come here?" Josephine asked. "You should have stayed at Larry's house, where you'd be safe."

"Shortly after they took us in, I caught him sneaking out. I followed him into the storm and demanded to know what was going on. He told me the truth about Dorcas and the house and there was no way I was going back to bed after learning how much trouble you were in. But now . . ." She shook her head and a tear ran down her face, free from threat of being wiped away thanks to Mary's bound wrists. "This was a mistake. I screwed up and put us in greater danger. I'm so, so sorry, Josie."

"Don't cry, my dear girl," Dorcas said, suddenly materializing beside Mary. She wiped Mary's tear away with her thumb, gently at first, before digging her long, jagged nail into her cheek. Mary inhaled sharply as her skin split apart and a rivulet of blood spilled out.

"Leave her alone!" Josephine shouted.

Dorcas smiled and looked to Josephine. She continued digging and dragging her thumbnail into and across Mary's face. "Or what? You'll get angry? You'll have a little temper tantrum? I wouldn't want that, would I?" She stopped torturing Mary, stood up straight, and licked Mary's blood off her thumb.

Mary let out a bottled-up moan and breathed heavily. Half her face was slick and red.

"I swear to God . . . ," Josephine said.

"How about him?" Dorcas said, interrupting Josephine. She had appeared directly behind Laurence and placed her hands on his shoulders. "Do you care if I have a little taste of Laurence?"

Before Josephine could answer, Dorcas opened her mouth wide and sank her sharp teeth into his cheek. He screamed loudly in pain, then screamed even louder when Dorcas tore off a strip of his flesh. Blood sprayed both from the hole in Laurence's cheek and Dorcas's mouth as she noisily chewed the raw meat. She swallowed, then shivered and sighed in pleasure. Laurence looked pale and sweaty, like he was near to losing consciousness.

"What the fuck is wrong with you?" Josephine yelled, desperate and near delirious with fear and anger.

"Nothing at all," Dorcas said. "I can already feel life coursing through my veins. Your sister's life, and his. Imagine how I would feel—

"—with a little bit of yours." Dorcas had disappeared and reappeared again, this time beside Josephine. She looked Josephine up and down, licking and smacking her lips wetly. Her eyeless gaze settled on Josephine's hands. "Let's see. From you, I crave a little more—more than blood, more than flesh . . . yes, a little taste of bone."

Josephine tensed in preparation for the worst, but the worst was so much worse than she could have imagined.

Dorcas gently tugged at each of Josephine's fingers, one after the other, starting with her right pinky finger, as she recited an old nursery rhyme.

To market, to market to buy a fat pig;
Home again, home again, jiggety-jig.
To market, to market, to buy a fat hog;
Home again, home again, jiggety-jog.
To market, to market, a gallop a trot,
To buy some meat to put in the pot;
Three pence a quarter, a groat a side,
If it hadn't been killed it must have died.

Dorcas had reached Josephine's left pinky, but didn't tug it. Upon uttering the word "died" she wrenched the finger sideways. It bent and snapped with a loud *crack*, and a jagged fragment of bone split through her skin.

White-hot pain seared Josephine's taut nerves, blinding her with fireworks before her eyes. Sweat broke out along her brow and she clenched her jaw so tight she thought her teeth might shatter. Somehow, she managed not to scream—she had a mad idea, the only thought she could presently contain, that she couldn't cry out in pain, that doing so would give Dorcas too much satisfaction.

Dorcas tightened her grip on Josephine's broken finger, then began to pull it, slowly but forcibly. The finger stretched out impossibly thin, far too elongated, and then reached its breaking point. With a series of loud snaps, Josephine's ligaments and tendons split. Her skin tore last, and her finger finally, blessedly, came free.

Although she had tried not to, Josephine realized she had screamed in the end, the moment her finger had been severed. The world took on a silvery hue and her hearing became muffled. She heard Mary and Laurence yell and cry, but it sounded like they were a great distance away, as if she was wearing her noise-canceling headphones. She found some small shred of comfort in the memory of her headphones, and more in the knowledge that adrenaline was pumping through her body and dulling the pain she should be feeling. *The body is an incredible thing*, she thought.

To which Dorcas added, "That it is." She held Josephine's finger up to her face and regarded it a moment before placing it longingly on her tongue and sealing her lips. She took her time as she chewed, the bones crunching like cracked walnut shells. Finally, she swallowed, and—without a hint of malice or sarcasm or intimidation—said, "Thank you."

Josephine's head rolled side to side and her eyelids fluttered. "Go fuck yourself," she managed to choke out.

Dorcas didn't respond to Josephine's taunt. Like a predator after feeding, she looked relaxed and utterly content. "That will satisfy me until the binding ceremony. And you, Mary, have given me a gift with your impulsive decision to return here. Once I've completed my preparations, I'll be paying your family a visit. Not as Dorcas, but as Dorothy. When a harmless but scared-looking girl shows up at their door and tells them you and your sister need help, they'll come running." Dorcas waved a hand at four wicker chairs, identical to the ones they were bound to, stacked against the wall. "I have seating prepared for them all. One for your father, one for your mother, and two for your sisters. The baby will need your chair." She pointed at Laurence. "But not to worry. It will soon be vacant."

Laurence glared at Dorcas defiantly, his jaw set and his fists clenched.

Mary glanced at Josephine's hand then quickly looked away and coughed like she was going to be sick. "My God, Josie. Are you okay?"

"I'll be fine," Josephine said hoarsely, hoping that would be true. She looked at the stump where her finger used to be and could feel it moving and bending even though there was nothing there but air. *Just like this house*, she thought darkly. *There and also not there. A phantom.* Blood pumped out of the wound with every beat of her heart, and Josephine felt a shred of strength leak out of her body with every fresh gush. She willed the blood to coagulate and, after a few more heartbeats, much to her amazement and relief, her stump stopped bleeding.

But Josephine maintained a hopeless expression. She didn't want Dorcas to know she was able to heal herself, or catch on to what she was thinking. Dorcas could read Josephine's *outside*, but she didn't always seem to be able to read her *inside*. And once Josephine had repaired some of the damage Dorcas had caused her, she had had an idea.

Helen, Josephine thought as she used her mind to search for her old friend, *where did you disappear to? Are you still in the house?*

There was a pause just long enough for Josephine to begin to despair before Helen's answer came.

Yes.

Do you still want to make things up to me?

Yes.

Good. I need your help, and I want to make things up to you too. If you help me, I'll visit you back home and tell you—the real you—the truth. Hopefully, I'll be able to put your mind at ease and help you find . . . I don't know, some relief, I guess.

What do you need me to do?

Dorcas lashed out and grabbed Josephine's face. She squeezed her cheeks, hard enough to hurt, and leaned in close. Josephine could smell the rot on her breath and see every scar inside her empty eye sockets.

"What are you thinking, girl?" Dorcas hissed.

"Too much pain to think," Josephine said quietly.

"I don't believe you. If only I could crack your pretty little skull open and scoop your thoughts out like a pot of stew. *You* stew." Dorcas leaned in closer still and inhaled deeply, as if that could somehow help her read Josephine's mind.

Josephine recoiled and focused on her pain, hoping that would be enough to mask her true intent.

After a moment, Dorcas said, "You're trying to summon help."

Josephine clenched her jaw and said nothing.

"Yes, you are. Foolish girl. Your family are the only people close enough for a low-level witch like you to be able to summon, and summoning them here will only bring them to me more quickly."

"Low-level *what?*" Mary said, but Josephine hardly heard her sister. She resumed communicating with Helen.

Don't come up to the attic. Instead, go to the basement.

But you said you needed my help, came Helen's reply.

I do, and I need you to go to the basement.

In her mind, Josephine saw Helen float through the purple door and down the stairs. Josephine hoped Dorcas wouldn't see Helen too. If Dorcas knew where Helen was heading, she would figure out Josephine's plan and would fly down to stop her. Josephine took the fact that Dorcas hadn't left the attic as a positive sign. Perhaps Dorcas was too focused on trying to find a way fully into Josephine's thoughts, or maybe she couldn't see Helen because, as a crisis apparition, she wasn't really there.

"Is that what you're plotting?" Dorcas asked, her face twitching up and down as she studied Josephine's face. "Of course it is. Isn't it? Tell me!" She grabbed the back of Josephine's head and banged their foreheads together.

Josephine bit her tongue, tasted blood, and closed her eyes. She felt sick to her stomach, but she had to remain focused on her task.

This place is horrible, Helen said. She was standing near the pile of rabbit bones. *What now?*

Do you see the mirror?

Yes.

Move it aside.

Helen did as she was told.

Look at the wall.

Helen made a disgusted sound. *There's a man's face. He's . . .*
alive.

Not for much longer, Josephine said. She didn't like asking
Helen what she needed to ask her to do next, but needs must.
I need you to kill him.

What?

I need you to kill him, Helen. I know, it's awful, but if it helps
you at all, he's going to die tonight anyway. And he's in pain. Think
of it as a mercy.

I don't know. I don't know if I can do that.

You have to. It's the only way to help me. He's the source of
Dorcas's power. I think if he dies before she performs her binding
ceremony, fusing me and my family to her house in his place, she
might die too. Again, but permanently this time.

Helen sighed. *Okay. How?*

Josephine used Helen's eyes to scan the basement. *There's a*
shovel beside the furnace. Use it.

Helen sighed again, but she didn't argue. She picked up the
shovel and regarded it silently. *Hit him with it,* Helen said.
It wasn't a question.

Yes. But you're only going to have one chance before Dorcas
catches on to what you're doing, so make it count.

Helen crossed the basement and stood before Mr. Lavoie.
She hesitated, but only for a moment. She looked like she might
throw up—if crisis apparitions *could* throw up—but she fought
through it and raised the shovel.

Mr. Lavoie's one exposed eye looked at her lazily. If he could tell what was about to happen, his face didn't show it. Josephine hoped that would make things easier for Helen.

Thank you, Josephine said.

Dorcas suddenly released Josephine's head and took three quick steps back. She clasped her hands together. "Ah," she said. "I *see.*"

Josephine didn't like that one bit. *Quick, Helen! Do it now!*

Helen pulled the shovel back, preparing to swing with all her might. But she screamed and dropped the shovel beside her.

It was the snake. Mr. Finger. He had slithered up Helen's leg and torso, then down her arm, twisting around her forearm.

"You see," Dorcas said. "Even if your mind is a mystery to me, you can't win. I have eyes everywhere." She tapped her temple, beside one of her empty sockets.

Helen ripped the snake off her arm and threw him to the ground, then raced upstairs.

Josephine fought through her desperation and came up with one last idea. She didn't stop to wonder if it would actually work. There wasn't time and she was out of options.

Helen! Go to my bedroom. The fire I lit earlier should still be burning.

Helen raced to Josephine's bedroom and stood in front of the fireplace.

What now? she asked.

Put all the remaining logs in the fireplace, Josephine said.

Helen did as Josephine asked. Sparks swirled in the air and the fire roared with renewed vigor.

Dorcas laughed.

The snake was in the doorway of Josephine's bedroom, watching Helen.

"You already tried burning my house down," Dorcas told Josephine. "Don't you remember? Do you honestly think she will be any more successful than you were?"

Sorry, Helen said. She floated into the air and Josephine wondered why Helen wasn't running away before she realized that Dorcas was controlling her.

A fourth chair slid into line with the other three and Helen was thrust into it. As before, the wicker bound her wrists and the chair's legs fused to the floor. Josephine hoped the chair wouldn't be able to hold a crisis apparition, but Helen gave up after a moment of struggling to no avail.

"I wanted to help you," Helen told Josephine. "I wanted to make things right."

"You did, Helen," Josephine said quietly. "You did."

Mary and Laurence looked at Helen but seemed unfazed by her sudden appearance. Josephine assumed they had both already seen so much that they had grown numb to anything slightly bizarre or unusual.

"Now you all see, once and for all," Dorcas said. "You're no match for me. Not even you, Josephine. I've been burned, killed, and yet, all these years later, I'm still here. And I'll still be here long after all of you." Dorcas waved her hand and the cauldron rose from the basement to the attic. As she continued to move her hands in the air, items from around the house—herbs, plants, water, trinkets, stones—flew to her. She fell into a trance and sang in an unrecognizable language as she worked. The snake slithered into the room, twisted between her feet, and settled beneath the cauldron, where he coiled his body into a tight ball. The hole in the floor remained open as Dorcas's items continued to float into the attic.

"I feel so foolish," Mary said.

"Why?" Josephine asked.

"I was blind to what was happening here. There were warning signs—I see them now—but I missed every one of them."

"Dorcas charmed you, Mary. She charmed the whole family. There was nothing any of you could do."

"How long have you known?"

Her sister's question caught Josephine slightly off guard. "About Dorcas? A day or two after we arrived, but—"

"No," Mary interrupted. "About you. About being a witch."

"Oh," Josephine said. "No more than a day. But like you said, there have been warning signs I've missed or ignored for most of my life. I can hear thoughts, and I can even move things with my mind."

"What?" Mary said in shock.

Josephine nodded. "Crazy, right?"

Mary contemplated that silently for a moment. Josephine began to believe that her sister was angry at her for hiding the truth so long.

But Mary didn't look angry. She looked sad. "I wish I'd known. There probably wouldn't have been anything I could've done to help you, but I would've tried."

"I appreciate that. I wanted to tell you, but I didn't know how. And I didn't want to freak you out."

"From here on out, no more secrets, okay? After all of this, I don't think there's anything you could say that would scare me."

Josephine didn't think they had a "from here on out," but she didn't have the heart to say so. "Deal. No more secrets."

Dorcas, still in a trancelike state, continued to add items to the cauldron while singing and chanting. The snake flicked his tongue in and out of his mouth rhythmically.

"Hey, Josephine," Laurence whispered.

"Yeah?"

"Can you get into her mind to stop her?"

Josephine shook her head. "It wouldn't work. She'd overpower me." She didn't bother keeping her voice down. She wasn't concerned that Dorcas might hear them plotting. In fact, Laurence's question was playing into her plan perfectly—the plan she had secretly devised earlier when she had asked Helen to throw the remaining logs on the fire.

Dorcas looked at Josephine and inhaled deeply, then sighed in contentment. "The air is filled with the stench of your desperation. I can practically taste it."

Josephine had banked on Dorcas assuming she had asked Helen to feed the fire in a last-ditch attempt at burning the house down. That way, Dorcas wouldn't know what Josephine actually intended on burning.

Her.

"Everything is ready for the binding ceremony," Dorcas told her familiar. "Time to lead the rest of the family here like lambs to the slaughter."

Dorcas hadn't sealed the hole in the attic floor, and Josephine had been keeping an eye on the fire in her bedroom. It had grown steadily until the flames filled the fireplace.

Dorcas slowly approached Josephine. "I'm going to enjoy your company these next fifty or sixty years, Josephine, as my house slowly consumes you." As she walked, she passed the hole in the floor.

Josephine knew she wouldn't be able to influence or control Dorcas, but she didn't need to. Instead, she closed her eyes and easily slipped into Mr. Finger's mind.

The rest happened quickly.

Josephine made him slither to the toe of Dorcas's boots.

Dorcas looked down out of curiosity.

And then Josephine made Mr. Finger transform back into his human form. He rocketed up, collided with Dorcas, wrapped his arms around her in a tight embrace, and jumped off the edge of the hole. They fell, entwined, straight toward Josephine's bedroom fireplace. Dorcas hit the back of her head on the mantel before landing on the burning logs. The fire roared up around them and Dorcas howled in pain. She kicked and thrashed, but Josephine put all of her mind and energy and soul into Mr. Finger's body, digging deep into her mental reserves to keep him pinned on top of Dorcas. Josephine knew she couldn't hold Dorcas forever, but she hoped she'd be able to hold her long enough.

Mr. Finger's body caught on fire too, but Josephine couldn't tell whether or not he felt any pain as the seconds and minutes slipped by. He didn't scream or fight as his skin blistered, bubbled, and slid off his body in thick slabs. Under Josephine's influence, he was as still as a statue.

Josephine was concerned Dorcas might try to enter Mr. Finger's mind to wrest control from her, but she didn't. Perhaps she was in too much pain to think of that. All her strength was focused on trying to get him off of her, and her strength was fading.

A moment later, Dorcas was weak enough that Josephine was finally able to enter her mind. It was a dark place, twisted, filled with hate and anger and images that Josephine would never be able to completely purge from her own mind. But she needed to tell Dorcas something, and she needed to ensure the witch heard her. She needed to ensure the witch *saw* her.

You shouldn't have only protected your house from burning again, Josephine said. *You should have also protected yourself. More than anything, you shouldn't have fucked with me and my family.*

Josephine got out of Dorcas's mind as quickly as possible and back into Mr. Finger's. Dorcas was little more than a blackened body that only vaguely resembled a human being, but Josephine continued to pin her down. She didn't want to take any chances.

Another moment passed before a cold chill racked Josephine where she sat in the attic, and she knew Mr. Finger was dead.

Dorcas croaked out a soft breath through her cracked, blackened lips. It sounded a little like words.

Silly girl.

But it wasn't words—it was just a breath. And it proved to be her last.

Dorcas died.

TWENTY-FOUR

The sun dawned on a new day and a new year. It was bright and warm and made it easy to forget the severity of the storm that had passed through the night before.

Josephine admired the beauty of the woods through the window in Laurence's kitchen. If she had ever been happier in her life, she couldn't recall. It had only been a week since they had driven from Amherst to Canaan, but that trip felt like a lifetime ago. It was as if her life had been cleaved into two distinct parts: Before Canaan and After Canaan.

I'm on the right side of that line, she thought to herself. They hadn't yet left Canaan, of course, but they would soon. The rest of her life lay ahead. She raised her feet onto the seat of her chair and hugged her knees to her chest. Her left hand was wrapped in the gauze Laurence's parents had given her before taping a piece to their son's cheek.

She'd done it. There had been many times she'd nearly given up hope, many times she thought she'd been beat, but she'd done it. It had cost her dearly—not only her finger; she felt like she'd lost a sliver of her sanity when she had entered Dorcas's mind—but she'd survived and saved her family. She'd burned the witch.

Laurence's parents—Mr. and Mrs. May—put a plate of bacon and eggs in front of Josephine and filled a cup with orange juice. She cleaned the plate in record time and washed the food down with the juice. She was almost as hungry as she was tired and sore. It wasn't until she had eaten seconds and thirds that she finally put up her hand and politely said she was full. The food tasted nowhere near as good as food prepared in Dorcas's house, and for that, Josephine was very, very thankful.

Mary sat beside her, and Josephine assumed she looked as rough—if not rougher—than her older sister. Dark bags hung beneath Mary's half-closed eyes. The bandage below her eye couldn't completely conceal how swollen and red her cut cheek was, and her hair was filled with dirt, bits of twigs, and ashes.

"More coffee?" Mrs. May asked Mary, readying the pot to refill her mug for a third time.

"Yes, please."

"I didn't know you drank coffee," Josephine said.

"Neither did I," Mary said.

They both laughed. So did Elizabeth and Allison. The four girls and Laurence were seated at the table while the four parents hovered around, serving food and drinks and refusing to let any of the kids out of their sight, as if Dorcas might return at any moment and snatch them away. Louisa crawled across the floor, happily chasing a dust bunny.

Mr. and Mrs. Jagger and Elizabeth and Allison had all woken with a start at the exact moment Dorcas had died, as if coming out of a terrible nightmare. In a way, that was exactly what had happened, only the nightmare had been real. The veil had been lifted, and they found a week's worth of repressed memories waiting for them. Dorcas, the house, Mr. Finger—the shadiness of it all came trickling in drip by drip, and each realization was more horrific than the last. All four got up and met in the Mays' family room, which woke the Mays as well. After a minute or two of panicked conversation, before they'd decided what to do, Josephine, Mary, and Laurence had entered the house, looking like they'd been to hell and back.

"Pumpkin!" Mrs. May had exclaimed in relief, wrapping Laurence up in a tight embrace.

Josephine had smiled at that as she gratefully fell into her own parents' arms.

The moment after Dorcas had taken her last breath, the fireplace she'd been burned in disappeared. So did the attic floor beneath the group's feet, and the walls, and the roof, and everything that had been in the house before the Jaggers had arrived, including the chairs they were bound to. Josephine, Mary, and Laurence plummeted like stones, but this time Josephine didn't need to choose who to save. She'd expected this fall, so she had had time to lift four of the trees from the basement to safely catch them. She watched in relief as Mary and Laurence were cradled within the branches of their trees, but the fourth tree was empty. Helen had disappeared.

Dorcas's body had disappeared too. They scoured the basement as snow fell on their shoulders, just to be sure that she wasn't hiding anywhere, but they found no trace of the witch.

Something out of the corner of her eye caught Josephine's attention, and she swiveled her head quickly to see what it was.

"What is it?" Mary asked tensely.

Josephine stared at the wall where Mr. Lavoie had been. He was gone. In his place, the cellar's stone foundation looked shinier and newer than the rest of the wall. Josephine hoped Mr. Lavoie was at peace, wherever he was. "It's nothing," she said.

"I still can't believe I could see this place with my own eyes," Laurence said in shock, "and I'm glad I'll never have to see it again. What do you think happened to Dorcas's body?"

"Probably the same thing that happened to Helen," Josephine said, but she didn't think that was quite right. They were both ghosts—sort of—but Dorcas had died and Helen hadn't. Josephine assumed Helen's crisis apparition had returned to her living counterpart, but she had no idea where a twice-killed spirit like Dorcas would end up.

It was as good a time as any to try to explain to the others that Helen had been some sort of ghost-of-a-living-girl who had been summoned to the house by Josephine, without Josephine's awareness or explicit intent. Laurence seemed intrigued, but Mary simply shrugged lethargically and said, "Whatever. Maybe I'll understand it later . . . but probably not."

Josephine couldn't blame her sister for appearing disinterested. After all they had been through, it was a wonder any of them were still able to stand, let alone think clearly. *I'm going to reconnect with Helen—the* real *Helen—when I get home,* Josephine thought. *Maybe, hopefully, it's not too late to make things right.*

She spotted a small pile of blackened scales in the dirt. "Found the lawyer."

She had seen Mr. Finger return to his snake form during the

fall. *Thank goodness we don't have to deal with a human body,* Josephine thought. *I wouldn't have had the ability to cope with that right now.*

Josephine and Mary looked at all their family's possessions scattered throughout the basement. Suitcases, clothes, toiletries, books—it had all fallen with them and was quickly being covered in snow.

"Should we pick everything up now?" Josephine asked without any great enthusiasm for the task.

"Leave it," Mary said. "It's only stuff, and it'll still be here when we return later."

Josephine studied her sister. A week ago, Mary would've died if one of her outfits had a single wrinkle, and now she was fine leaving everything in the dirt.

Seeing Josephine's look of surprise, Mary shrugged and said, "Guess my priorities have changed."

"I'm exhausted," Laurence said through a yawn that caused him to wince and cover his wound. "Let's go back to my house and try to get some sleep, and hopefully never wake up."

Josephine knew it was a joke, but she wasn't afraid of the intensified aches and pains she knew she'd feel whenever she'd wake up. Life was a blessing, and she felt fortunate that she and her family still had it.

She had slept, but only a little. Josephine woke with a start every fifteen minutes or so. Shortly after the sun had risen, she gave up trying and shambled into the kitchen, where she had allowed Mary and Laurence to answer most of their family's questions as they ate breakfast. There were a lot of gaps in their telling of the events, gaps only Josephine could fill, but there'd be time to fill them all in later.

Mary sipped her third mug of coffee and Louisa finally caught the dust bunny she'd been chasing across the floor. She stuck it in her mouth with glee. Mrs. Jagger picked her up and tried, but failed, to retrieve the gray clump of dust and hair before Louisa swallowed it.

"Oh, well," Mrs. Jagger said with a shrug, setting her youngest daughter back down on the floor. "I hope it tasted good."

Josephine smiled and laughed with everyone else, then let her gaze drift back through one of the kitchen windows. Her eyes fell upon Dorothy's—no, Laurence's—fort. It looked so picturesque among the snowy evergreen trees, but the sight of it made her feel sick to her stomach. She'd fallen for Dorothy's lies. She'd trusted her. But the thing that hurt most was that Josephine had genuinely liked Dorothy.

Don't beat yourself up, she told herself. *Dorcas was deceitful and cunning. She would've fooled anyone.*

Laughter filled Josephine's head; it sounded uncannily like Dorothy's. Josephine blinked, shook her head, and looked around the room as a tremor of panic began to rise from the pit of her stomach.

It was Allison, laughing at something Elizabeth had said. Not Dorothy. Of course not. Dorothy—Dorcas—was dead. Gone. And she could no longer harm Josephine and her family.

Mrs. Jagger suggested that it was time they hit the road. No one argued. The van was still in town, but a quick call to the mechanic's shop confirmed that it had been fixed and was ready, so Mr. May offered to drive Mr. Jagger to pick it up. He dug

Laurence's old car seat out of the basement and they took Louisa with them.

As they cleared up from breakfast, Mrs. Jagger thanked Mrs. May for taking them in. Mary and Elizabeth thanked Laurence for everything he had done, then stepped outside. Josephine and Allison remained with Laurence.

"I don't know where to begin," Josephine told him. "If not for you—"

"I know," Laurence said with a put-on smile. "I was pretty heroic, wasn't I?"

Josephine laughed. "You were. If not for you, well, we probably wouldn't be having this conversation right now. Thank you."

"You're welcome. Thanks to you, I won't have to worry about Dorcas haunting the woods anymore, and no one else will . . ." His words trailed off and his smile fell.

Josephine didn't need to get into his mind to know what had bothered him. "I'm sorry I wasn't able to help Mr. Lavoie."

"It's okay. There was nothing you could do. He'd been there too long and now he's in a better place. At least, I hope so."

Josephine smiled sadly. "I hope so too."

They hugged, and Josephine left Allison and Laurence alone to say their goodbyes. She joined Mary and Elizabeth outside. When Allison stepped outside a few minutes later, she smiled and told her sisters she and Laurence had exchanged numbers. Everyone had the decency to not joke about them being boyfriend and girlfriend.

"I've got something for you," Josephine said, reaching into her backpack and pulling out Allison's necklace.

"My harmony ball," Allison said in delight. "Where did you find it?"

"I kinda, sorta borrowed it." *To trick the family into thinking you had gone missing.* "Sorry."

"No need to apologize." The ball rattled and chimed as Allison put it on. "You must have had a good reason."

Josephine was relieved to hear no trace of sarcasm in her sister's tone.

Mrs. Jagger joined them and they set out through the forest. Mrs. May and Laurence waved goodbye as the Jaggers left. Before long, the Mays' house and Laurence's fort could no longer be seen behind them. Josephine pointed out the pentagram carvings on the trees as they approached the remnants of Dorcas's house. Mrs. Jagger gasped when the cellar came into view.

"I expected the house to be gone," she told her daughters. "But seeing it with my own eyes is still . . ."

"Unbelievable?" Josephine offered.

Mrs. Jagger nodded. She looked like she had aged ten years in one morning. "I'm so sorry about what happened to you, Josie." Her eyes darted to Josephine's hand.

It still throbbed, but Josephine knew she'd learn to live with it. "Thanks, Mom. I'll be okay."

"If I could go back to the beginning of the week, I'd—"

"I know," Josephine said with a hunch that there would be many variations of this conversation in their future. "It's not your fault."

Mrs. Jagger hugged her daughter tightly. "All the same, I'm sorry."

Josephine closed her eyes tight and enjoyed the embrace.

They collected whatever they could salvage of their personal belongings from the basement as quickly as possible. Josephine uncovered a broken piece of painted porcelain that she recognized from the statue of the tree with the door and the pentagram she'd bought.

"What's that?" Mary asked.

"Nothing," Josephine said. She tossed it back to the ground and covered it with snow using the toe of her boot. Doing so uncovered Louisa's lucky rabbit's foot. She picked it up and pocketed it.

Mr. Jagger and Louisa returned in the van shortly after the others had lined up all their personal belongings on the driveway. They loaded everything in the trunk and took their seats. Josephine remained outside on her own, telling her family she needed a moment. No one asked why.

She saw the forest. She saw the cracked stumps of the trees she'd felled with her mind. She saw the unusual gap in the woods where a house should have been, but no house stood. She saw the basement's stone walls. She saw the smooth surface where Mr. Lavoie had been. She saw the space that once held rabbit bones and spiderwebs and a broken mirror but now only held four broken trees and a blanket of snow.

She saw Dorcas.

The witch rose out of the ground in the basement and floated up into the air where the second floor had been. She pointed a long, accusatory finger at Josephine.

"I accuse *you*, Josephine Jagger," she said. "I accuse you of *witchcraft*, punishable by death."

Josephine blinked . . . and Dorcas was gone.

"Get a grip, Josie," she told herself.

"What's that, sweetheart?" Mr. Jagger asked through his open window.

"Nothing," Josephine said with a shake of her head.

"Ready to go?"

"You have no idea." Josephine took one last look at the world around her, breathed a sigh of deep relief, and got into the van. As she sat down, she stepped on something hard and lifted her foot, revealing her broken headphones. She kicked them under her seat with her heel, eager to buy a new pair as soon as they were back home. She'd learned a lot about her abilities the past week, but not yet enough to feel completely comfortable with them. There had been several times her powers had nearly harmed her family. And she craved the peace of mind she found in slipping the headphones over her ears before bed.

She handed Louisa her lucky rabbit's foot and the baby cooed in delight.

Josephine didn't fully relax until they'd pulled out of the driveway and onto the road, and even then, she still felt a little tense. But she gave herself permission to feel that way for as long as it would take, even if it took a lifetime. She imagined it would.

Josephine saw her mom and dad in the front of the van, Mary and Louisa in the two middle seats, and Elizabeth and Allison in the back row beside her. And she was happy. She could see that they were happy too. Having seen that, she slipped the net over her brain.

"I almost forgot to turn on the GPS!" Mrs. Jagger said.

"Never mind that," Mr. Jagger said.

"But . . ."

"Let's just drive," he said with a reassuring smile. "We'll be fine."

Mrs. Jagger relaxed a little and returned her husband's smile. "Okay. Let's just drive."

They drove through Canaan, past all the small houses, Wayne's

Lanes & Jo's Grille, the gas station and mechanic's shop, the motel with its neon VACANCY sign, and the restaurant where Grace had told them about Pauline's Boutique. *Sorry for taking my dollar to New Hampshire,* Josephine thought with a sideways smile. Park Street was ahead on their right, as was the sign pointing to the Alice M. Ward Memorial Library.

"Turn here," Josephine told her dad. She picked up her backpack and rifled through it.

"Why?" Mr. Jagger asked, obediently doing as he'd been asked.

Josephine found what she was looking for. She pulled *The Kirkman Guide to Witchcraft* out of her bag. "I need to return this to the library."

"Wait, something just came back to me," Mary said. "I stole that book, didn't I?"

"What?" Mrs. Jagger said in shock. "You stole a book? I could see Josephine doing that, but you, Mary?"

"Thanks," Josephine said to her mom. She turned to Mary. "You didn't steal it. You borrowed it. Without a library card, sure, but the librarian let you."

"Phew," Mary said. "I don't want the Canaan Library Police to chase me all the way back to Amherst."

Her dad parked the van close to the library and Josephine hopped out.

"I'll be right back," she said. She was about to walk to the library, but then she paused and turned back around to face the van. She'd had a thought. Something she wanted to do.

She lifted the mental net and reached out to her father. She bore her mind into his and filled it with a mix of emotions: confidence, satisfaction, and, above all else, happiness.

You're not a failure. You're going to figure things out, you're going to find a new job, and we're all going to be okay, she thought. She knew he wouldn't be able to hear her words—that's not how her influence worked—but he'd get the essence of her thoughts. She broke off contact and wrapped the net back around her brain.

"Honey?" Mrs. Jagger asked her husband. "Are you okay?"

He frowned, but then his expression softened, and he smiled. With a nod, he said, "Better than okay. I feel great. Ready to get back home and start fresh. You know what I mean?"

Mrs. Jagger returned his smile and stroked the hair on the back of his head. "Yes, I do."

See? Josephine told herself. *You don't need to be afraid of your abilities anymore. You can use them for good.*

She walked up the steps to the library's front door and slipped on a patch of ice. She managed to keep her balance and regain her footing, but she dropped *The Kirkman Guide to Witchcraft*. It opened to a random page in the middle, revealing the beginning of a new chapter. A chapter that Josephine had only skimmed before, not read.

Chapter Seven: Witch Bottles.

She read the beginning of the chapter as she stood back up. A sinking sensation spread through her entire body.

Witch bottles are made of stone or glass and date back to at least the 16th century. Their usage was most common in the United Kingdom, but the tradition spread to other countries, including America and Canada.

Josephine skimmed over the next few paragraphs until another section caught her eye.

Typical witch bottles might contain a number (but not necessarily all) of the following: bent nails, thorns, broken glass, wood, or samples of the witch's blood, urine, hair, or bone. When biological contents could not be obtained, items of significance to the witch could be substituted.

Josephine skimmed a little farther, her eyes settling on the next page. She stopped breathing. Although she was alone, it felt like someone had snuck up behind her and squeezed her throat.

The two most important steps to ensure the intended witch is trapped within the bottle are:
The bottle should be buried as close as possible to the witch's home, lair, or dwelling. Better yet, it should be buried inside the witch's home.
The bottle must be buried by a good witch.
If these steps are followed and the contents are appropriate, the witch will be trapped within the bottle. It should be noted that witches trapped within bottles will remain alive until released. Therefore, witch bottles should be handled with the utmost care and concern, and should never be dug back up or damaged in any way.

An imaginary lightbulb turned on above Josephine's head. *Click-click.*
Oh no, she thought, nearly dropping the book a second time.

Of everything she had just read, one sentence in particular had made such a strong and immediate impact that the words felt burned into her brain.

The bottle must be buried by a good witch.

Like me, Josephine thought. *I'm a good witch. And I buried the bottle. And I buried it in Dorcas's basement. And she told me what to fill it with. And she knew. She knew what I am.*

She always knew what she was doing. Everything was part of her plan. The witch bottle was her backup plan, in case I beat her. She played us all—especially me—like a fiddle.

Mr. Jagger rolled down his window and leaned outside. "Everything okay?"

Mrs. Jagger stepped out of the van and looked at Josephine in concern.

Josephine looked from her parents to the book and back to her family again. She shook her head.

It should be noted that witches trapped within bottles will remain alive until released.

"Baba," Louisa said.

"What is it, Josie?" Mrs. Jagger said. "You can tell us anything."

Josephine covered her eyes to think.

I didn't kill Dorcas. I helped her cheat death yet again.

She wanted to speak, but found she couldn't form the words. Not out loud. That would make them real. And this couldn't be real.

Click-

But it was real.

-click.

All too real.

Josephine finally found her voice, but it was little more than a whisper. "I'm fine. It was nothing more than a bit of a slip on some ice, but I'm okay now."

If she repeated it enough, maybe it would be true.

I'm okay now.

If she convinced herself the book was wrong and Dorcas was gone, nothing bad would happen.

We're all okay now.

If they got out of Canaan and never returned, the past would never be able to catch them.

Everything is going to be okay now.

Plink!

Something red and wet had landed on the open book. A drop of blood. Josephine felt her nose, but it wasn't bleeding. She scanned the air above, but saw nothing. The blood soaked into the page on witch jars, then furiously scribbled across it, as if someone were scratching out the words, using the blood as ink.

Josephine knew she must be controlling the blood with her mind, but she wasn't aware she was doing it.

And if I'm doing something without being aware, she thought as her stomach dropped, *I'm still not in complete control of my abilities.*

She rushed to the library and returned the book through the drop box, relieved to be rid of it, then hurried back to the van. The sun had slid behind a dark cloud, and Josephine suddenly felt a chill rack her body.

Her family talked and listened to the radio as she silently stared through the window, watching trees and houses as they bled past in a blur. Time passed and the miles racked up, but she still felt so far from home. Too far.

She tried to make herself sleep, but her mind was racing and there was nothing she could do to slow it down. She couldn't stop thinking about the book, and the blood, and the voice in her head saying her family was no longer okay—she was a threat to everyone she loved, and always would be.

She had to remain vigilant.

I'll never stop, she promised herself. *I'll never rest. Forever and ever after.*

After an hour or two, she finally began to drift off. As her eyelids closed, she thought she caught sight of something, something in the woods, something following them . . .

But she was tired. Bone tired.

Josephine's body shut down and her brain turned off.

Lights out.

Click-click.

And in the darkness of her mind, she dreamed.

AUTHOR'S NOTE

They say it takes a village to raise a child, and writing a book is no different. *House of Ash and Bone* would never have been completed, let alone seen the light of day, had it not been for the dedicated efforts and caring support of many.

Although I've published many books before, this is my debut young adult novel and marks the first time I've worked with a new publisher in thirteen years, making me feel a little like I was starting out all over again. The entire team at Tundra Books took me under their collective wing and made me feel like part of their family from day one. I can't imagine a more fitting editor to have worked with on this book than Peter Phillips, whose continual support and vision took these pages to eerie new heights. The countless conversations we shared about horror movies and modern board games were a most welcome bonus, and I'm already looking forward to hearing what you're going to recommend I watch and play next.

Shannon Swift, the book's first test reader, applied her keen attention to detail to make several brilliant suggestions, and for that I am grateful. Copyeditor Linda Pruessen and proofreader

Erin Kern went through these pages with a fine-tooth comb, untangling several knots and polishing the prose to a high sheen. And author Deke Moulton gave their opinion on an important and sensitive matter, which I valued dearly and appreciated more than words can say.

The cover artist, Julia Iredale, did an incredible job capturing the sense of foreboding lurking just inside the house, and I can't look into Dorcas's hollowed-out eye sockets without feeling my skin crawl. And the designer, Emma Dolan, brought so much creativity and care to the overall look of the book, ensuring every little detail (the hand-carved pentagrams!) perfectly reflected the world of the story.

No book—no matter how appealing—will find as many readers as possible if not for the attention of a dedicated publicist. Stephanie Ehmann was a fan of the book from the start and brought an abundance of energy and passion to sharing it with the world. The fact that you picked up a copy is likely thanks in some way to her, and so I, in turn, owe her a debt of gratitude.

Remember when I said this book wouldn't have seen the light of day without some people? At the top of that list is my good friend and fellow author Vikki VanSickle, who opened a window for me shortly after a door had closed. I don't know how I'll repay her, but I'll figure something out one day.

I can't possibly leave out rock band Queens of the Stone Age, despite knowing they're unlikely to ever read this. I listen to music as I write and pick a different band or musician for each new book, and QotSA was the band for *House of Ash and Bone*. The book's title is a nod to their song "Burn the Witch," which includes the lyrics "Burn the witch, burn to ash and bone."

Their haunting, brash, daring music colored every page of this novel, and the two will forever be intertwined in my mind.

And finally, my family. My parents and in-laws, Terry, Shirley, Carol, David, and Georgette, for a lifetime of love, support, and encouragement. My siblings and their partners, Steve and Nathalie, Mike and Karen, and Stephen and Ulli, for their selflessness, generosity, and good humor. My kids, Charles, Bronwen, and Fiona, for teaching me more about life and happiness than I'll ever be able to teach them. And my wife, Colleen, for everything. And no, that's not hyperbole— I owe it all to you.

House of Ash and Bone includes brief references to real events—and people—of the Salem witch trials. Dorothy Good, daughter of William and Sarah, sister to Mercy, truly was the youngest person accused of witchcraft during this devastating period of American history. At the age of four, her name was incorrectly written as "Dorcas" on the warrant for her arrest, but that's where the similarities between what we know of the real-life Dorothy, and the Dorothy in this book, come to an end. Twenty-five people were killed during the trials, including nineteen executions, and it goes without saying that all those accused of witchcraft were innocent. The trials serve as a warning for how awful humans can be to one another, and yet, more than three hundred years later, we're still repeating many of those same mistakes. Much like the fairy tales Josephine Jagger reveres, we continue to tell stories of Salem and witches. There are many reasons for this, but the one I'm most drawn to—the one I like best—is that we hope for a better future. Through the telling of these stories, we hope to win the battles raging inside of us. As she's driving back home and drifting off to sleep on the final page of this book, that's all Josephine wants—to control the beast within, to be a better person, and to protect her family without bringing them any further harm.

The rest of Josephine's story is unwritten, but I, for one, like to think she achieves her goal and leads the life she wants to live. And I hope that you, dear reader, lead the life you want to live too. For even in the darkest of stories, there is light to be found.